THE
STORY
I TOLD
MYSELF

THE
STORY
I TOLD
MYSELF

ARVASHNI SEERIPAT

The Story I Told Myself

Copyright © 2024 Arvashni Seeripat

ISBN: 979-8-9896509-0-3 (print)
        979-8-9896509-1-0 (ebook)

Published by: Arvashni Seeripat
               39 Wilson Drive
               Morristown, 07960
               NJ, USA.

Writing Coach/Editorial: Deborah Ager, Radiant Media Labs
Editorial: Melissa Stevens, Purple Ninja Editorial
Book Design & Production: Catherine Williams, Chapter One Book Design, UK

Printed in the United States

Acknowledgments

The Story I Told Myself is the realization of my lifelong dream of becoming a novelist, a dream I didn't dare acknowledge to myself. But sometimes when others hold up a mirror to our dreams, we can see them clearly. Shivesh Haripersad, my brother, and John Sanchez, my professional coach, held that mirror up for me.

Shivesh, our daily frivolous, fun, and intense conversations infused this book with the essence of the mystical, brought a realism to the story, and gave me the courage to take the next step all the time. John, I clearly remember the day you said, "You have a book or two in you." Your belief in me instilled a confidence to make big choices and to keep moving forward.

As a first-time author, I knew very little about what makes an idea a manuscript or what makes a manuscript a book. Enter Deborah Ager, my coach who helped me take ideas and make those ideas into a narrative that told a story that was meaningful to me. Thank you, Deb, for your tireless work with this fool (me!) who is filled with abstract thoughts and ideas!

Melissa Stevens and Catherine Williams joyfully endured the journey with this new writer. Melissa's editing prowess gave the manuscript its final form, and Catherine's eye led to a book cover and final book design that I love! I am so grateful to have three powerhouse women help me shape this novel.

I have a family where love, support, and honesty live in abundance. To my parents, Rishi and Geeta, the stories you shared with my brothers, Shivesh and Vishal, and me throughout our childhood are the backbone of this book. They are the basis from which these characters emerged. Thank you for the stories and for your unconditional love. I feel it in every breath I take.

To Preyasen and Linda Rungasamy, thank you for taking the time to read the manuscript and for the hours spent discussing the story and its evolution. Pre Mama and Linda Mamie, your positive words and energy always leave me with an optimism that raises my spirits.

My gratitude comes full circle and with a bursting heart for my husband, Pravir and two sons, Armahn and Aryan. Thank you for sitting through endless readings, discussions, and my obsession with writing this novel.

Pravir, thank you for sharing my joy and for helping with the research when I went searching for obscure information. Your work helped anchor the book in a world we can relate to. My son, Armahn, used his talents to create videos for social media marketing. These are super cool, thank you! And to my youngest son Ary, you are one amazing guy with your unwavering support. The laughter, the tough conversations, and the togetherness inspires me every day. I love you guys!

My ancestors left India to come to South Africa more than a century ago. I am eternally grateful for the opportunity to tell their stories.

Note from the Author

The story of the Indian diaspora during the 1800s and early 1900s is one that is not often told or held in the collective memory. In a world where sugar trade decided economic powerhouses, Indians were cheap and often abused labor that the British exported globally. Some were sent to the Indian Ocean Island of Mauritius, others to the Caribbean, and 152,184 were sent to South Africa. These men and women were not free. Lured by a promise of free passage to the green fields of Port Natal, they left their homes and villages for what they believed were better economic opportunities, but little did they realize that they were bonded into a life that no one could thrive in.

The diaspora has been successful around the world. World leaders, statesman, religious leaders, business leaders, and just good human beings have emerged from this slave-like start. We also have our despots, but who doesn't? We were so busy building lives and communities, promising ourselves that we would never allow ourselves to go back into the yoke of poverty that sometimes we forgot to pick our heads up and remember how we got here and how incredible our people are.

My fellow Indian diasporans have told their stories beautifully. This is my attempt to tell the story of a courageous people who came as indentured laborers to South Africa from the 1860s to 1915. Those original 152,184 individuals are now about 1.56 million in South Africa. This story is a fictional tale set in a contextual reality. It follows the sweeping journey of a young woman, Shivali, accompanied by her two children, Hari and Uma, from India to South Africa as they attempt to unpack the nuances of their lives.

Many brave authors have told the stories of indenture in South Africa, and my hope is that many more will write the stories of their ancestors. I am just adding to the collective of our lived experiences. My ask is that you read with forgiveness. While this is a contextual reality, some of the details will not match exactly for various reasons, including author choice and ignorance of details. Either way, I apologize from the outset.

Thank you for joining me on this journey. It is with joy and pain that I share this story of my people with you.

Contents

Chapter 1

Shivali's Shadow's Freedom

1887

No one came here anymore. The temple priest and the old, embattled bull in the dusty, gray courtyard were the only willing visitors of this place. The priest didn't see me, or maybe he didn't want to. I had walked past him in the village, and he conducted my wedding, but would he even know what I looked like? My head was covered throughout the ceremony, and all the days after that. Beyond the man I married, no one had seen my face for years. For them, I was just the shadow that accompanied him. During the marriage ceremony, the priest spoke of being each other's shadow. He made it sound so romantic that we would always be together. He didn't mention that one of the shadows, me, was silent, empty, and dark with no detail or color. I was the air that no one saw, least of all my husband.

The side gaze of the old bull held just the slightest hint of sympathy. He stood like a prophet, attracting a following of flies that attached themselves to his leather. The gray giant stood against the courtyard wall that provided the only shade outside. His sympathy was coupled with a look akin to judgment as his languid eyes assessed me slowly in rhythm with his chewing of the dry grass. I

1

watched him too. I would take the sympathetic look of the animal, if only to say that I existed. I was worthy of the judgement, though. This bull knew what had happened and what was to happen. This bull had witnessed all my visits to this deserted temple.

I closed my eyes, allowing the judgment to rain upon me as I remembered the inner sanctum of the temple. Unlike other temples, this one had no statue to make offerings or to fall at the feet of the deity and beg, "Please protect me. Please save me." The only symbol of holiness was the black stone rising from the floor, snaked by milk and water with tiny flowers and leaves floating gently in the shallow channel surrounding the stone. Three white horizontal lines cut the dark stone, creating a startling contrast. I knew that when I opened my eyes, that was what I would see. But if I kept my eyes shut for just a few moments longer, the bull wouldn't judge, I wouldn't just be a shadow, and I could close off the world a bit longer. I waited some more in the welcoming darkness.

Shadows were never lonely, at least that's what I thought because they always had a body to keep them company. The body that was meant to be my lifelong companion brought only fear. The only place I had found release from the panic of his everlasting presence was this temple that no one visited, where only the temple priest and the old bull sat vigil for errant souls like me.

The stillness of the temple embraced me—tight and safe—and beckoned me with its dark, shadow-filled center. The shadows had become my only friends, faceless outlines welcoming me with open arms and holding no judgment. The absence of light allowed me to relax the tenseness in every fiber of my being. The darkness provided safety. I wasn't sure why. If a home was where you felt safe, then this was my only home. In my mind, this was where I needed to be. Even I didn't recognize the person who stood here now. This wasn't the Shivali I was before I married him. That Shivali no longer lived. This Shivali was only his shadow.

Even though the darkness usually calmed me, today my body was rock hard, rigid, and my heartbeat stumbled like a drunken, broken soul—sometimes in full flood, sometimes in slow motion. I tried to do what my *baba* (father) taught me: "Breathe, Shivali. In through your nose and out through your mouth." But this wasn't the moment for Baba's lessons, because I could not breathe. I needed the calmness of the temple to quiet me. How was it that everything around me could be still and calm when I felt so unsteady? Today wasn't an "every day" day of fear. Today's terror held a special grip, and it wasn't fear of him.

I opened my eyes expecting the accustomed darkness only to realize that I was still standing on the first step outside the temple, in the cast of the evening sun, in full view of the bull. No shadows welcomed me yet. The priest was nowhere to be seen. I didn't think he had even registered our presence at the temple. As usual, he didn't see me. No one did. Entering the temple was the only thing to do. Because of what I had done, and what I was about to do, I might repulse even the shadows. What if the only acceptance I had known in recent years turned its back on me like the others? Where would I go?

I wasn't alone there. Tiny hands squeezed my shaking fingers, breaking my self-absorption. Tears rapidly spilled, attempting to escape the turmoil that was my heart and mind, only to fall onto the dry hands of my children. They had witnessed so much today. Too much for small children. Too many adult things for a brave six-year-old girl and a tough four-year-old boy to endure. It was too much for *me* to endure. Uma and Hari should be playing in the courtyard of their home, not standing with their mother in front of her temple begging for some peace.

My Uma was slightly built, just bones and hard edges, and she could blend into any place. Her face was sweaty and smeared with dirt. Her dress was green, but now it carried the brown of our surroundings, and it was streaked with a red that threatened us all. Darling Hari was a small boy with chubby cheeks, knees, and elbows. His eye was swollen an ugly red and purple, closed, and bigger than what his eye should be for his small boy face. Both the children held onto my hands like the last leaves of autumn clinging on to a tree that didn't want to let go. The wind was blowing. They felt it, but they held on tight. What I had to do could not have an audience of children. Especially not my children.

"Uma *Beti* (daughter), please sit with Hari here against the wall. There is a bit of shade, so it's not so hot." I tried to lead them to the courtyard wall. The bull still looked at us, chewing his grass, not moving but fully aware of these three frightened humans.

"No, Mama, please don't leave us here alone. Let us come with you. We don't want to be alone!" Uma's little girl voice held my words in my throat as she pulled at my hand and forced me to look at her. "Please, Mama, I don't want to be without you."

My poor baby girl was stronger than she knew, and she didn't want to leave me alone.

"I want to come with you, Mama." Hari buried his face in the pleats of my *sari*. "I don't want to sit outside. The bull is looking at me and I am scared of him."

I kneeled in front of Hari. "Please, *beta* (son), sit here while I go into the temple. Uma Beti, please keep him with you. I'll be back just now." Uma squeezed my hand again. "The bull is my friend. I've seen him often. He won't do anything to you. Don't be scared my darling boy."

Their frightened faces followed me as I led them to the far side of the courtyard. Quietly, they sat against the courtyard wall. Even when asking to come with me, they didn't scream. My children were muted by the day's events. Their silence didn't stop the tears, though. Contrasting streaks of brown skin and shades of red and purple created a pattern across their faces. I was amazed at how their wet faces still looked at me with full trust—trust that I would keep them and us all safe. I didn't know how to tell them that I didn't know how. Their hands sought each other, and they comforted each other. All the while, the bull vigilantly kept watch and gently went about eating. The sympathetic hint was now focused on the children. The old bull knew who really deserved his sympathy, and who deserved his judgement.

His judgment rooted me there, even as the small hands had let go. The look of the bull brought with it the memory of what I had done and a fear of what I was about to do. I wasn't asking if I should do this. It was the next step after what happened earlier this afternoon. This was the end. My mind had been in the temple so many times, and it knew the way in, but my feet betrayed me. The cold metal blade tucked under the folds of my sari and pressed against my breast became the calm I needed. It had served so many purposes today, passed through so many hands, and yet it still called me to complete its work—to finish the work of this life.

The voice in my head said, "Shivali, you know what to do. Finish what you started. This is the end of this, but not the end of you. Finish this and start something new." Was this my voice or the God of this temple? Or were the shadows speaking to me? I wasn't scared of the voices. I was scared of me and what I had done. More than that, though, I was terrified of what I was capable of.

"Shivali, enter the temple. This is your place. You know it, and it knows you. I know every inch of your pain and suffering, and I love you. Finish what you started. It is time for you to be free. You have to do this for yourself," the voice urged.

My feet were still heavy, but I needed to finish this now. My companions, my shadow friends called me again. They always witnessed my pain. Now they were asking me to free myself from it. Knowing that I wasn't alone, and I was with those that loved me, I slowly brought my head, my heart, and my hands together, and the energy of belonging somewhere gave me a tiny confidence to enter the temple. As I entered, I stared at the black granite, and my fear ebbed and flowed. The tiny orange and yellow marigolds floated aimlessly in the channel of milk, whispering a promise to kiss my pain away. I wanted the swirling leaves to rain solace on my frightened mind or take away my fear, but I knew they couldn't.

The afternoon removed the crushing fear of death but brought with it a new dread. This afternoon I made sure that his fists, teeth, and feet could not inflict any more harm on the shadow that stood silently ready for his wrath. This man that I married and stood in anonymity with for years was no more. The things I did earlier had to have a conclusion for me and for him.

During my marriage ceremony, three symbols were placed upon me to show the world that I belonged to him. The mark of a married woman in my culture was your husband placing *sindoor* (orange powder) in the parting of your hair. My hair was parted, and he marked me for the duration of this life and the seven lives together that marriage inflicted upon me. I watched widowed women have their sindoor washed off in public, like the death of their husband was a stigma for them to bare, placing the responsibility of his death squarely on their shoulders.

My hair was considered his pride, and I was forbidden to cut it. Otherwise, how would I part it for him to show off his prize? Widows were required to cut their hair, and if they dared protest, it was cut off for them. What use was beautiful hair but to entice your husband? Why would you want or need that hair when the man you married was no longer here?

Beautifying yourself for him was also your wifely duty, and bangles worn on your wrists provided the decoration that you carried with you everywhere. When he wasn't here anymore, why did you need to have beauty with you? I had worn my bangles for more than seven years. I displayed all the symbols, but he had nothing. Nothing was asked of him, and I could not mark him as mine during the ceremony. Only animals needed to be branded, not men. Perhaps the old bull looked at me with sympathy because I wasn't human enough to remain unmarked. His judgement came from how I saw myself, or perhaps how I was *about* to see myself.

I removed the cold steel and held it in my hand. Blades were used to mark animals and people. This blade had known its role well. The coolness of the metal had warmed just a bit from my body heat and cooled enough from my actions. The orange evening glow reflected on the steel, revealing its darkened age and its surface, covered with a mixture of blood and sindoor. The sindoor from my forehead found a place on the blade. I knew how it got there. I had wiped the knife against my hair as I stood over the body. Blood and sindoor were one, making a sort of rust-like color. I couldn't distinguish what was blood and what was sindoor. That was good. I didn't need a sindoor parting anymore.

Exhaustion crept through me. While my body felt heavy before, now every step required massive reserves of energy. These were the final steps for closing the marriage rituals. It was hard when your body said, "Please, no more. I am tired." But your mind said, "Finish this now, today." Daily my body won out. Today my spirit knew it wouldn't break anymore.

Besides, my Shiva was waiting for me by His black stone. The Shiva for whom I was named. My name was Shivali, which means "Beloved of Shiva." The water and milk offered themselves to me. I cupped them and washed my hair and what was left of the sindoor from my head. The rest was on the blade. The flowers and leaves gracefully cascaded over my forehand as they ran down my face, leaving streaks of orange powder, white milk, and dirt. I washed my own sindoor out. He had marked me, but I unmarked myself. Anyway, I wasn't a wife anymore. He was dead.

Not much in the way of bangles left; he broke them when he

threw me against the wall. They looked desolate and lost strewn across the floor. Maybe that was the sign? Where there were once seven on each wrist, there were now just two, one red and one green. These were the handcuffs that must come off. Shiva offered himself as an altar to rid myself from these beautifying shackles, and I willingly accepted the invitation and broke the bangles on the stone. They fell like petals, neatly settling at the base of the stone and mixing with the small flowers. I took the offering of milk and flowers, and I gave the offering of bangles. The next time I decorated myself, it would be for me.

Strangely, the last ritual that I gathered my strength to perform wasn't one that I would have wanted for myself. But I wanted to mourn my old life properly. I wanted to rid myself of everything that he owned on me. My hair gave him a place to mark me. It held his pride, and his ego went with his life. The darkened knife that killed him still had another task to complete. Even though I wouldn't have wanted this, it didn't take too much will or hesitation to decide this was what I needed to do. As I held out my hair and hacked away at it, the blade sliced easily through the dark silk. Even the steel had no hesitation in doing its work. Strands of black fell around me, and just like the offerings of bangles, I made a tribute of my hair.

The widows in my village covered their shaven heads in white saris and hid their faces. They wore no color—not in their hair, not on their bodies, and not on their wrists. Color wasn't for you; color was for your husband's pleasure. Otherwise, why would they strip you of all the color once he was gone? Men didn't stop wearing color when their wives died. They just carried on with their lives or remarried. They were never marked as property, so they never had to rid themselves of their markings.

The three external signs of my married status were gone: no sindoor, no bangles, and cut, rough hair. This marriage was no more, and I was no one's wife anymore. But I wasn't colorless. I accepted

Shiva's offering of flowers and milk, and that colored me for now. I had finished it. I felt complete but lost. I belonged nowhere, to no one, and to no place. We couldn't go back to the village or the house. I was sure they would find his body soon, and they would be looking for us. That they would kill me wasn't even a question. What use was I? Death didn't scare me. The idea of the children all alone, or with his family, scared me. I would not leave my children with them.

The temple's calmness held me tightly in its arms, providing comfort while my exhaustion crushed me. I conducted all my widow rituals on my own, for myself, on myself. As I collected my strength, I thought about the silence of this temple. The silence had settled into the cracks of the walls, filling the spaces with its essence. The temple felt full even when it was empty, and I knew that no one would come near me anymore, because I was full even though I was no longer a shadow. I closed my eyes again, letting the silence fill all the cracks within me.

Walking back to Hari and Uma was easier than walking into the temple. The courtyard was as deserted as earlier in the day, but it now also held the fears of two children. They sat still in the court-yard, their small dirty hands intertwined and heads touching under the watchful gaze of the bull. The bull looked at me as I approached them. His eyes spoke of a sadness and a joy. His eyes reflected mine, and I was grateful for his gaze. I nodded a thank you to him. He watched my children while I rid myself of all my markings, yet he was still marked as an animal.

Uma stroked Hari's hair as his head dipped onto her shoulder. This small boy's eyes could not fight sleep much longer, but my Uma would not let herself give into the cleansing sweetness of sleep. She was always vigilant, alert, fearful. Looking at them, the first post-widow-ritual sobs escaped me. They were so innocent and tiny, yet they lived in an adult world filled with pain. My heart hurt and my throat constricted. I wanted to preserve their innocence as much as I could, but what I exposed them to today would never allow innocence to exist again. What they watched and what they did! This life would never be the same for them. I wanted Hari to have a chance to be a man that never spoke his mind with his fists. I wanted Hari to love deeply, unlike his father and grandfather. I wanted Uma to have a chance to be a woman that never lowered her eyes in fear or cowered in the dust of the corners. My tears were prayers—prayers that the choices I made today would give them a chance to be something more than this village would allow them.

As I approached them, passing the watchful eyes of the gray bull, their faces were drawn painfully tight, the whites of their eyes looked so much bigger than they should. Uma roused Hari with a slight shake of her bony shoulders.

"Hari, Mama is here. Get up, Hari baby."

My little daughter was my son's mother without even thinking about it. Their faces were filled with fear, and the pain I saw was for themselves and for me. I must have looked frightening to them with my cut hair, bloody wrists, and dark streaks all over my face. Would they hide from me? Would they want me? That was a new horror to be contemplated and made me even more anxious. Would my children still love or want me? After all that happened today? Yet they didn't turn away from me. Instead, both walked toward me, hand in hand. Uma's small hands looked ash white she was holding Hari's hand so tightly.

Hari let go of Uma to take my wrists in his hands. "Does it hurt, Mama?" His tiny voice asked such a big boy question.

"No, darling. The pain is gone. It is just blood."

Hari nodded, used his dusty shirt to wipe my wrist, and then kissed it as I kneeled in front of him. "It's not so bad, Mama. It will get better soon."

Hari's acceptance of the situation and of me drew fresh tears, and I let them flow. When did my children become my comfort? I felt like I was a child in the presence of two adults. This wasn't how it should be, but this was how it was.

"Sit, Mama, and rest for a little while. You look so tired." Uma combed my hair with her stubby baby fingers. My beautiful, sweet Uma, always looking for order in chaos. "Don't worry about Hari, I will watch him. Sleep a little bit."

I closed my eyes with worry. These two children were the only things I had in this world, and I had so much faith in them. I knew we would be safe, someday; we were together. But I didn't know what to do next. We needed to leave this place and find somewhere to hide or live, but for how long and to where? I also wasn't sure I could do this on my own. I had Uma and Hari, but I was all alone, and I didn't even know if I wanted to do this. I was so tired.

"Close your eyes, Mama. Uma Didi and I will watch you." I heard Hari and Uma's voices as I drifted off, tired, satiated, and scared. The evening had passed, and it was night. I was no shadow tonight.

Chapter 2

Shivali's Tainted Pearly Moons

How long had I been sleeping? I woke up in darkness. The children had drifted off, but I could still see the tension coiled rigidly in their bodies.

"Beti, get up."

Someone was shaking me. Who was touching me?

"Wake up now. It's not safe here for you or the children."

My eyes struggled to see the temple priest standing in front of me. I could feel the urgency in the shiver of his hands.

"You have to leave here now," he said.

I looked at him. Did he know what I had done? What if he did, and he was going to tell them? Oh! I have to leave here and leave him. My entire body panicked, and the priest sensed my terror. I pulled away from him and instinctively moved toward the children.

"Don't be scared of me, daughter. I don't want to scare you or the children."

He put out his hand as if to show that he was no threat to us. But I trusted no one. Besides, he didn't even acknowledge me when I entered the temple.

"When I saw you earlier, I was in a hurry to do my evening *puja* (prayer) at home. I thought you just came to pray. But when I came back, I saw the sindoor, the bangles, and the hair. Beti, you shouldn't have done that in the temple. It is not the place for that."

His words were warning me, and yet his eyes crinkled deeply with an outpouring of concern and resignation. He was wrong. The temple was the *only* place for all that I had to do.

"Don't worry," he said. "I'll clean and cleanse the temple, but I can't stop what will happen if the village Brahmins find out about this." His tone told me that he was worried for himself too. "Luckily, almost no one comes here anymore. They all go to the big Krishna temple that the Brahmins built. They get all the donations there. That temple has money. People pray there. You are one of the few people that ever comes here. I have seen you many times."

The quiet was punctuated by our conversation. Even though it was low, it was enough to signal a change in the courtyard. The children stirred, but the bull was still asleep. There was nothing significant for him to get up for.

"Whenever you come, you are crying, beti. You are the Brahmin's wife, isn't it?"

He knew me, and here I thought no one knew me.

"He is not a good man. He stopped people from coming here because he wanted people to give money to the other temple he built, not this one. He is not a good person. I saw your face; he is not a good husband." The priest stopped and looked at me. "He *was* not a good man?"

His eyes softened with care and some interest in the life of his competitor. He was an older man, past his prime according to my dead husband. He was stooped, grey, and kind. His kindness had not passed its prime, though. My husband never had that.

I nodded slowly and bowed my head in shame. "*Pundit-ji* (respected priest), he was a very bad man. I killed him this afternoon. I killed my husband." I had told someone now. I didn't know what was going to happen. The priest could call people to take me away, but I told him because he knew already. He saw all the remnants of my marriage I had given to Shiva, and he hadn't called anyone.

"You must leave this place now, beti. What is your name?" He asked me a question that no adult had asked for seven years.

"Shivali," I whispered, and he smiled knowingly.

"Shiv-ji's beloved. That's why He is here for you, beti. You and the children have to go now."

"I don't know where to go, Pundit-ji. I don't know what to do next. Where can we go? I have no money and no one to help me."

"Wait here. Don't go anywhere. Wake the children and get ready, but don't leave, please. I am just going into the temple." He was already running back into the dark inner part of the temple. "Wake the children!" he shouted over his shoulder as he entered the sanctum. "Quickly!"

My instincts took over and I trusted him. I woke the children, and they sat up immediately. My wrists were sore. Every part of my body protested but moved. Hari reached for Uma's hand. He was slow, though, and Uma grabbed his hand first. They took care of each other. The bull opened his eyes but didn't get up. He just watched us, and even though I couldn't see his eyes properly, I could feel his tenderness.

The priest came back very quickly. "Shivali Beti, take this," he said, shoving some money into my hands.

I couldn't take the temple's money!

"This is temple money," the priest said, "and it is for the person who comes to pray all the time. It is meant for no one else but you and your children."

I took it, even though I shouldn't have. What choice did I have? I had nothing; he had made sure of that.

"You must go now. In the morning, the whole village will be looking for you. They will find you and kill you. You know that. You must go!"

"But where will I go, Pundit-ji? I don't know where to go." I spoke pathetically, clasping the money in my hands. I was helpless and fell to my knees in front of him. "I don't know where to go."

"The train leaves in the morning for Calcutta from the next village, Dwarpur. Just after sunrise. If you leave now, you will be there to get the train. Take it, beti. It takes about three days to get to there. I heard that in Calcutta ships are leaving for a new country, South Africa, and then to a place called Port Natal. You can work there in the sugarcane fields. You must try and get onto the ship with the children. No one will know you there. You can escape this. Go, beti. Go now!"

The only other option was to stay here and die. If they found me, they would kill me. I didn't even want to think about what they would do to the children.

"Thank you, Pundit-ji. But can I clean the temple first?" Even though I knew what I had to do, I couldn't forget that I had in some way desecrated my Shiva's temple.

"Don't worry about the temple. I'll do what needs to be done. You go now! The ship will take you to this new land, but you have to cross the *Kaala Paani* (black waters) first. Just take *Paramatma's* (God's) name and cross the sea, beti. Don't worry about what anyone says."

Just the sound of the words Kaala Paani filled me with terror, but that was a fear balanced against the horror of this place. I touched his feet. This priest was one of the only people to show me kindness. Murderers like me didn't deserve compassion, but I needed to feel someone touching me with a little blessing. His hand on my head gave me courage to take a step again. I tucked the money into my blood-soaked blouse, and we left the sanctity of the temple.

We took two hours to reach Dwarpur. Each step carried with it the heaviness of the past and the fear of the future. The station stood on the outskirts of the village, and one dusty platform made up the entire train station. The bulbul birds were the only visitors that early in the morning, so no one asked us where we were from or why we looked like we had just escaped from a prison. If they asked, they would have asked the right question. We did escape from a prison, where the warden was now dead. Hari and Uma didn't ask me where we were going until we reached the station. Poor Hari, his legs couldn't carry him, so Uma and I took turns. Uma wasn't much older than him, and yet the strength in this small girl was just beyond my comprehension.

If I had come in the day, I don't think we would have gotten onto the train. The ticket seller was still sleepy, so he just took the money and gave me my tickets. He didn't even see me. Today I welcomed the invisibility.

"Where are we going, Mama?" Uma finally asked after we bought the tickets and found a place to wait. The train would arrive in a half hour. We sat far from the ticket office so that no one would see us.

"We are going to Calcutta on a train, beti. It's a big town far from here and near the sea. The pundit-ji said that there are ships that go to South Africa and a place called Port Natal. That's where they plant sugarcane, and I can get a job for us. We don't have to worry about this village ever again."

"I have never been on a train before," Uma said quietly, more to herself than to me or Hari. "Is Calcutta a nice place?" Her eyes were wary.

"I don't know, Uma, but I think it would be better than here." Honesty was the only offering I had to give her.

She nodded, and again spoke to herself. "We can be in peace there."

"I am hungry, Mama." Hari tugged at my hand and looked at me. "My stomach is making lots of noises." His free hand rubbed his tummy.

My babies! They hadn't eaten anything since yesterday morning.

But there was no food around us. Everything was closed, and no one was selling anything to eat.

"No one is here yet, Hari. Drink some water, and we can eat as soon as someone comes with food, or we can eat when we get onto the train."

Every train station had a tap just outside the platform for the villagers. We walked to the tap and Hari and Uma drank to stave off their hunger. I took the opportunity to clean myself and the children. Tears, blood, sweat and dust had settled heavily on us. As the station woke, a few more people came onto the platform, and fruit and vegetable sellers set up their mats. I gave Uma some money to buy fruit. Guavas and bananas kept Hari and Uma's hunger at bay. I would survive a bit longer. The children needed to eat first. I needed us to get onto the train.

The train arrived in a cloud of smoke. No one beside us boarded, and that meant peace and freedom until the next station. We found seats tucked away in the back. We would have three days to sit quietly and hope we faded into the scenery. When the train moved, Hari was very excited. None of us had been on a train before. Uma and I carried the worry of being caught, and Hari carried the excitement of adventure, covering up a fear that I could see building in him every time he grabbed Uma's hand. The harsh *click-clack* of the train slowed into a rhythmic background noise, and Hari and Uma fell asleep after the excitement of boarding waned.

Cockroaches kept me company as I waited for the ticket collector to arrive, trying anxiously to cover my face with my dirty sari. The insects casually continued with their explorations of our seats as I watched. One cockroach sat where the window met the steel of the train. I wondered if he was looking for an escape like us. Or maybe it was a she, and she was looking for a place to lay her head. Back and forth, the insect roamed, trapped in the train like us, looking at a life outside but stuck in this one. Once the collector punched our ticket, I relaxed for a bit. Hopefully, we would be left alone. Sleep first, and then when the children woke, we would have to find food. The bananas and guavas would run out soon.

I drifted into a welcoming sleep for the first time in days, but sleep brought its own demons.

I couldn't remember the last time I felt this safe—tightly rocked in warm embraces and softly lulled to sleep. I wanted to stay like this forever. The warmth was tempting me with a forever sleep. I wanted to close my eyes and stay tucked away in this corner of the floor for all my days. But that feeling was interrupted by a sticky dampness that rolled down my neck, burrowing itself into the opening in my blouse and making a pool under my breast. I watched the blood quizzically. Where was it coming from? Certainly not my body? I couldn't feel anything. My blouse couldn't contain the pool, and the blood seeped through the fabric.

The embrace was warm, and yet it moved. It became more urgent.

"Mama, open your eyes. Mama! Please!" Uma's tiny arms squeezed me awake. Her high-pitched six-year-old voice lead me back to her. Why was Uma waking me? We were all sleeping on the train. We were safe.

"Uma? Why are you waking me? Sleep child, you must rest."

"You are bleeding, Mama! Please, Mama. Look at you!"

Except we were not on the train now. I was in yesterday afternoon's nightmare, reliving each moment with my children. I could hear Uma's sobs locked within a whisper in case my husband heard and knew I was awake. If he thought I was alive, the pain would start all over again. Uma's cries were like the spaces between words, blank; but without them, no meaning could be communicated. She spoke to me in those whispered sobs between words.

I was barely alive, but alive. My opened eyes were covered by the haze of the midday sun. There was fire in my mouth, and it burned hot, burned blue. My nose was wobbly. I knew it was dislodged from its place. I blinked rapidly to clear the haze and saw pearls lying on the floor, glistening in the sun. The discolored whites mixed with the dust and blood. The purity of the whites was painted by the filth around it, tainted forever.

The back of my hand reached out to wipe out the fire in my mouth. And then I realized in growing horror that the pearls on the floor were my front teeth, lying like a broken necklace waiting to be crushed under a careless foot. My teeth were not the only broken tokens on the floor. The crescent half-moon of my bangles made a tangled pattern strewn across the dust. Red and green colored the floor in a way that I had never been allowed to own color in my life.

I could feel tiny erratic quivers coming from beneath me. Hari quietly shivered as he hid buried under me. My arm ached terribly but not enough to stop me from lifting it to check on Hari. My baby boy's beautiful eye was swollen shut. The angry red colors were a sign of danger, and for years, no one had seen or listened to these signs that flashed everywhere we turned. Today, in the dusty golden glow of sunlight, this little boy, whose only indiscretion was to be born my child of this man, hid in my sari folds. Hari often paid the toll of his birth with his body and spirit.

No one escaped this man's madness. Not even his blood. The anger and the fists got worse every day. To the world, we were his family. To him, we were the bodies he owned, and he used us to appease his anger every day. Very early on in our marriage, I learned that my blood would be sacrificed to his fists. I didn't know that if I were not enough, anyone within reach would suffice, including his children.

As I tried to pull Hari out from under me, Uma helped me. Hari refused to show his face to the world. My child hid his face and hoped that his life was small enough so that no one noticed him. He burrowed into me, his one normal eye wide with fear. The darkened patch of his swollen eye shadowed the despair in my heart. My sari was no protection for Hari's fragile body, and my body was no shield against him if he reached for Hari again. Uma saw my pain and held my hand, creating a bridge for my broken soul. Uma and I were twin bridges that arched over a history of tears and a river of blood. Her hand was hardened and rough. *When had it become so rough?* While her one hand built a bridge, the other held an old steel knife. It was dark with age and had seen life beyond us. *Where did she get that knife?*

"Uma, where did you get this from?!" I was angry and thankful.

"I took it from under *Dadi*'s (paternal grandmother) carpet when she asked me to clean her room. Don't be mad, Mama. Please don't be mad. I took it because we needed something to help us. No one helps us. Everyone just watches him hurt you."

I couldn't argue. Her innocence and honesty were hard to refute.

"Mama, please take it. Please. You need to take it now," Uma whispered urgently through her tears. "I am scared. What if he comes back?"

We all feared him even more because he was this way stone-cold sober. This man had anger in his veins, and cruelty was his lifeblood.

Tainted pearly moons called out to me in my own voice. "Now, Shivali. Take it. And if he comes at you again, finish this before it is more than your teeth and your blood. Before Uma's and Hari's become the next spirits and bodies he injures."

Our shuffling and whispering awakened the beast, and he burst into the room. I smelled his rotten breath as he exhaled on my face. I knew that a blood sacrifice would happen here today. He aimed a punch at my ear, but I knew that he was coming this time, so he only managed to graze me. The ringing made me sway wildly, even in my seated position. But this same position gave me an open view of his neck. He swung with so much force that he stumbled forward, bringing him closer to me. I plunged the knife into his fleshy neck over and over. It was surprising how soft his neck was. The beast would be so thrilled to see how much was spilled. Blood shot from his vein and hit the walls like a jubilant offering. The same veins that carried his cruelty sprayed his evil all over the walls. Blood covered the twinkling of pearls and moons.

He collapsed in front of us without a word. I had killed him. His blood covered everything—the walls, the floor, and me. It glued my hair together and soaked my clothes. As I lifted my hand to wipe the blood off my hair, I realized that I had the knife in that hand. It now wore not just his blood, but my sindoor too. I thought the children had escaped him, but the look of abject horror on Hari's face told a different story.

"Hari, Uma, we have to get out of here before anyone sees us." The children didn't even drop a tear of sorrow for this man that fathered them. Too many tears of pain had been shed throughout the years.

"But you have blood on your face and clothes, Mama. You have to wash that off first and change your sari. Let me get you some water. Stay here." Before I could even respond, Uma was out the door. This six-year-old was too old to be a child. While she went for water, I grabbed the only thing of value besides my children, my *Ramayana* (Holy Book of Ram) from its hiding place at the back of the cupboard. This book that brought me solace and my children were the only things to call my own.

The thud of the train stop brought me out of my nightmare. We stopped at another village to pick up more passengers. The sun was much higher in the morning sky now. This station was much busier than Dwarpur, and the food sellers were in full sight. I sat up with the previous day's images still in my mind and the feeling of the wind behind us as we ran to the temple. That was the only place I could think of going to. The safety of the temple was what we needed, even if it was just for one night. I could still feel the slap of the metal blade against my breast, peaking from its place in my blouse.

I decided to get up and get us some food. The children were still fast asleep. They slept properly for the first time in two days thanks to the rocking of the train. I was too tired to sing lullabies, but they were too tired to hear them anyway. They trusted me, and even in sleep, their tear-dried faces showed the weariness of life. I didn't want that anymore. Weariness wasn't a garland we wanted to wear.

"Uma, I am going to get us some food. Stay here," I whispered, even though they were asleep. My baby girl nodded but didn't open her eyes. She tightened her fingers around Hari's hand. The sellers had their own business to conduct and didn't pay much attention to me. Some *roti* (bread), water, and bananas should keep us full until we reach Calcutta. I knew how to keep our bellies full, but would I know how to rid my soul of the stain of killing my demon husband? This new land of Natal might teach me how to do that.

Chapter 3

Hari's Red Guavas

Uma *Didi* (my big sister) always got the best of everything. Even today, Uma had the best seat. It must feel so nice to have the cool window against her head. I wished I could put my head on the window. Maybe then the pain in my eye would go away. I tried to rub the ache away, but it was still there. Mama said that by the time we reached the big town, the pain wouldn't feel so bad. She showed me on my fingers that it would take two more nights and half a day to reach the town. That felt far away and so long for my eye to hurt so much. It felt like the time Ram, my bestest friend in the whole world, dropped a rock on my foot. That took so long to get better. Even longer than when we waited for Diwali. At least Ram tried to make it better by rubbing my foot. Baba wanted to hurt me. Mama said that Baba couldn't hurt us anymore. She wouldn't let that happen. I believed in my mama.

I missed Ram, though. I wondered what he was doing now. Ram liked to eat, so I was sure he was eating guavas with Sakshi, my other best friend. She's a girl, so she can't be my bestest friend. I liked guavas too. The white ones but not the red ones. I didn't like red at all. The white guavas were Ram's favorite too. Sakshi didn't like guavas—I always saw her spit them out. But Sakshi had no one to play with, so she ate guavas and played with rocks like us.

Ram, Sakshi, and I were going to build our own house with rocks when we got big. It would have a room for me, for Ram, and for Sakshi. Sakshi got so mad when we told her that her room was the kitchen. We had so much fun making her mad—her eyes would get all big and dark like clouds. Clouds without rain, though. Sakshi didn't cry, but she could hit hard. Ram accidentally dropped the rock on my foot because we were fighting with Sakshi, and she hit him so hard that he started crying for his *maya* (mother). Would they build the house without me? Maybe they would make a room for me even if I was not there.

Sakshi's sister Madhu was getting married next month. I heard Madhu telling Sakshi that there would be horses, elephants, *mithai* (sweets), and so much food! *Laddoo* was my favorite mithai, but I didn't think we were going to go. Mama said that we were going to go on a big boat. She said that the boat could take a hundred people. A hundred people! I wonder what that many people in one place looks like. I had never seen a hundred of anything. *Would there be mithai on the boat?* I looked up at Mama to ask, but she was sleeping. Her head was covered, but I could still see the blue marks on her face.

When I looked at her, I was a bit frightened and held my breath. She reminded me of the old witch that scared everyone. She lived at the edge of the village. Sakshi said she ate children and was still so thin because of magic and that she lost her teeth crushing the bones of small boys. Ram and I never wanted to cross her. Today Mama looked like the witch, all blue and black, with some missing teeth. Her hug tightened, and I felt safer again. This was my mother, not a witch. She didn't eat little boys. I buried myself in her sari and made myself as small as I could.

I was still mad at Uma Didi for getting the best seat. She thought because she was big she could tell me what to do, and I must always just take what was left. *Just wait for when I grow up, Didi, and when I build my own house.* When I get a job and I earn money, I will not be the last one to get everything and the bad seat on the train.

"You hungry, Hari baby?" Uma Didi leaned over Mama to ask.

I was not a baby! But I was hungry, so I nodded, but not too hard because my eye and head still hurt.

Uma reached into her pocket for two guavas. I whispered to her, "Let's share one? Mama must also be hungry." Even though we ate the rotis earlier, I was still hungry. Mama didn't eat anything. She would be hungry when she woke up.

Uma Didi nodded, and we shared a red guava. I didn't like the color red. Next time, when I am big, I will buy white guavas for Uma Didi and Mama.

So many people got on and off the train. Maybe this was what one hundred looked like? A family with two boys came onto the train late in the afternoon. They were nice. They gave us samosas and chai and the boys even showed me their toy. Mama didn't want to take the food, but I wanted to eat, and I think Uma wanted it too. The nice mother lady made us take it. She was very pretty. Like how Mama used to look. She didn't look like that now. They didn't stay long. When I woke up in the morning, they were gone. Mama said they got off in the night while we were sleeping. They could have said goodbye. I liked playing with the boys.

The other people frightened me, especially how they just looked at us. The one lady wrinkled her nose like we smelled. I started to say "Hey! What are you looking at, lady!" But Mama shushed me. Everyone always shushed me. I thought Mama scared a lot of people. When I felt scared of her, I buried myself deeper in the folds of her sari. I felt safe there, but sometimes I felt pokes. Mama's bones could hurt!

Mama shook me awake excitedly. "Hari Beta, we have only half a finger left to go! Soon we will reach the big town!"

The big town! I tried to hide the shivering. It had not stopped since Baba hit me. No one could see that my body was trembling. I just felt it inside me. Didi didn't even feel it when she held my hand, and she held it a lot. I was scared of the big town. I didn't know this place or these people, and I was lonely and missed Ram and Sakshi. Didi didn't play at all. She just fed and cleaned me and took care of Mama. I felt safe with her. But I would like to have fun too. Maybe this trip would also be fun? Maybe there would be children on the boat to play with? That would be nice!

The last part of the train ride was taking forever. Mama and Uma were silent now, and the carriage was full of hot, sweaty, and smelly people. At least we were not the only smelly ones! So many people crammed together, and all of them were waiting to reach the big town. We were not used to being crammed together with strangers.

I closed my eyes again, and I had a dream. I dreamed of a house of rocks, with three rooms and a kitchen. With friends and guavas, only the white ones of course! Of weddings and laddoos. I dreamed of boats, green fields, and a little peace.

Chapter 4

Shivali's Kaala Paani

I didn't think about what we would do once we reached Calcutta. My own family would rather see me and my children dead before they accepted a widowed woman with two children back into their holy, priestly home. I was a stranger to them now. No, not even a stranger. A stranger would be more welcome. After all, all visitors were God. I was the pariah that would be better off dead.

I wondered if his family had found his body. Had they washed all the blood out and made it pure again? Were they surrounding him, crying for the wonderful man he was? After all, he was always showing affection, especially when embracing your neck to draw out your breath. He gave gifts directly to our faces. Perhaps the sweetest words were spoken through clenched teeth, whispered as you felt your life start to leave your body. He was the husband, and by default, they thought him wonderful and pure. Their funeral ritual would remain unfulfilled, as who would burn on the pyre with him now? His soul would forever remain without his *saathi* (life partner), untethered and lost.

Not us. And not that life, especially one that was linked to the sacrifice that his fists demanded. And Uma would not be safe with them. If they didn't marry her off immediately, I knew what fate would be in store for her if they had a say. At least with me, Uma would have the chance to live a life without fear, and Hari would lead a life where his worth wasn't linked only to him being a man. The judge of his karma would not be his gender. So many rushing thoughts flooded my mind, making an already crowded space almost impossible to move around in.

When we got off the train, the smell of fish was the compass to follow. My eyes immediately watered before my nose recognized the smell. Reaching the port was the easy part. Everybody in Calcutta seemed to be heading to the port. The thronging crowds brought their own heady, stinky mix of smells. Uma and Hari hung onto me with all their strength. This wasn't a place for children, but it must be a place where Uma and Hari tasted freedom from this life. Few women and even fewer children stood in the crowd. Where were the wives and the children? The throngs were moving in one direction. It looked like a covering or shelter of some sort. People were all trying to get in. Since I didn't know what to do, that was maybe a good place to start. I heard some people say that some men had waited for months to leave. *Months?!* How long would we have to wait?

We couldn't stay in one place for too long or we risked being caught. The fear that lingered in my belly crept up into my throat. What if they found us here? Did I make a mistake by bringing the children to this place? His family were going to find us and take the children from me. If they found me, they would torture me. Death would be better. What if they took Hari and Uma back to their father's family? What had I done?

I was so busy counting my mistakes that I didn't feel Uma's hand leave mine. My hands suddenly felt very empty. Hari was here hidden in my sari, but where was Uma?

"Uma! Uma!" The panic and fear mingled in my throat and filled my mouth with a sour bile taste. "Uma!" I couldn't even hear myself above the crowd's noise. How would Uma hear me? *Bhagwan* (God), help me find Uma!"

I was so scared that my legs wouldn't let me move from where I was standing. Moving was out of the question because the thick throng of hot bodies prevented it. My eyes darted around the crowds, lingering on the tops of heads, burrowing into the walls of brown, but I couldn't see my Uma. Even my twirling on the spot did nothing to help me find her.

I felt the side of my sari being pulled hard and insistently. I started to speak before I looked down toward Hari. "Hari! Let me find Uma!"

As I looked down, Hari said, pointing straight in front of us, "There is Didi, Mama!"

Uma pushed against the bodies as she weaved her way toward us. "Mama! They are saying they need more girls on the boat. They have enough men, but the boat won't leave without more girls."

Uma tugged at my hands and looked up excitedly at me. I was so relieved to see my girl and yet so mad! What if I had lost her too? What if I had lost my only ally, even if she was just a child?

My face twisted with a mix of anger and relief. "Never leave my hand, Uma! We don't know these people or this place." Anger held my love at bay. "What if I lost you!" Uma didn't know that she was both my child and my strength. What would a child know about that?

"But they are saying that they need more girls!" Uma said. Her wide smile revealed her happiness at having found us a way out.

"I don't care! Don't leave my hand! Don't go anywhere without me!"

"I'm sorry, Mama. I won't go anywhere. I just heard them say that they need more girls, so I went to hear them."

Joy hovered tentatively on Uma's face as she waited for my reaction. My gaze softened. She was just trying to help, but the fear of losing her overpowered any notion of gratitude.

"I don't want to lose you, Uma. You are my *jaan* (my life). If I lose you or Hari, I lose my life. *Aatcha* (understand)? Let's stay together."

I felt the tremor of excitement in Uma's hand as we pushed through the crowds. Forcing our way through the people was hard work, and the bodies crushed against ours. The migration of the crowd moved us forward. I could see the front desk, and only a few more people stood in front of us. I saw only one other lady in the line around us. She was two people ahead. She was tiny, with shiny black hair that hung just below the drape of her pink sari. The sari sat on her head tightly, closely guarding the secrets that her mind might hold. I shook myself out of my daydream with a laugh! *Why do I assume everyone is holding a secret?* I couldn't see her face. I wondered why she was here. Was she here with her husband or alone?

"Move! Move back! We first want to see the working men," a guard said. He pushed the woman aside and pulled two men in front of her. "Let the Saab see them first. These men are built for work, not making babies!" His voice sounded like crushing stones, heavy, hard, and dusty.

I pulled Uma and Hari closer to me. These people were not nice. I could feel Hari's body tremble as a slight whimper escaped my little boy. Uma's hands felt sweatier, but she didn't say a word or make a sound. She just held on tighter to my hand. The guard looked at the lady with a leer.

"Can you even have babies? You are so small! Maybe I will find you tonight and teach you a thing or two," he said, grinning as he grabbed her waist.

Everyone heard him. Everyone saw him. Some men laughed, and some men shifted their eyes to the ground. But no one said anything, except the pink sari lady.

Her body may have been small, but her voice was large enough to fill a ship! "Touch me again, and I will cut off your arm. We will see how and what you teach me when you have no hands!"

As she turned around, I caught a glimpse of the most beautiful lady. Her dark heavy brows, smooth forehead, and brown skin were so delicate. I was trapped in awe and so ashamed as I watched her. I had lost some teeth, had a broken nose, hair that I hid, and I had no voice. She was everything, and I was nothing. Nothing with two children. The guard giggled. That was such a weird sound coming from such a large man.

"Don't worry, I will find you tonight. You can teach me then." He giggled again, and his belly rippled with excitement. He winked at the lady and left after making sure that the working men were in front of her. She was now just in front of us.

"Insolent man! I hate these guards," she mumbled under her breath as she turned toward us.

The day was dull and humid. A very Calcutta day. She lowered her eyes and smiled at Uma and Hari. "So nice to see young people in this place! Hello, I'm Tara."

"Tara!" I said the name under my breath. *Tara* meant star in the sky. And she looked like a star, bright and strong.

"Are you just going to look at me, or are you going to tell me your names?"

Tara's words carried a tune as she spoke. I didn't smile back because I didn't want her to see my broken teeth. But I wanted to talk to her.

"I am Shivali, and this is Uma and Hari, my children."

Tara smiled at the children and me and held out her hand. "So good to see another woman. There are not many of us here. As for children, I think you both are the first I have seen in this place."

I was scared to let go of Uma or Hari's hands to take hers. I just looked at her. Did she see the fear and pain in my face or the relief of having someone acknowledge us and talk to us as human beings?

Tara squatted in front of us, pulling up her sari slightly to make the squat easier. Her head was still covered even as she lowered herself. "Hello, Uma and Hari. I am also going on the ship, just like you both and your mother."

Uma looked at her skeptically, but Hari tugged free from my grip and hugged Tara.

"You are coming with us? I am so happy! I thought we were going alone," Hari said. "Mama said a hundred people are going on the boat. I want to see what a hundred people looks like!"

Hari's chatter made Tara laugh out loud.

"Will you be my friend, Hari?"

"I have two friends already: Ram and Sakshi. But you can be my friend too."

"Call me Aunty Tara," she said as she laughed with Hari.

Uma stared at Tara. I could feel Uma's need to hug her, too, but my girl held back and pulled Hari back gently.

"It is ok, Uma. Aunty Tara is a nice lady." Uma relaxed a little bit, but my watchful girl didn't let her guard down fully.

"Are you here alone?" I asked Tara. She seemed to be alone. No one was with her, and no one had been around for all the time we had been behind her in the line.

"I'm married. We came together to get onto the ship. We've been waiting for over a month for it to leave. I haven't seen him for the last two weeks. I got tired of searching and waiting for him. First, I thought the guards took him away or he died, but one of the boys from our village that came with us told me that he left to go back to the village because he got scared. He left me here and went back with a friend he met here. I am not going back to the village. The village means going back to waking up and taking care of everyone and everything, because I'm the *bahu* (daughter-in-law), while no one worries about me." Tara's voice was flat and low without emotion. "This morning, I decided that I was going to the ship alone and that's why I am in this line. I'm lucky that we met."

I liked Tara. I wanted to be like her. Not Shivali. A nobody. Tara hugged me and I let her.

"They need women for the ship to sail. It won't sail without enough women. So, I'm still going."

"Will they take children?" I asked her. I was happy to hear women could go, but children must also be allowed for us all to go to this new land.

"I think so. Especially boys. I heard someone saying that they can work once they grow."

The line moved forward, and soon it was Tara's turn in front. According to the nameplate on the table, the controller's name was Iqbal Siddiqui. It was written in Hindi and Urdu. I understood Hindi but not Urdu. Everyone around us called him *Iqbal Saab* (sir). He was a slight man, thin and tall. I could see his bones sticking out on his collar. His face was lighter brown than most of the people here, and his eyes were kohl lined. The lining took nothing away from the sternness in his face. He wore a long white shirt over English pants, and he was wearing socks and shoes while everyone else wore sandals. His bony neck carried a locket that sometimes got lost in the caverns of his neck. You could see he was uncomfortable when he squirmed in his wooden chair. He looked even more uncomfortable with the jacket that he had on over the shirt. The makeshift covering offered him shade while we all stood exposed. Lucky the day was dull.

"I think his backside has too many bones," Hari whispered to Uma. I smiled behind my hands but still told Hari to keep quiet.

"Are you not already cleared to go? Where is your husband?" Iqbal Saab asked Tara.

"He's gone back to the village, but I still want to go to work."

Iqbal Saab waved Tara to the side. "Yes, but now you will travel as a single woman, and the conditions will change for you. No more house when you land in Port Natal. You will have to stay with all the single people."

Tara turned and winked at me. "We can stay together? Me, you, and the children?"

I nodded and smiled, relieved. We made friends quickly with Tara and now we finally knew someone.

When it was our turn, Iqbal Saab confirmed that he needed more women and girls to join the trip. Hari could come as well. We were going to the new land, but we all needed a medical checkup first. The doctor couldn't care if I was well or not. He checked my teeth—what was left of them—and told me I was fit. Fit for what, I wondered. I had been fit my whole life, but not for the things I wanted.

From that moment on, Tara, Uma, Hari, and I stayed together. We found a space in the corner of the yard away from the crowds, but here you could never really escape them.

Now we waited. Iqbal Saab was generous with his time, and he checked up on us often. I didn't feel this special even on my wedding day! I heard the other ladies say that he was scared that the women would leave, so he kept a close eye on them. The people we were with all spoke excitedly about the money they would earn and send home. Many talked about when they would come back home after five years. They called the arrangement "indenture." Slavery was outlawed but now, legitimately, we could be herded like cattle for five years of paid labor. All we had to do was put our thumbprints on the contract, and we would have housing, money, food, and clothing for the next five years and return home when our indenture period ended. Most people had heard a story about someone who had come back home, so we accepted this to be true. The Coolie Law number fourteen that the English passed in South Africa made it possible for Indians to leave their homeland yet made slavery nearly legal with no consequences.

I didn't know this when I left, but I got to know it more as the years passed.

That night, the guard came looking for Tara. He was drunk. You could see it in his walk and smell it on his clothes. Tara told him to leave. She wasn't afraid of him, but he wouldn't go. He tried to grab her, but she bit him on the cheek hard and broke the skin. He screamed so loud that the children woke up. I gathered them, and we sat very quietly as Tara pushed him away. He left, but even Tara said that he would come back. Of this, we were sure! He had already marked Tara as his property.

What we didn't expect was him coming back with another guard the next night. He wasn't drunk this time and was ready to take what he thought he was owed. Tara screamed for me to take the children far away. I took them deeper into the corner. The darkness provided more cover. So much noise, and yet no one said anything or tried to help. There was definite curiosity about what was happening. I saw faces peering out of corners, from behind shawls. Curiosity wasn't action. No one wanted to confront the guards. That just spelled trouble.

Uma said, "Mama, we have to help!"

I just held her down and covered Hari and her with my sari.

They took Tara away. The guards cackled about teaching her a lesson tonight. After moments of madness, everything became silent. Uma looked at me. "Why did you not help? Why did you let them take her away?"

How did I explain to Uma that I had to make choices for us to survive even if it meant we couldn't save our friends? I saw the anger in Uma's eyes when she asked the question. A little more of the joy was stripped away from her small face.

It was early morning. The time when the sky blushed pink as it welcomed the sun into its home. When my eyes opened, Tara was sitting in front of me. Was it even possible that such a tiny body could look even more shrunken? Tara almost disappeared into the light, and she sat there for more than half the day. The children avoided her. The aura of sadness held onto her like a cloak. When Tara finally got up from her spot, she looked for Uma and Hari first. They both crept into her lap and sat with her for the longest time.

Tara looked at me and said, "I'm fine. They can take everything, but they can't take what isn't theirs. I'm determined to get on the ship."

Tara and I held hands and hugged, and sadly I realized that being a woman in this world meant sacrificing so much and still knowing what wasn't up for auction—my courage, my determination, and my children.

The days played out the same for weeks. We spent the days waiting for the evening and spent the nights waiting for the morning. The holding yard was large and fit more people than I had ever seen before. More arrived every week. We knew that Iqbal Saab was waiting for the full number of men and women before the ship could sail. I noticed that when people first came to the yard, they wore bright colors. Red, orange, green, and blue, but all the colors looked brown after a few weeks. The color was stripped from us as we waited. We became a sea of brown that lacked any consideration of humanity, just merchandise to be traded. People arrived gaunt and became even thinner waiting for the ship to leave. Was this because we ate very little or because we lost a bit of our souls in this place? The merchandise must be healthy, yet we ate only once a day. We were given rice and dhal on most days with an occasional vegetable. Most people complained because they were used to eating fish. I saw fish sometimes cooking in the corners. People traded themselves for food. The children managed to scavenge a bit of food here and there.

THE STORY I TOLD MYSELF

Uma somehow always came back with something more. I was more comfortable with her wandering a little away from us now. She wandered with Tara and had become good at finding vegetables growing around us.

The nights carried anxiety for Tara. The guard came at least every few days, and we didn't know which day he would make an appearance. This carried on for a few weeks until one day we stopped seeing the guard altogether. After a few weeks, we heard that he had died. They said he went mad and started frothing like a dog. He couldn't hurt Tara nightly anymore. That was all that mattered. But she still had to deal with what happened. Her smile was still there but was vacant and hollow now. She and Uma searched for food together and helped us stay fed.

There were few women, but we had started to see more coming into the holding yard. Most were nice. Mostly they stuck to their husbands because the yard was scary for an unattached woman. Tara made friends with most of them, and slowly we all tried to make the food go further, last longer, and feed more bellies.

Every night music was played with songs sung of stories in faraway places, of lovers waiting to be reunited, of lovers wanting to share one more moment with their beloved. My favorite was "*Balam, ek raath rahi jaana* (Lover, stay for one more night)." Tara liked this song and sometimes I heard her humming it. I often wondered if she was thinking about her husband or maybe someone else? I liked the song because it was playful, but I didn't lament for my husband at all.

I, too, had a song to sing, one I performed in the arena of my mind. A song of betrayal, a song of adventure, a song of a new beginning. No one heard this song. But it was strong. The song bound us, gave us hope, and brought us a joy that was scared of the unknown journey that lay ahead but still thrilled for the adventure that we would have. Another song lamented among the people. This was a song for the tainted souls that left their land of birth and crossed the ocean to start a new life. A lament for the loss of purity now that we were breaking the bond that had anchored our souls to this land of gods. Our very existence was linked to our land of birth. When we crossed the forbidden Kaala Paani, what would happen to us through the cycle of life and birth?

The rituals had already begun.

"Madam, let's do a prayer for you and your children so that your souls remain pure, only two rupees."

What did they know? My soul was already tainted. I killed a person. No ritual was going to take that away from me or my children. Where was the ritual to save us when he was demanding blood?

Had someone said "Madam, two rupees and we can take away the threat to your soul from murder," I may have considered it. The temple priest told me not to be afraid of the Kaala Paani. I believed him. This Kaala Paani may have been the place to lose my soul, and for that, I was grateful.

These rituals were meaningless to me, but I already knew we would be doing this in the new land. We worried more for our souls in the afterlife than we cared for the people around us. This would be a new way of living. I wondered if our souls would reattach to this land when we came back. But I didn't think the three of us were coming back. Our souls would forever remain on a new path.

Four months passed as we sang, lamented, prayed, and hoped that no one would come looking for us. We were lost in the crush of Brown bodies waiting for a power to tell us if we could go on living, go on breathing. Uma, Hari, and I had one shining hope: Tara. She made this all bearable. Tara had begun vomiting. She thought no one saw her and didn't say anything about being sick. I didn't say anything either. *Maybe she's pregnant?* After seeing her color drain even more and her eating slowly stop, I finally said to her, "You have to eat, for the baby at least."

Tara's hallow laugh was different from earlier. "This is not a baby, Shivali. The guard gave me his illness. Soon I will go mad like him. Promise me that you won't let me froth at the mouth for all to see."

On the day Tara died, Uma went out on her own to find some more food. She didn't see Tara die. The other guards took her away very quickly, and we didn't even get to mourn her. That was the way of the holding yard. We only had tradeable value. When Uma asked about Tara, I told her that Tara had died.

Uma looked me straight in the face and said, "She was our friend, Mama. You could have helped her."

Uma was right. Maybe I could have done more that night.

The days passed as we tried to keep Tara alive in our minds. When we had enough women to make the quota of twenty-five percent, the SS *Umzimkulu* was ready to leave with all of us on board. The year was 1887, and we were severing all our bonds with our birth land. Hari, Uma, and I huddled together as we found a place to sit on this English ship leaving for a land of hope: South Africa. The ship was packed to capacity, a wash of fabric from dhotis and saris everywhere on the lower decks, all still a dusty shade of brown.

Hari asked Uma, "Is this what a hundred people looks like?" His eyes widened in surprise.

"More like three hundred, Hari, I think." Uma fidgeted with her hair.

Three hundred people would be all together here for eight weeks. Their noise had its own strange rhythm—an orchestral hum that was made up of ritual, fearful prayer, excited chattering, and silence. *Let's hope the Kaala Paani cleanses my soul from my crimes.*

Chapter 5

Uma's Secret Blue Stories

Shanti and I were best friends. We always went to the river. The stones there were big and flat. We stretched out on them and looked at the clouds while our feet dangled in the cold water. Shanti had funny toes. Her baby toe was small and stubby and overlapped her other toe. She hid her feet in the water so that no one would laugh at them. I laughed anyway because her toes were very funny! I loved putting my feet in the water because it felt like someone was rubbing them. The water was so relaxing. On a hot and sticky day, it felt so cool, and I loved hot and sticky days.

The river was my most favorite place in the whole world. I can't remember a time when I didn't know about this "Neel" river, the blue river. The water was so brilliant blue, the same color as the eyes of the strange man that came to talk to Mama once when Baba was gone on the farm. Mama didn't even look at him. I didn't understand anything he said, but his eyes were strange. That was the first time that I saw someone that looked so different from us. Baba was so angry that day because he didn't want Mama to talk to anyone. He said that talking was for people with brains and not for Mama. But he told Shanti's father that the English were looking for people to work on a sugarcane farm far away. He said that the man was a *firangi* (foreigner)! Shanti told me, and we both wondered if firangi was a good or bad word.

When Baba got angry, I would go to be alone by the Neel River. But mostly I played with Shanti. Shanti and her family lived close to us, almost our neighbors. They were close enough for us to hear Shanti's father scream at her mother, and close enough to hear the pots falling all over but still far enough for Hari and me not to hear what he said. All the fathers in the village were so angry. Shanti's mama and mine were always scared.

There was a patch of soft, light-green grass, just one small patch. A giant peepal tree (sacred fig or bodhi tree) gave the grass shade and made it the best spot for us to play. The sun played hide-and-seek with the leaves of the peepal tree. The grass looked so pretty when that happened. The rocks of the river were so close to the grass patch. We played so many games! Hide-and-seek (like the sun and leaves), and we had fun playing in the river. We loved to dry off on the rocks when we were done dangling in the water. Sometimes the sun was so strong that the grass got dry and hard, but the peepal tree leaves still played with the sun.

My favorite time, though, was when Mama came to our spot under the tree. She told us about kings and queens and about a warrior so strong he could swallow the sun! Mama loved to tell us about Krishna, the cow herder who danced with all the girls in the forest and played his flute for his best friend Radha. Shanti said we were the girls dancing with Krishna. Mama sang and clapped while we danced. I wanted to be like Sita, the goddess queen who is incredibly strong and powerful.

When she could, my mother brought her book—her voice when she read was so mesmerizing. She sounded like she was singing. The book was sometimes hard to understand, and that was when I loved my mama the most. She told us the stories so that we could understand the lessons of the Ramayana. That was the thing about her, her stories were pretty, and I understood them. We didn't tell anyone that Mama read the story. It was our secret. Mama said if anyone found out, we wouldn't be able to come here and hear stories anymore. No one would allow us, and I knew Mama was right. We saw how angry Baba got just when Mama talked to anyone. Shanti, Hari, and I didn't tell anyone.

Hari brought Ram and Sakshi there sometimes to hear the stories too. Mama told Ram and Sakshi not to tell anyone. We all loved listening to Mama's stories because everyone else was too busy to be with us. We would all keep the secret if it meant we could have Mama all to ourselves. I didn't like it so much when Hari brought Ram and Sakshi, though. They had their own secret place to play, and Shanti and I had ours. But I did like it when Sakshi brought mithai for us—then it was a good day. Even the birds loved it when Sakshi brought sweets. We listened to stories, ate sweets, and played in the blue water. If we left a few crumbs, the birds would swoop in to eat them and leave just as fast! Hari and I loved watching the birds. Shanti feared them because she thought they might peck her. She was mad; the only thing the birds would peck at was the crumbs. They would leave, but they always came back. They never left us forever. Even Shanti liked that about the birds.

I thought about the Neel River a lot. I missed the blue water, the green grass, the tree, and my mama's stories under the tree. I missed Shanti and her funny toes. Mostly, I missed us looking at the clouds and imagining being queens and dancing to Krishna's flute.

We were surrounded by blue now, but the big water was blacker than blue in the nights and sometimes in the day too. There was no grass or trees, but at least Mama still had stories to tell us. We heard stories from others too. Last night, I heard a short man with the big, bushy beard say that it was his birthday. He was happy, and his friends were happy. They laughed and danced. His laugh sounded like thunder and wind as his words rolled over the black waters in waves. I heard him talk about the *khet* (farm) of his family and how hard he had worked on the farm. He told the others about how many girlfriends he had before he got married. Their laughter and scoffs were loud. He told everyone how much he loved his wife. She was the best wife ever, and better than all the girlfriends! The men called him Gopal.

Mama tried to stop us from hearing what they were saying, but they were so loud! To distract us, Mama told us the story about how Krishna the cowherd was born in the thunder, rain, and lightning. When I closed my eyes, I thought I was back by the Neel River. The same feeling but a different place.

"Mama, do all the queens, kings, and gods have to have something bad happen to them first? Sita, Ram, Krishna, everyone has something bad happen to them. Is this the only way for them to be queens and gods?" I asked.

This was troubling me. Even in the stories, for anyone to be very happy, they must first have had so much sadness and trouble. Their mothers and fathers must have betrayed them or left them. Mama said that sometimes people have hard things happen, but it makes them stronger, and then they know how great they can be. Then they know that they can be queens, kings, and gods. I didn't know if I really wanted to be a queen like Sita then, because I didn't want more bad things to happen to us. I didn't want to be great. I just didn't want to keep secrets anymore or fight so much to just live.

Mama, Hari, and I watched the men from our spot on the deck. The ship had five levels. The open deck was where the captain and workers watched the sea. The deck immediately below was where the English men stayed. It was the officer's quarters. Only certain Indians were allowed to go up to that deck. The officer's deck also had the officer's dining room and lounge where the English ate, drank, and were happy with no sad times or troubles. I heard the birthday man say that the lounge was the best room he had ever seen. All leather and carpets. With large chairs and lots of books. Even Mama said she would have liked to have seen the books!

Below the officer's deck was the kitchen. There the food was prepared for the officers and the Indians but in separate kitchens. The one for the officers was smaller than the one for all of us. People complained in whispers that the officer's kitchen had all of the best food that we didn't get to have. I would have liked to taste some of that someday. The Indian kitchen was huge with large pots to cook for more than three hundred people. We were used to eating rice and dhal. In the beginning of the journey, we had some vegetables, but that finished halfway through the trip. I liked yellow dhal. It was easy to eat, and I felt full, but it would have been nice to have something else. I thought about Aunty Tara often. I liked her so much. She was like Sita, a warrior. I liked how she and I would go out into the holding yard to find something else to eat. She also had bad things happen to her. Was she a god now? But no one was praying to her.

The floors below the kitchens were where the Indians slept. The fourth deck was for all the single men. No women and children slept there. It was so crowded and very loud. Often, we heard fighting. That deck couldn't fit all the men, so some of them slept on the fifth floor with the women, children, and married couples. The married couples were nice, except when fighting happened. Broken noses and open cheek gashes were common for us to see. We had claimed a small, dark and damp space against the wall, and that was ours now.

Each adult person was given a straw sleeping mat and a thin blanket when we boarded the ship. Adults only because they would be able to work and that made them valuable. Hari and I had no mat to sleep on or blanket to cover ourselves. It was so hot on the lowest deck, so we didn't need a blanket. Hari and I slept on the mat, and Mama slept on the blanket. I used to love the hot and sticky days, but this was just too hot. The nights were the worst when we couldn't sleep.

When it was so hot in the day, I sometimes tried to take Hari on the open deck. But Mama told us never to go without her. Hari and I would go for a little while before Mama came back from her job. Mama didn't know that Hari got scared in this place when she wasn't with us. It could get so dark, and so we walked about just to do something or just to be in the open air. Oftentimes, Hari and I didn't leave the spot at all during the day. Then, we played games. We imagined we were building the house with Ram and Sakshi. We talked about what we would do when we reached the new land. Hari wanted to plant a white guavas farm. We laughed so much because we didn't even know if the new place would have guavas. Hari asked me what I wanted. I didn't know. Maybe a river with a tree. And no trouble. (I didn't tell Hari that.)

When they gave us the mat and blanket, the man helping Iqbal Saab also told Mama that she would work cleaning the Indian kitchen. They told Mama that her job was to scrub the rice pots clean. Every morning, Mama went to work. She came back late because they had to clean the pots for the next day. Mama did her work scrubbing the kitchen and came to find us when she was done. She brought us food, which we ate quickly. Mama said we were fortunate that she cleaned the rice pots because rice got stuck to the bottom of the pot and got hard and dry, and no one ate that. Mama cleaned out the pot and kept the hard rice. That kept our bellies fuller, but we were always hungry. We probably looked like the birds we used to watch eating by the river. They ate so fast, almost afraid that someone would take the food away before they finished. Hari and I loved to watch the birds play around the trees and the river. They flew away but always came back. *Are we like the birds? Maybe we are leaving our home, but we will come back someday?*

Aunty Tara was always on my mind, especially when I took Hari on our walks around the boat. She was so fun, and she always made sure that we had enough to eat, to smile about, to laugh about. Hari and I walked and talked to keep him from feeling scared but also to find something extra to eat. We went walking one day, and I wanted to see the officer's deck. I knew they wouldn't let us in, but maybe we could see from the outside? We were so small, and no one even knew we were around. Also, the boat was so busy in the morning that no one even noticed two birds fluttering in their path. Hari's hands shook with excitement. As we stood outside the entrance, Aunty Savitri (the birthday man's wife) saw us. I thought she was going to be angry with us. Mama was always angry when we did something she said not to do, but Aunty Savitri just smiled and said children need some fun. She took us into one of the rooms. I had never seen anything like it, and I couldn't believe the big, white bed! The floor had a soft, gray carpet—not like our hard floor. We didn't stay long. Aunty Savitri said we must not be there for too long in case someone found us, and then we all would be in big trouble! Before we left, Aunty Savitri gave Hari and me something from the table. It tasted like mithai. Our first taste of English sweets! Hari and I remembered this taste forever. But we never spoke of it in front of Mama, and Aunty Savitri didn't say anything either.

I don't know when it started happening, but I started to pull out my hair whenever I got scared. It made me feel safe to do something. I was looking at my hand now, and my hair was once again in my palm. No matter how much I tried, I couldn't stop pulling out my hair. Mama got so mad with me when she saw the patches, and she said no one wants to marry a bald girl. That didn't sound like a bad thing. I didn't want to ever get married. I didn't want to be like Mama or Aunty Tara. I wanted to hide myself and be safe with Mama and Hari forever.

Mama's tummy had been sore twice on the ship. This trip was so long and just felt like it would never end. When her tummy hurt, there was always blood everywhere. When Baba used to look for her,

46

Mama always tried to hide her blood. We were always hiding—the blood, the stories, the officer's deck, ourselves, and even the knife. If we hid ourselves, then nothing bad could happen to us. Not everyone wanted to be a god or goddess. It was too hard.

Chapter 6

Shivali to Coatwali—Her Sky Gaze

I don't know when I stopped looking at my feet. Before, it was easier not to make eye contact with anyone. If I looked up, I never knew what was coming for me. When I got married, even my brother told me never to raise my eyes. Women didn't need to look up. What was there to look up to and to look forward to? Children? Those came from down below. It was never our place to look up. That was for the men in our home. My place was under my husband's feet. I lived in his shadow, as his shadow, and when he knocked me to the floor, the dust in my mouth reminded me that my place was under his feet. But now I saw blue sky and water. I couldn't remember when I started looking up. When I started seeing the open sky and more than the black emptiness in the tomorrow.

The breeze felt soft on my skin and tasted salty on my tongue. The smell on the open deck was one of freedom, and the cacophony of loud sounds was so welcoming in its overwhelming obscurity. The open water, stretching out for miles in front of me, comforted me. The warmth of the sun on my face reminded me of Baba when he held my chin in his hand, firm, hot, and always present. I was guilty of such a sin, yet I was so happy when I felt the sun. Its orange and gold tried to forgive me every day and gave me hope that we could start again and live again. But every night I relived my actions, my sin. Once we crossed the Kaala Paani, would I be freed from the nightmare torture of killing my children's father? If my soul was no longer pure, now that I was crossing the Kaala Paani maybe his death didn't matter anymore? When I felt the sun on my face, the guilt receded and didn't consume me. That was the work of the night. The job of the day was hope and a prayer for my children's changed destinies—not for my tainted soul.

No one looked at me. I disgusted everyone. Fear came later. Disgust defined their first thoughts of me. I had lost some teeth, and my nose had not healed well. The sun couldn't reach some parts of my face anymore. My nose was bent in the middle, and the tip bore toward my left hand. My hair had grown out, but I cut it again. People were afraid of my short hair. *Is she a woman without her long hair?* All these definitions of who I must be and what I must look like to be accepted by them. Sometimes I thought it would be easier just to be what they wanted: long-haired, quiet, eyes cast down, hands down, illiterate, and manageable. But I was, for the most part, all that. That got me here, though. A woman who killed, a widow, and a mother with two children searching for safety. But I hated what that made me. I must have been something else.

I liked that they were afraid. They stayed away from me. I heard the other people whisper that my eyes were the most frightening, because they were huge, dark, and round. It was good that they knew what they looked like. It meant that these eyes were not downcast and looked them in the face. These men couldn't handle eyes that met theirs directly. My eyes held my secrets buried deep, hidden from view. The deeper the secrets, the darker and wider the pools. Even Uma and Hari were scared when I was angry. When I was angry, the secrets morphed into demons that tried to escape through my eyes, widening the pools and exposing my torment.

The fifth deck was a violent place. Fights among men and the rape of women and men were regular events with consequences that would haunt us forever. Fights over food were commonplace, and they could get nasty. I saw men stabbed badly over a spoon of extra rice. Some men (and women) started to notice that I was bringing the charred, blackened, hard rice back for the children. You noticed what your thoughts were focused on the entire day, and sometimes you saw what wasn't there. Everyone was hungry, hungrier than they should have been. The English had a funny way of keeping us healthy when we ate so little. And the children got even less because no one knew what price the farmers were willing to pay for them. It was funny how the life of a child hung in the balance when someone was weighing up how much they were worth.

I remembered a story that my baba used to tell us about a king who gave his subjects the value of their queen in gold. Every year, after harvest, he would make the queen sit on a scale, and they would weigh up the gold to balance it. The heavier the queen, the more gold the people got. It was in the people's best interest to keep the queen fat, so they fed her all the time. You would think it was in the English's best interest to keep the children fed, but their value, their weight in gold, hadn't been established yet. Funny thing this "value." Uma and Hari were invaluable to me but of no value to these English. What was valuable and to whom?

What the men didn't know was that I had been watching them too. I heard their mumblings, and I saw their feverish glances at us. I knew that we would have to be ready. I always kept the knife not far from me. My darkened savior was always by my side. The tension grew over a few weeks because two young men kept watching us. Hunger was escalating for everyone. With hunger came anger. The knife sat snugly against my breast. Ready in wait, not for *if* it was needed, but for *when.*

The day I had to use the knife was a rough day. My stomach churned like the seas that boiled over for the entire day. No sun, just wind and rain. I returned to our place on the deck around the same time that I came back every day. It was late, and I knew Hari and Uma would be hungry. I had just gotten to the deck when one darker skinned older boy grabbed my hand, pulled my sari, and tried to grab the wrapped rice. I stabbed him in his arm. But I didn't just stab him; I twisted the knife deep as I looked into his eyes. Blood erupted from the wound, and he screamed.

I waited for everyone to rush at me, but everyone was used to fighting so no one did anything. And I didn't say anything. I didn't scream or shout. I just twisted and twisted the knife. Deeper and deeper until I found the bone, and then I stopped. Hitting the bone awakened me from my trance and made me realize what was happening. The boy had stopped screaming and had fallen to the ground, whimpering. The young boy, not more than eighteen years old, hungry, and frightened not only of the English but also of this woman who protected her children. Savitri and her husband, Gopal, came to us tentatively, scared of me and scared for the boy. Savitri held my hand gently while Gopal picked up the boy, carried him in his arms, and took him to his mat. His friend hid in the corner shivering and was too scared to speak.

"His name is Mohan, Shivali. His friend is Madan. They are just children." Gopal spoke over his shoulder as he tried to make the boy comfortable.

I saw the disgust in the set of his shoulders. "I know that I hurt the boy, but what could I do, Savitri?"

She didn't answer immediately, just held my trembling body. I couldn't stop my shaking. Savitri knew about Tara, how she died, and what happened in the holding yard.

"I have to protect my children," I said. I saw Uma and Hari looking at me. Hari's eyes were wide with fear and shock and ringed with red, but Uma's eyes showed nothing. She walked up to me, took the knife, wiped it, and gave it back. Then she sat down next to me and held Hari tightly, their hands melting into one. Uma scared me. She was emotionless. *How could she just wipe the knife and not cry or show any fear?*

Savitri said, "Let me go check on the boy and make sure he's ok. He's just a boy. Shivali, you shouldn't have done that."

I held Savitri back and asked her to sit with Uma and Hari. "I have to talk to him, Savitri. I must make this right if I can."

I walked to the boy. He was still whimpering and taking shallow breaths. He tried to get up, to run when he saw me coming toward him. But Gopal calmed him down, or rather held him down. He was in no condition to stand, let alone to go anywhere.

"I'm sorry I hurt you, son. I didn't mean to hurt you so much, but I'll do whatever it takes to protect my children and myself."

The boy fainted, and I wasn't sure he heard anything I said. Baba had told us that the best thing to do when we got a deep cut was to put fire on it so that it burned up all the demons that might sit in the wound. I told Gopal, and he rushed to the kitchen to bring some of the lingering coal. It took some time for Gopal to come back. In all that time, the boy lay in my arms, Uma and Hari sat with Savitri, and stillness enveloped us all. His friend just blended into the shadows of the night. I cleaned Mohan's wound, pressed the coal in the cut, and wrapped it tightly with a cloth. He screamed like I had stabbed him again, and my tears finally came for the damage I caused this child. The wound might get infected, but the bone wasn't broken, so I would clean it often. His screams stopped abruptly as he passed out. My tears took longer to stop, and when they did, they promised to weep only when Mohan was better. Silence enveloped us all once again.

Later that night, I heard Mohan screaming in pain or maybe fear. Perhaps both. Gopal and Savitri brought the two boys to sleep near them. I saw them clearly now—motherless children trying to survive on this ship, trying to survive this journey, hoping the new land would bring more hope than the journey. It took a while for Madan and Mohan to trust me. Trust and friendship with the children came much easier. Uma and Hari made friends with these boys. Every evening, I opened Mohan's wound, cleaned it, and checked for infection. Mohan's left arm would always be slightly weaker, but it healed well over time. He stayed away from coal and knives. I came to know from Gopal that Mohan's parents didn't know that he had left for Calcutta. Madan was Mohan's cousin, and they both had run away together. Gopal said that they left because there was nothing in the village. Starvation was a real monster, and many would rather face an unknown fate than certain death. The charred rice fed four more mouths from that day forward. Gopal, Savitri, and the boys. Gopal, Savitri, and I ensured the children ate. Our stomachs filled watching their hunger appeased or at least lessened.

Mohan never lost his fear of me. His body trembled whenever I was near. His shoulders stooped even when he ate. He ate like a scared bird. Madan was scared, too, but with less trembling. One morning after the wound healed, I sat down next to Mohan. It was early, and everyone was sleeping. The fifth deck was cold this morning. I always rose earlier to make sure Hari and Uma were prepared for the day before I went back to the kitchen. Not too much to do, but it was something for me to feel like I mothered them. It had also become my routine to check on Mohan and then Madan even while they were asleep.

On this day, Mohan had awoken earlier. When I sat down next to him, I could sense his terror. His skinny body trembled, but he didn't move away. I took the hand of his scarred, weakened arm in mine, and brought it onto my lap. His hand was limp, too afraid to carry any strength, too afraid to put up any resistance, or perhaps too afraid to let someone be a comfort. I let my hand be the strength to hold us both. I cast my eyes down at our intertwined fingers and then looked at Mohan. He had long fingers, like he was meant to play the veena or sitar (Indian musical instruments). His nails were dirty, and this boy trembled beside me, the woman who stabbed him.

"I am so sorry I hurt you, Mohan. I was scared you would kill me, and no one would be left for my children. I was scared that you would hurt them. I never wanted to cause you so much pain." Tears flowed as I held his hand. A man's hand with a boy's tremble. A musician's fingers with laborer's nails. "I am so sorry. Forgive me."

Mohan stared at me for a long time, and then sobs slowly racked his body. His fingers tightened around mine. Slow sobs released tidal waves of loneliness, of fear, and of sadness. I held him for the longest time. As we sat together, I thought that nothing was as it seemed. Right could be wrong and wrong could be right. The moment determined which was which. Mohan and Madan were hungry children trying to eat, and I was a mother trying to protect my children. Who was right and who was wrong? And who was I to judge or give justice?

Between sobs, Mohan told me about his mother and father. That he and Madan came from the same village. They were cousins. They ran away from home to go to work on the sugarcane fields in the new land. Their parents didn't know where they were. They didn't tell them that they were leaving, but now they missed home and wondered if their parents missed them. Mohan told me he missed his *maiya*'s (mother's) roti and chai. I held him tighter and let him cry for his mother. I hoped Hari never had to cry for me with so much sorrow.

"I miss Maiya so much. I miss *Pita-ji* (Father). If I could go back home today, I would."

I sent a silent message to Mohan and Madan's parents. "Your boys are safe. As much as I can, I will look after them with at least roti and chai and let them know a mother's love as best I can."

As days passed, Madan and especially Mohan slowly lost their fear of me. They were the best storytellers, albeit with a lot of exaggeration. They told the story of the wild woman from the fifth deck to other men, and the story spread that I wasn't afraid to hurt anyone, that I stabbed Mohan with a knife, and that I almost severed his arm. He had the scar to prove it. I encouraged Gopal to say that he saw this too. It made the story even more credible. What Madan and Mohan did for me with their stories I cannot repay. They created a fierce, scary Shivali, one that everyone kept away from. This story and the way I looked made it hard to make friends, and honestly, I liked it that way.

I thought this ship might be safe, but women were not safe anywhere. Since there were so few women on this ship, we were easy prey. It had been weeks since we had seen land, and it was making the men crazy in the head. They were drunk often. The officers liked to give the men alcohol at the end of the day. They liked the men being dependent on them. That was when they were at their most frightening, and no one was safe from the madness in the head. Savitri said she slept with only one eye shut because she knew men roamed the ship at night, even on the fifth deck. For once, my looks were our savior. I didn't think anyone would come looking for me, but I was always scared for Uma. She was only six years old, but dealing with men who were crazy in the head meant we must be careful. We slept together, all seven of us with Uma, Hari, Savitri, and me in the middle and Madan, Mohan, and Gopal around us.

I knew that Uma and Hari sometimes went for walks on the officer's deck. When Savitri told me that she found them on the deck, I was so angry! What if something happened to them? What if they got caught? I rushed to scold them, especially Uma. She should have known better. When I thought I lost Uma in the holding yard, my heart couldn't survive. It was Gopal who stopped me from scolding Uma again.

"Shivali, Uma is a good girl. Let her be. We will watch over her. This little girl takes on so much."

Savitri and Gopal promised me that they would watch over them. Mohan and Madan kept a close watch on my two children as well. They shared the effort to keep them safe. But truth be told, I was also curious about the officer's deck. I also wanted to see the rooms that Savitri and Gopal spoke of. So, I went to the deck early one morning when I knew the officers were having breakfast. I couldn't believe that this world existed on the same ship on which I was travelling. Anger and curiosity took turns playing with my mind. We didn't even have enough mats for the children to sleep on, but here, on the same ship, were rooms with beds and carpets. Why was that even possible? *Are we not human too?*

And then I was fascinated by the lounge. Books lined the walls. How I wished I could read them. These books were in a language that I didn't understand—English. I vowed that one day I would learn how to read English. This room filled with books was almost as precious as my Ramayana, the one I almost left behind. The only book I ever had. My baba's gift to me. I spent longer than I should have in the lounge. I saw a coat lying discarded in the corner, and I picked it up, just to look at it. And I couldn't put it down. The brown dusty coat wouldn't leave my hands. My mind, already fractured with anger and curiosity, splintered again with temptation. I left with the coat tucked under my sari. The forgotten coat was now mine. I hadn't heard anyone ask for it. I told Savitri that I took the coat. She was worried someone might know it was stolen, but no one missed it. Like so much on the ship, those who had so much didn't know how valuable their things were, while we who had nothing valued even the charred rice at the bottom of the pot.

I had never had a wool coat, or a wool anything. I didn't wear it on the kitchen deck, but I wore it when we were on our sleeping deck. It suited me and went with my short hair. Hari called me *coatwali* (coat lady) mama. Uma laughed and that's what she called me too. When I put on the coat, I felt so protected and shielded. I felt capable and strong. Some people asked why I wore a coat and where I got it from. It only took a few looks of my scary eyes, and people left me alone. I scared them with my damaged face and my coat.

Wearing the coat made me feel like the person I was before I was married to him. That girl was always smiling with beautiful pearl teeth and learning all the time. All girls and boys were taught to read. My father made sure of that. He taught us himself. He always wore his coat and dhoti when he read the stories of Ramayana and *Mahabharat* (great Indian epics). He made sure that we could read the verses ourselves. He always said our salvation lay in being good people who did good for others and who always sought to learn and grow. He wanted all the girls to be able to sing the Ramayana. But we knew that we would be married off as soon as we came of age, so we learned to read, write, and sing for our in-laws. In my case, though, a daughter-in-law who could read and write was dangerous.

My baba died when I was fifteen years old. I was married off then. No one wanted a burden in their home. Another mouth to feed and another body to clothe. All teaching stopped then. I couldn't even practice what I knew already. No one wanted their daughter-in-law to know more than their son. I had to know my place—lower my eyes and feel the dust. Uma was born ten months after my wedding. Any suggestion of reading, or even knowing anything, was met with a counterforce of brute strength delivered personally and directly to any available part of my body, especially when the first child was a girl.

It was a little better when Hari was born. There were celebrations that a boy entered their home, *puja* (prayers), and relatives all coming to bless us for bringing a son into their family. The only blessing I had was from my children. Some of my most joyous times included sitting by the Neel River with Uma and Hari and their friends, telling them stories, singing them songs, and reading them stories. All in secret. Even they knew this was a secret to keep. Sometimes

I wondered how we managed to keep everything quiet. Sakshi, Shanti, and Ram could have told their mothers. I think they may have, but their mothers said nothing. Uma and Hari would never have said anything to him. They knew better. Shanti and Uma loved listening to the stories the most. They loved to act out the dramas of the story over and over again.

My coat reminded me of the time with my baba, of knowing that I was worthy of love. Worthy of learning. I didn't think I would ever take it off. I asked Savitri for Gopal's old dhoti. I thought I would wear a dhoti, too, like my baba. I could feel his strength flowing through me when I put it on. I felt like both a mother and a father. I provided for my children, and I kept them safe. I wanted my daughter and son to learn to read and write, like Baba wanted for me. Standing in the sun with my coat and dhoti, I felt like we would have a different life. I didn't know what working with sugarcane would be like, but I could learn like I learned to read the Ramayana. Like I learned to hide my knowledge. Like I learned to hide my guilt.

More than eight weeks had passed on this ship. We were all much thinner than when we boarded. That's after we had thinned out in the holding yard. The winds blowing across the ship's decks could easily knock us over. Everyone had rings around their eyes—rings of commitment to this journey, this Kaala Paani crossing, and rings that came with the promise of a new land and a new life. The ship would exit with more souls than when we boarded. Sex on a ship gave rise to many pregnancies—children conceived over water, destined to be born in a new land. Where would they belong? India, South Africa, or the ocean? Who knew whether they came from crazy in the head or from love. Did it matter? Megha, one of the pregnant girls, told me that she was raped. Megha was one of the single young women on the ship. She was planning to have the baby and give the baby away if anyone would have it. Megha was a lovely, sweet, bubbly, petite girl when she came onto the ship. Today's Megha was sad and quiet. Today's Megha had seen another side of life and of men.

I saw the captain's first man packing up the captain's belongings. I didn't understand the English men too much, but I could feel that we must be reaching Port Natal. The excitement on the ship was growing. People were talking about what would happen when we arrived. Neither dark eye rings nor near starvation could hold back the palpable feeling of a new start. Gopal and Savitri were also excited but were more scared and nervous now. Savitri heard the officers discussing in the lounge that not all couples would get to stay together. Indian marriages were not legal, so it was easy to separate them at the port. Gopal said that he would rather die at the port, but no one would take his Savitri from him. Hari and Uma both asked me if we would go back home. Hari spoke about Ram and Sakshi. Uma whispered Shanti's name in her dreams. My heart cried for their loss of home and their childhoods. The same heart sang for their future and for new dreams. Durban, the port city of Natal, South Africa, was our new home.

Chapter 7

Hari's Holy Water and Dhotis

Sticky hot. My back and hair are so wet. The heat reminds me of our village at home. When Ram and I used to play, my hair was always wet, especially just before the big rains came. Sakshi used to say that Ram always looked like his mother put the whole pot of oil in his hair. I don't think Ram liked that, but it was funny! When it rained, all our hair looked like we put a pot of oil into it! Mama and Ram's mother didn't like us playing in the rain, but we always snuck outside. Sakshi couldn't come often to play in the rain, because her mother was strict.

I held one of Mama's hands. Uma was holding her other hand. Last night Mama packed all that we had. Uma held the bag, which was really Mama's sari, with all our clothes wrapped like a present. Two pairs of short pants and two shirts for me, two dresses for Uma. Mama was wearing her new coat and dhoti. *Do all other mamas wear saris only?* All the aunties on the boat wore saris, but my mama didn't, not so much anymore. At first, she wore a sari every day on the boat. Then only when she went into the kitchen, now only her coat and dhoti. I couldn't remember when Mama last wore a sari. Sometimes she looked more liked the uncles than the aunties. I felt like she was our mama and baba. We didn't talk about Baba or all the blood at all. When we were in the holding yard, Uma asked me if I missed Baba. I told Uma I didn't want to talk about Baba or the train with anyone. Even Uma. Uncle Madan asked me about our baba one day. I told them that we don't have a baba, and then I went to sit with Uma Didi. They were nice, but I didn't want to talk about Baba that day, or at all.

I wanted to carry the bag and I tried, but it was quite heavy. I could barely lift it! We didn't have very many clothes, so why was the bag so heavy? I asked Mama. With a smile and a wink, she said she had three precious jewels to take everywhere: Uma, me, and her book. I didn't know that Mama had brought her book on the boat. *When did she do that?* All I remember from that day was running to the temple and then running to the train station. I tried to remember when she would have picked it up, but I couldn't. But I was my mama's precious jewel. I liked that! I loved Mama's stories from the Ramayana, but I didn't want to be hidden like the book. The bag also had another dhoti. I was too scared to ask Mama if that dhoti was also a jewel because it was hidden.

Mama took that dhoti from the men sleeping across us on the boat. Aunty Savitri saw Mama. I saw her, and Uma did too. Everyone else was sleeping. I was trying to tell Mama to put the dhoti back, but Uma held me tightly, digging her fingers into my arm. Uma said we must keep Mama taking the dhoti a secret because, if we said anything, they might take Mama away. My arm was still so sore, and Uma's finger marks were still there. It was a purple color now. Uma held me hard. Lucky, I didn't say anything loudly, and Mama was still here, not like Aunty Tara. If Mama went away too, Uma and I would be all alone in this new place.

The sky was gray, and the wind was like fire. The waters around us didn't look green with white foam on top. It smelled like the holding yard in Calcutta, like fish. So many people waited in line to get off the boat, but we were still so far away from the shore! How were we going to get to the land? I couldn't see properly, but I heard people saying that we were far from the land. Madan and Mohan were there with us, too, standing in line. Madan said there was a smaller boat that would take us there, so we all must wait our turn. I hoped we got on the same boat with uncles Madan and Mohan. I liked Uncle Madan; he talked a lot and was nice. He liked me to tell him about Ram and Sakshi. He also made games to play with me and Uma. He described all the weapons that God had, and we guessed which one. Ganesh with a pen. Ram with a bow. Krishna with a flute. My favorite was Shiva with his snake because it sounded like my mama's name. Uncle Mohan was quiet and sat more with Mama. Uma said that Uncle Mohan missed his mama. The man in front of us smelled like the cowshed at home, and the heat held the smell in place where we were standing. I could see the back of his dhoti—all dirty, brown, and wet and stuck to his big legs. I could see through the dhoti and see his hairy legs! Something fell on my forehead. The second drop hit my cheek as I lifted my head to see what it was, and the drops were from the man.

When Baba used to make us pray, he used to sprinkle holy water on my head and face to bless and purify us before we started praying. We weren't praying, but water drops were falling on me. I hoped this wasn't a blessing before we got onto the land. Not with this stinky man's sweat! Mama said we were pure, and we didn't need to make ourselves more pure. I wiped the sweat off with the back of my hand, but my hand was wet too. I tugged on Mama's hand. I was trapped between his legs and Mama's dhoti.

"I can't breathe. The man smells, and his sweat is falling one me," I told Mama.

"We're almost at the end. Little while more. Put your face against my dhoti. Just keep walking," Mama whispered quickly.

I turned my face into Mama's dhoti and let her push me forward. Was she not feeling hot and sweaty in her coat? I could see her face shining. Little more and we would be off the boat. Uma was also trying to move forward. I could see her face too. It was scrunched up, and her cheeks looked filled with something. Her eyes watered, like she was trying to keep that thing inside. She was trying to hide that she wanted to vomit. I wondered if it was the heat, the smell, or the long line that was making her feel sick. Her eyes, though, told me she felt like me. Uma had Mama's eyes. They looked like storms, and when she was mad, the storms were wild. We both just wanted to get off the boat and get away from all the smelly people. Uma also liked to talk with the uncles. But today Uma wasn't talking with Uncle Madan and Uncle Mohan.

The uncles were not troubled by the heat. They were busy talking and laughing with the other people in the line. They seemed excited and asked lots of questions.

"Do you know how they will decide which plantation to send us?" Uncle Madan said.

"When will we know where we're going?" asked Uncle Mohan.

"Do you think we can choose to be together?" Uncle Madan sounded very hopeful and a little scared, I think.

I hoped the uncles were staying with us. They made everyone smile. Especially Uncle Madan. Uncle Mohan, not so much.

The noise changed as the line moved. As we got closer to the end of the boat, I could hear more shouting. The voices sounded scary, like everyone was angry. I hid my face deeper in Mama's dhoti. The pushing stopped, and Mama said, "Uma, Hari, let's get on the small boat. That boat will take us to the land."

Another boat! I didn't want to get on another boat! I was stuck on the edge. My feet wouldn't move. I wouldn't let them. No more boats.

"Hari, just move!" Mama said. Her eyes were mad and round. "Now! Hold my hands. Uma, hold the bag and don't lose it!"

Uma told me not to be a baby and to do what Mama said. Uma was always bossing me, but she was a baby too! Before I thought about what I was going to say to Uma, I stumbled into the boat. The people were pushing, and Mama was trying not to fall with me.

Uma caught me and held my face in her hands. "Soon, Hari, baby, we won't have to take a boat again."

I let Uma Didi hold me as Mama got on with us. Didi put the bag into my lap. It was so heavy! Mama held us both tight. At least the breeze felt nice. It was still smelly, though. I looked for Aunty Savitri and Uncle Gopal, but I couldn't see them. I wondered if they went before us or were maybe coming after? So much was different from home, and now this was different from the first boat. Everything was changing all the time.

When I was so scared, Uncle Madan told me to think about Ram and Sakshi. He said that I smiled when I talked about them. Were they building our house? The one with the kitchen and the rooms for Ram, Sakshi, and me? I wanted to see the house, but I didn't want to get onto a boat again. Maybe they could come and visit me here. When we grew up, maybe we could build a house here together. Uma could stay in our house if she wanted to. Our house would have a lot of space, not like the boat, and a big garden so that no one would have to bury their faces in dhotis or be held so tightly so that we didn't fall. Uma was holding me tightly, just like how I was holding Uma.

I could see the shore now. There were trees everywhere! Everything looked so big and green. There was a big shelter with lots of people outside. Mama said we were here now, and we could get off this boat. No more boats. *Ever.* I heard some voices say, "Let's get the babies off the boat first." Who were they calling a baby? I was my mama's big boy, my mama's jewel! I tried to tell Mama I was not a baby, but she just told me to *chup* (keep quiet)!

Mama got off first onto a big wooden landing. I could see she was trying to stand straight. Uncle Mohan handed Uma and me to her. The boat was swaying way too much. The men were standing, and it was making the boat rock from side to side! Mama took me first, put me on the wooden floor, and then took Uma. Why did I feel like I was falling? My legs and my stomach were all funny. Uma vomited right in front of me. It was the first time I saw her vomit. Mama cleaned Uma quickly with the bottom of her dhoti. I thought her dhoti would smell of vomit now. But Mama didn't care, and anyway we must move quickly.

We fell into another line, just like when we were on the boat. But this time, there was no Uncle Madan or Uncle Mohan in the line. I didn't see anyone we knew. I held Mama so tightly I could feel the material of her dhoti crush in my hands. My head ached. It was so hot. The puddle of smell just became a detour. The line still moved around the vomit and snaked toward the tables with men in front of the big building. There wasn't much talking, like when we waited for the boat. Everyone was quiet. Their eyes looked hopefully at the building. I didn't see any other boys and girls. Uma and I saw a few small boys and girls on the boat. But mostly, their parents didn't let them play with us. Uncle Madan said they were missing out on playing with me, so he was going to play the most with me.

The line ended at a large desk. Lots of people, only men and mostly White people, were standing around the desk. So many White people. Even more than in Calcutta. The head man sat on the desk, and he was the one speaking the most. There was another man standing next to him, and he was the one that was speaking to all the people that came off the boat. When it was our turn, Mama tried to answer the questions, but we didn't understand what the man was saying.

His hands looked so funny. They were smooth like the butter Mama made from the milk. Slightly yellow and looked so creamy. *What kind of hands are those?* They looked like baby hands. Mama said this was where the sugarcane grows and that all the people here worked with the sugarcane. *Will I have butter hands, too, when I work with sugar cane?* My hands already looked like brown sugarcane stalks and not like butter! His eyes were different, and I liked them. They looked like the color of the brown stones in the Neel River. Smooth, like the light going through the stones. He looked like a happy man.

The Indian man spoke after the cream-colored man spoke. He looked like us, and Mama understood what he was saying! I could hear Mama say her name.

"My name is Shivali. Father's name: Tewari. Village: Ishapur."

She said my name. Then Uma's name. They asked Mama where was Baba? She said we came alone. We had no one with us. When Mama said that the people started talking a lot and quickly. We couldn't understand what they were saying. The Indian man took us to another place. He was pushing Uma and me. Mama told him to stop, but he just pushed us even more until we were in a large room. There were some ladies there. Just ladies and us. I heard the man ask Mama why she was wearing a coat. Why was she wearing a dhoti? He laughed and said maybe Mama was a man. When he left, the other ladies came to talk to us. They said that they were also waiting here. After all the men had a plantation to go to, then only would they come for us. I hoped we didn't have to stay too long there like in Calcutta. That was long. I saw Mama talking to an aunty—I think her name was Megha Aunty. I saw she was crying, and Mama was wiping her tears. The ladies spoke nicely to Uma and me, but we were so tired that both Uma and I just wanted to sleep. They gave us some food when the sun was setting but it didn't look or smell nice.

"You must eat, Hari!" Mama scolded me, but my tummy was still sore, and my head still hurt.

"Leave me alone! I don't want to eat!" Mama forced me to eat a little, but it was Uma who fed me. Uma Didi and I tried to eat together. One bite for me, one bite for Didi.

Lucky, it was just one night. The next morning the men took us to the place where people were calling our names to get onto a cart.

Their words were drowned out by all that was around me. All I saw was green. Everywhere you looked there were trees and more trees! It wasn't like home where it was brown with few trees. There was dust all over, but the trees were so big. And I could hear loud noises. They made me feel more scared. *How am I going to live here?* I looked at Uma Didi, and she was also looking around us. But she looked happy. Her eyes were calm. Maybe because she vomited and felt better? Was she not scared like me? I held her hand tighter. I held Mama's hand tighter too. We couldn't tell anyone Mama took the dhoti. Uma Didi and I couldn't be all alone in this green, new place where we didn't know anyone.

Chapter 8

Uma's Birds-of-Paradise

1897

More than ten years had passed since we landed in this English colony of Natal. This land, as sweet as sugarcane, was our home. The sugarcane waved in the wind and looked as vast as the Kaala Paani. Green cane stretched as far as my eyes could see. But my heart stretched back to the Neel River's blue hues. Colors that were light when the waters delicately washed over the stone, and dark in the deeper parts of the river—just like our lives, light in some parts and deep dark and hidden in others. My recollection of our home was now more like a slightly open door with streaks of light bringing flashes of memories, enough to tease the sharp, rough, bloodied edges of my mind to be a tenant, but not enough to hold a permanent space there. Even fleeting glimpses left my memory of the Neel River and clouds unchanged. Sometimes I could smell the grass and the river. The hint of spice and the scent of the mustard fields smelled different from the grass of the green cane. The air smelled sweeter with the perfume of all the flowers. There were times when I caught my breath because I could feel the water over my toes, and a smile ploughed its way through my heart, tickling my lips when I thought of Shanti's funny toes.

I loved my new home, and I was especially fond of our garden in front of the house. I liked the green expanses of gardens more than the oceans of sugarcane. Here, the purple and orange flowers stretched toward the sun and stood tall. I imagined each flower in love and competing for the sun's attention. Who could feel his love first? Who could reach the sun first?! Each flower created space for the next as they formed a ring around our house. Mama planted marigolds at the edge of the fence, and the circular shape of their petals reminded me of little laddoo balls, ready to be plucked and eaten. The marigolds made the fence glow radiantly.

At sunset, our home was bathed in gold dust. It was almost ethereal, as though our house belonged in the story of the Ramayana. And the old wire fences! Tiny pieces of old paper and cloth gently decorated the fence. It was the fence that gave me my first streak of memory; the pieces of cloth and paper reminded me of the prayer flags on the temples around our village. Just like the prayer flags of others became the prayers of everyone, so everyone's trash became our decoration.

Our house was small. There was a tiny kitchen dominated by a hearth, a sitting room that became a hall for all, and two bedrooms, one for Mama and one for Hari and me. The veranda was my favorite part, and it stretched around the entire house. That was where I liked to watch the sunset and bask in the glow of the marigolds. Here, we were hidden from searching eyes. The solitude of a life among the sugarcane had gifted me a full head of black hair. Even after all these years, fear had never left my body and had nestled deep enough not to play hide-and-seek with me. Fear was a permanent resident. If I ever allowed myself to say it out loud, I would say that I never had a say in what or who was permanent in my life. But like old friends or known enemies, we lived side by side in my mind. The dormant seeds of my life had sprung among the rain and sunshine of Natal, and this place had become my field to plough new dreams.

The day we landed here in Durban, I vomited out the entire trip across the ocean. The fear had kept itself wound deeply within my body. Hari's mouth twisted with disgust when I threw up at his feet! Poor Hari, I knew he was so frightened. This new place with its green trees and hot winds scared him. All these new people were confusing, with so many languages spoken. Even more frightening than the boat. When one of the men was asking us if we had a baba, I couldn't understand what he was saying.

"Mama, I don't understand what these people are saying. Why don't they speak like us?" I asked.

"There are so many people here, and they come from all over. We're the only people from our village. So, we might not understand all the time what they're saying."

But Mama knew that all of us speaking different languages was also causing more anger and fights. Misunderstandings, annoyance, and anguish of not being understood made everyone on edge. That was bad, this was worse. More tongues, some that sounded so alien. Not even like an Indian language. I was scared too. The people were so different. Even the Indian people. The men were loud and angry most of the time. There was no kindness in how they spoke to us. Hari said they spoke to the horses better than to us. These men held the start of our new life in their hands, and they shouted. They didn't care for the adults, and they didn't even see the children. They shoved everyone onto the carts. The carts were big and pulled by horses, and they were filled with about thirty people.

Mama was one of only three women that were on our cart. The other two aunties looked young. Mama said Megha Aunty was going to have a baby, and the other aunty's face looked like ours—scared, nervous, and not sure what was happening to us. Her uncle held her hand through the whole trip. Mama held our hands. No one held Megha Aunty's hand. She didn't have a husband. Now I know what happened on the ship, but back then I didn't even ask why Megha

Aunty didn't have a baba. Not having a baba was normal for us. There were no Uncles Madan and Mohan, no Uncle Gopal, or Aunty Savitri. I wondered where they went. They were our only playmates on the boat. Uncle Madan played lots of games with us. More with Hari, but I liked to watch them play. It made me feel calm, and for a little while I could forget all that was happening. Uncle Mohan was quieter and liked to be more with Mama. Although that came later. In the beginning he would not even be in the same place as her. He acted like the air she breathed was poisoned, and he would die if he breathed the same air.

I thought about Aunty Tara a lot. She was my friend. I loved her like I loved Shanti. I missed her. How I wish she were on the cart with us! So many times, I wanted to talk to Mama about Tara Aunty, but Mama's eyes didn't allow you to ask these questions. I knew Aunty Tara would make a joke and make us laugh. She would maybe have said that the big man's belly was like a rice pot! Or that he smelled like the cows after a hot day, sweat mixed with pee. She would have taken away the scariness just by making us feel happy. I loved my mama, but she wasn't a happy person. She didn't play or make us laugh. She was always so serious. All the people talked to Mama, so she was always busy with everyone. I wished she would play and laugh with us like Aunty Tara. But Aunty Tara was gone.

Later as the years passed, I learned from the other coolies that the Coolie Law passed in 1859 long before I was born, and it made it possible for the English to bring in Indian workers to work for five years in Port Natal. They had to "contract" for two terms, so it was only after ten years that they could even start to think about going home. This "law" was all about labor and not about people. What it didn't talk about was giving people dignity and respect.

"Shivali Tewari! Come on, let's go! Get on to the cart." When the tall Indian man, the *sardar* (farm overseer), called our names to go to Thompson's Farm, Mama, Hari, and I were too tired to ask where this place was. We just wanted to reach the place we could finally call home and sleep.

"Come on, let's get onto the cart quickly," Mama said. She wanted us to hurry, but Hari's legs were tiny, and he was tired.

"Wait! I thought your son was older. This boy can't work, and your girl is useless to us on the farm! You are useless, all of you!" The sardar's face was red, his eyes narrowed with accusation, and his voice boomed with a rage that made both Hari and I jump. That was probably the first and only time he saw or acknowledged us.

Mama tried to tuck us behind her as the sardar's face twisted into an ogre's when he spoke. "We paid for able men who could work a full day, not children that we would have to feed. This is nonsense! You are not getting on the cart!" He forced us to the back of the line. His massive body was a wall that we couldn't cross. There was no place for burden, only a place for workers.

But the sardar didn't know my mama.

"Sardar-ji, please can we talk without the children and all these other people?" Mama looked around at all the people staring at us and begged him. "Please sardar-ji."

Reluctantly, he took my mother by her right elbow to the side, away from us. The other women whispered to each other. Nobody knew what was happening.

The sardar listened to Mama. I could see her talking, and he reached out and touched Mama's face. She turned her head, and I saw the look of disgust. At the time, I didn't know what she said to the sardar. We just got onto the cart. Years later, I learned that Mama promised to cook for all the men every evening and work on the farm in the day. She made herself able and valuable by promising to fill the stomachs of men so that they could work harder. I wasn't sure what else she promised.

I still didn't know how the sardar agreed to that, but we got onto the cart. I wished I had seen more of the trip as we made our way to the farm, but Hari and I slept most of the way. The motion of the cart sang us its lullaby as we made our way to Thompson's Farm. The song of the cart was punctured by the sobs of Megha Aunty. She cried all the way there. I tried to speak to her, but she wouldn't even look at me. Megha means cloud, and Megha Aunty felt like a dark cloud. Now I know more about how scared she was. Back then, I was so tired I just wanted her to keep quiet. Mama woke us up when we arrived at Thompson's Farm. The road from the farm entrance to our house was long, dry, and stony. We had traveled so far, over black waters, on trains, yet it still felt like safety was just always so far away.

The last part of this journey seemed the longest and never-ending for me. The sardar showed us the owner's house as we passed. It was a massive white house with beautiful orange, purple, and blue flowers in the front garden. The owner's family stayed there. Two older boys and three younger girls. As we passed their house, I wondered if the girls like to play queens and warrior princesses like Shanti and me. Maybe they had a Neel River where they could look at clouds and sit on the green grass. There was lots of green grass in this place. I thought my Neel River was the best, but I was sure they had a nice one too. Did the children stay with their mama and baba? I wondered what their baba was like. Was he a monster, or kind? Like the uncles on the boat?

The sardar said the older son just returned from London. Where was that? The name sounded so funny in my mouth. Was he like my sweet Hari? Kind, funny, and naughty? And did he love his sisters like how Hari loves me? Did his sisters love him tight so that no one could ever hurt him? Time would play its games with me as it always did, and these answers would all reveal themselves. Later, I would learn that those orange and purple flowers were called birds-of-paradise, and the blue flowers were Hydrangeas that every-one called Christmas flowers. They were now my favorites. The first flowers I saw in Port Natal. Those flowers were my first welcome into my land. They made me feel like a warrior princess was being welcomed home. Hari was happy that the flowers were not red, until he saw the bougainvillea and hibiscus that grew against the fences. The red bougainvillea waterfall fell with grace and abundance over the fence, and the hibiscus was like stars with bright yellow centers. We laughed when Hari declared that he would never have red flowers in his garden and made us all promise not to have red flowers in ours. I teased Hari and said I wanted the waterfall of bougainvillea, and he got so upset! He started to cry, and I had to calm him down. He even made Mama promise that I would not wear red at my wedding. I didn't say anything. I am not getting married. Even a head full of hair could not convince me.

I had seen White people in India, but I had never seen huge Black men. Their skin looked like the polished black stones that I saw next to the river. They were so tall. Most of them smiled as we passed by in the cart. Large grins filled their whole faces. Their eyes were curious, warm, and happy, like Aunty Tara's! I loved their eyes, and I fell so in love with these beautiful people. They all looked like they were in the sun the entire time. We could see the sweat rolling off their bodies, and it made them glisten in the glow of the sun. But there were some men who seemed to be angry with us. We had just gotten here, why would they look so angry?

I was so tired that I didn't worry about that too much. We would learn that these men were just afraid that we would take their jobs. The sardar and owners sometimes played that trick with them, making them think that we were here to take the work. Black men didn't want to work on the farm, and when they did, they did so grudgingly. So, seeing these foreign, Indian people coming to work on the sugarcane plantations wasn't a good omen for them. They didn't want us to be friends at all. It didn't help that the English treated us all like we were not human beings. Hate changed over time as there was enough work for everyone, and we realized we liked each other, but the seeds of hatred were constantly stroked by the English and continued throughout my lifetime. Hari and I grew up alongside Black men and White men. We grew up knowing Indian and Black women, but somehow White women were not too much a part of our lives.

The cart rolled on with its tired and weary load. I closed my eyes some more. I just wanted to sleep. Sometimes I wished I never got up and I could sleep like this forever. Mama's lap was the perfect resting place. Even the excitement of a new home couldn't overcome my exhaustion. Hari seemed to gain a new energy. He was so fidgety. I just wanted him to stop jumping. The cart swayed every time Hari jumped up. The sardar screamed at Hari to sit down. His voice was like a lion's roar, and he brought the fear up into our throats. Hari got so frightened! He sat down rather quietly, and I was secretly happy that he did.

A Zulu man was sitting with us in the cart. He smiled at Hari, eyes crinkling, and his teeth looked white and sparkly. He placed his rough finger against his thick, pink lips, inviting Hari to keep quiet. Uncle Zweli and Hari would remain friends from then on. A Zulu man from Port Natal and a small Brown boy from India both excited and confused by this new land.

Chapter 9

Uma's Spice Bride

1890

Dust and mud, sweat and spice were what I recalled most about the first years on the farm. Mud covered our walls with its comforting earth, and the spice's perfume decorated our home with pride. Spice was the bride of Port Natal, settling into a new home, making a picture-perfect place even more beautiful with its new flavor.

Most of the workers stayed in large, mud-brick houses with many rooms, but with few bathrooms. On Thompson's Farm, there were ten line houses, with each house holding ten to twelve people—ten people when there were only adults, but twelve with children. Our house had twelve people. It was the last house, which meant that it was the furthest from the river, but it also had a large open grassy area next to it. The area was wet most of the time, and we were always muddy when we came back into the house. This became Hari's playground, and he would spend hours playing outside. When he came in, Mama would always shout at him to clean up. But she was working on the plantation most of the time, so Hari came in, and I cleaned up so that Mama wouldn't be mad. I didn't understand why Mama would be mad because she was always dusty when she came back from the sugarcane, but I cleaned anyway. We didn't want to make Mama angry, especially when she was always tired.

The mud was wonderful—it was wet enough to let things start to grow, but dry enough so that the plants could continue to grow, and fun enough that Hari and I could play among the green plants. Hari's favorite game was *ghar-ghar ki khel*, or house-house game. In this game, Hari and I built a house with a kitchen and two rooms. Hari would bring sticks and we would use the mud to make the walls. I would always decorate the house. Hari was always quick to tell me to only use the white and orange flowers. He didn't want any red ones. We would play that Hari would go to work in the day, and I would stay at home. And our friends would come to visit, especially Sakshi and Ram. But I didn't want Shanti to visit. I would be too sad if my imaginary Shanti came to visit since my real Shanti wasn't here. So, we played with imaginary Sakshi and Ram.

"Didi, when I grow up, I want to marry Sakshi."

Hari always said he wanted to marry Sakshi, but I think he wanted the mithai more than the wedding!

"Sakshi is not here. She is in Ishapur. That's far away," I said.

"I know, Didi. Maybe when I am older, I can go back home and marry her? Do you think she will remember me? I don't want her to forget me. I don't want Ram to forget me either, but I don't want to go on another boat."

I didn't want Shanti to forget me either. Hari and I just held each other tight, next to our house.

"They won't forget you Hari. I think they will remember all the fun you had together and all the games you played."

I secretly hoped Shanti also remembered the river, the stories, and the warrior queens and princesses. Nobody here knew how much fun we had. No one here knew how happy we were with our friends.

The big house had a kitchen area that took up most of the space in the middle of the downstairs floor, and the kitchen housed two fires throughout the entire day. We used one firepit for cooking meals and another for boiling water to drink and wash. With so many people, heating water and food was a full-day affair. One of the uncles we called Dada Uncle always made the fire before everyone else got up. We called him Dada Uncle because he was so old, and we didn't know his real name. He didn't smile and never spoke to Hari or me. His narrowed eyes and frown made him look mad, and we kept out of his way most of the time. There was enough anger everywhere, we didn't need to make more. And anyway, Hari and I always had our own funny things to laugh at. We didn't want anyone to frown at us or make an angry face when we laughed. Mama's job was to put the fire out at night. Once a month, Dada Uncle would clean out the *chulas* (firepits), and he would be covered head to toe in soot and ash. Mama told us that Dada Uncle was a nice man, but I couldn't see why. Even if I woke up before him, I never came to the kitchen until the fire was made.

The married aunty and uncle had their own house close by, but behind all the big houses. When I asked Mama why they lived separately, she said, "They're lucky, Uma. They get to live alone because they're a married couple."

"What about us, Mama? We are three people. Shouldn't we also have our own house?"

"We don't have a baba. We can only have our own house if we have a baba. But anyway, isn't it better like this?"

"I wish we had our own house. Sometimes so many people make Hari scared." I didn't know how to tell Mama being with so many people scared me sometimes too.

"Don't worry, Uma. Hari will be safe, and so will you. At least we don't have to worry about anyone hurting us." Mama said that without malice or hope, but with relief and faith that it didn't matter for us.

I liked living with all the other uncles; they were good to us. The nice ones played games and made jokes with us, and the uninterested uncles just smiled. Dada Uncle just frowned and sometimes grunted. A game Hari and I played was that Hari would imitate Dada Uncle. He would pull up his pants, push out his lower lip, and make a big frown. His eyebrows came together to make a small triangle in between his eyes. I would act like Mama and scowl back with a bent nose and missing teeth! My teeth weren't really missing. I just put the charcoal from the fire on my teeth. Then we would both cackle like the crazy people we had seen on the boat. We made sure that no one saw us because Mama and Dada Uncle were the sternest people in the house. They would surely shout if they saw us.

Every day, Mama and the men went to work in the fields. Hari and I stayed at home. The workers (all of us) were called *coolies* (laborers). Everyone, including the sardar, called us coolies. My job was to clean and sweep, keep the fire going in the day, and cut the vegetables for Mama for the evening. My main job was to take care of Hari. The job was all right, and I didn't mind caring for him. What I didn't like was cleaning the toilet, which was a wooden structure behind the house. Everyone used it in the morning and evening. The sardar told us that we had to clean that every day, or we would get sick. If anyone got sick, we'd get no pay or food. Ten people using it every morning wasn't fun. Flies flew around my face as I cleaned. It was horrible all year around but got especially bad in the Durban summer. The wet of the heat and the smell always made me want to vomit.

One day in February, the smell was so bad that I couldn't get close to the toilet. That day, I vomited and didn't clean it. Hari also wanted to vomit, and when he wanted to use the toilet, he went into the fields. When Mama came home, she grabbed me by the arm and made me clean it before anyone could go in the evening. I hated this! I wanted to run away. I was sure the owner's children didn't clean the toilets for everyone. Why did I have to clean? But I also knew how hard my mama worked. Tears crowded my eyes as I cleaned the toilet. First, I had to scoop up all the waste from the hole in the ground and carry it in a bucket to the big hole behind the open field. Mama told me that all the waste must be covered by sand. I was crying so much that I couldn't lift the sand with the spade.

A heavy, brown, wrinkled hand took the spade from me and quickly covered all the waste with two large shovels of sand. Dada Uncle didn't say a word. I still had to wash the area with water and leave new water for everyone to wash with. Dada Uncle came with me to bring the water back. He washed the toilet while I vomited in the backyard. On that day, all the vomit that ever existed in my body left me. Dada Uncle let me vomit and helped me clean. He never told Mama that he helped me. I never told her either. After that day, every morning when I woke up, I would go and help Dada Uncle make the fires. He never smiled and neither did I, but my heart was grateful to this wrinkled man. He was my family too, but it troubled me that Dada Uncle didn't have his own family here. He was too old to be alone.

One early morning while we worked alongside each other preparing fires, I asked him, "Dada Uncle, where is your family? Are they in India or on another farm?" I didn't ask if he came alone. I knew what it felt like to be alone, and I didn't want to make him feel bad.

Dada Uncle didn't look at me, but he said gruffly, "My parents are dead, and my older brother and both sisters are all married with their own families." His hands were busy with the wood, but he still answered my questions. "They must have grandchildren."

"Did you not get married and have children?" I was curious about his life.

He stopped placing the wood in the firepit and looked at me with a sternness that looked more sad than angry. The lines across his forehead deepened as he looked past me. We had to leave the people we loved. Dada Uncle could have left his people too.

His voice wavered as he said, "I loved someone once, but no one would be happy with us together. People couldn't just accept that we loved each other." He wasn't talking to me; he was focused on something in the distance.

"Why? What happened?" I said.

The moment passed and Dada Uncle's eyes found me again. "Uma Beti, that is something that is in the past. Let's leave that to be where it is. I have my memories, that is enough for me. Besides, I have you and Hari. You are my grandchildren," he said with a rare smile. Dada Uncle spoke lightly, but his whole body told the story of his memories.

We never spoke about his love again, but it made me very sad to think he couldn't be with the person he loved.

The open muddy space behind the house was where we grew vegetables. The rations that the plantation supplied were so small that it was almost impossible to survive on rice and dhal only. Dada Uncle planted the vegetable garden so we could eat more pumpkins in the winter and tomatoes and potatoes year-round. I heard him tell the others that the seeds for the garden came from the owner's wife through the main house cook. The cook was a coolie that lived in the servant quarters next to the main house. His name was Unni. His full name was Unni-Krishnan Korrapati, but everyone called him Unni. He was older than Mama, but way younger than Dada Uncle. He was a rather short man with a round face. It was from all the rotis he ate. His face even looked like a roti! He had thick lips that had an even thicker covering of hair over his upper lip. The mustache was always wet with small food bits trapped inside it, and he smelled like oil. I wondered if the oil they used in the owner's house to cook was different from ours. Was that why Unni smelled different?

Unni gave the seeds to Dada Uncle. He said that the owner's wife sent the seeds to all the houses. All the houses had small gardens behind them. We knew the other people in the houses next to us and sometimes even shared vegetables when we had a lot so they wouldn't go to waste. The gardens of this place were fruitful, and we often had lots of vegetables, more than we could eat ourselves. Mama asked Unni why the owner's wife would want to give us seeds. They gave us rations and that was so little, so why did they care?

"She likes me a lot. The madam trusts me because I do everything for her," Unni said, his round face shining like he had rubbed it with the oil from the curry. "You are all lucky that you have me working in the main house. Without me you would have no vegetables. You eat well because of me."

Mama said Unni was full of himself and always believed he was more important than everyone because he worked in the main house, but never mind, we would take the seeds.

"The stomach knows no pride," she said.

I didn't understand that, but I knew that at least we ate vegetables with our dhal and rice.

I liked to do my job well (besides that one day of cleaning the toilet) so that Mama would not have to worry about anything, but it was boring to be at home the whole day. That's when Hari and I would take long walks, sometimes to look for the purple and orange flowers. Oftentimes, we would find ourselves at the owner's house. Their children played like they had no chores to do, especially no cleaning toilets. They certainly didn't have to cover everybody's daily waste with sand. The children looked much older than us, especially the boys. The girls looked slightly older than me. We liked to watch people being happy and having fun like how Shanti and I used to. Their garden wasn't full of mud or vegetables, but it had loads of orange and purple flowers and long patches of green grass with a fountain they'd play in on the hot days. The end of the garden had a huge tree. I didn't know what type, but the leaves were a really dark green, and in the spring the flowers were plentiful and pink. The biggest branch had a swing attached to it. How I longed to swing in it. It reminded me of our tree by the Neel River. Three large dogs roamed the front lawn.

The first time we walked past the house, we stood far away from the house and just watched everyone.

"Do you think they like to play house-house game?" Hari said. He was always talking about the house-house game! I also wondered what games they played.

"Maybe, I think they also like to play on the swing and maybe with the dogs?"

"I think so. Didi, do you like dogs?"

"I like them, but I have never played with one. Their teeth look big and sharp! I wonder if they bite. I might be a bit scared of them!" I said.

"You are such a scary ninny!" Hari laughed at me, his eyes crinkling in the corners and his teeth flashing white and broad. The top middle two were missing now!

At least twice a week, Hari and I would walk to the main house and watch from afar. We walked in the afternoon after the chores were done. Did they go to school in the morning? Hari and I stopped going to school ever since the day at the temple. But Mama never forgot that we needed to read and write. She still tried to read to us daily, but sometimes she was so tired that she forgot. Finding the time was hard for Mama. Some nights she disappeared and came back late. I knew it was late because it was usually after I couldn't keep my eyes open any longer waiting for her to come back from wherever she went.

The day was colder. Maybe July. Colder, but not cold. Durban rarely got cold like Ishapur in the winter. Hari and I were so bored, so we took our walk, shivering. Our bodies had become used to this warm climate all the time. The owner's wife was sitting on the veranda in the rocking chair. She was thin. Usually, she wore a cotton dress that came to her ankles. Today, she had a shawl around her shoulders. She was cold too. Her large eyes were crinkled either from age, being in the sun all the time, or from laughter, and her mouth was pink. Her hair was golden, like the color of the sugarcane juice that runs out of your mouth when you first bite into it. That always smelled sweet. Did her hair smell sweet too? Well, if it did, it would be a heavy smell because she had a lot of hair! She tied it in a knot at the top of her head, so her neck could stay cool. This place was always wet, even when it was slightly cooler.

She stared right at us with her bright blue eyes. She always looked like she was knitting something, and today was no differ-ent, except she saw this Brown girl and her Brown baby brother. She waved. Hari was quick to wave back, but I got scared. What if Mama found out? Would she be mad that we took the walk? I remembered how mad Mama used to get when she found out that we used to walk around the boat alone. She waved again, but this time I held Hari's hand so he wouldn't wave back. We left so quickly that she couldn't follow us. Of course, she knew where we lived. Maybe she didn't know how we lived, or maybe she did. That first wave broke the ice. Hari and I would see her often when we walked to the main house. She would wave every time. After a while, we started waving back and moving closer to the house. The main house stopped being so scary, and we stood close to the low, white fence, watching the lives of others unfold in front of us. A life without toilet cleaning, without fire lighting, without hiding, lived openly.

One of the sons came over to the fence to say hello whenever he was around. He was older than everyone and was always reading or talking to the others. He had black hair, and his face was the color of butter. He was maybe six feet tall and slender, and he always wore long pants and short sleeve shirts. He was the one the sardar told us had come back from London. He was eight years older than me. Sometimes I saw him play cards on the veranda. Often, we never saw him. The cook, Unni, would tell us that he went away to Johannesburg to work. It took me a long time to learn the word Johannesburg. I hadn't heard it before then. Unni spoke as if this was his son that worked in that town! So much pride for someone that wasn't his. Many people, including the sardar, spoke about this place, *Johannesburg*. Dada Uncle said that was where the *sona* (gold) for wedding chains came from! I wondered what that place was like. Maybe, one day, I would visit Johannesburg.

The first time the son saw us I tried to run away, but Hari pulled me toward him. He said these people were nice. "We must be friendly. They could be friends, Didi! I want to make friends."

I recall that first conversation so vividly.

"Hello, you two! What are you doing hiding behind that palm tree?! Come on over. What are your names?"

His voice sounded like he had small stones in his mouth that washed the words as they came out! It was so different from all the voices we were used to. His mouth was wide, and his teeth were white and straight. His face was covered by a closely cut black beard. Dark brows framed his blue eyes, just like his mother's.

We were just learning some words in English, so neither Hari or I understood what he said! He saw that we were confused and spoke in Hindi. This he had learned from the sardar, but I found that out much later.

Hari told him our names, but I didn't want to talk to him. His voice was soft, his eyes twinkling, and his words kind. His smile was big, and his hands carefully held the mangoes that he offered us from the garden tree. His fingernails were clean.

Hari was such a boy and grabbed the mango. The owner's son offered one to me, and I saved it for later. Hari ate his mango right away. I knew he would want mine later! We never stayed long. Just long enough to watch this family, say hello, and eat mangoes when it was mango season. Sometimes we just sat outside the low, white fence watching them. Whenever we heard that the owner's son was back home, we would walk to the house to eat mangoes and talk to the kind man that went to Johannesburg.

Chapter 10

Uma's Silent Breaths

1892

Sand, sweat, and cane green were Mama's evening makeup when she returned from the sugarcane. Most days, it was just as the sun was setting. There was no time for Mama to even think about washing first—that was an after-cooking activity. These were the times when her dhoti looked brown and dirty. Mama's second job started when she returned, then she would cook rice, dhal, and vegetables for everyone. Occasionally, someone brought a goat or a rabbit. She said she read the Ramayana, so she couldn't eat anything that breathed and wouldn't touch them. Over time, that changed, and Mama cooked and ate fish. I heard her say that her father would be so angry with her!

Hari said, "Lucky he is dead then!" Hari loved to eat fish and goat but not rabbit, which seemed like eating a pet.

"Hari! Don't speak about my baba like that! He was a good man." Mama's voice was sharp and pointed, but not angry. "Your *nana* (grandfather) was the best man I ever knew!"

We didn't know our nana.

"You think I will ever know someone who was the best ever?"

Hari looked at both Mama and me. He paused for a few seconds then said, "Mama, I think you are the best ever!" Hari hugged Mama tightly. I watched them. I didn't know anyone who was the best ever.

The uncles in the house left just before it got bright and came back as the sun was setting, sometimes with Mama and sometimes after. The days were long, and the work was hard, but the smiles were genuine and broad. The nicest were Uncle Madan and Uncle Mohan. When we got to the house that first evening, we didn't see them as they were out learning about the cane. We got to the house and fell asleep—all three of us—in the one room we were given. Hari held Mama, and I slept at her feet. We were so tired and hungry. But tiredness won the battle and hunger had to wait for the morning. It was Mama who saw Mohan first. Mama dropped to her knees when she saw Mohan and she cried. Mohan grabbed Mama's coat, and they hugged for the longest time. Hari and I watched them, but we didn't wait for when we could also hug Uncle Mohan, we just ran to him. People we knew! Our people! When Uncle Madan walked in, I hugged him. Hari began to cry and then stepped in for a hug.

They told us that when they got off the ship, they were immediately put onto the cart for Thompson's Farm. Uncle Madan told us that Mr. Thompson had bought almost all the labor on the ship SS *Umzimkulu*. Mr. Thompson was a rich man, and his farm was the biggest in the area. Uncle Madan said that Mr. Thompson's father owned the farm first, but he used to plant wattle wood. Only when the ships started coming to Port Natal did Mr. Thompson start to plant sugarcane.

Uncle Mohan and Uncle Madan missed their mothers so much. Mama was their mother, too, not just Hari's and mine. Mama made roti for us with our flour ration and chai. The roti and chai comforted Uncle Mohan. They made boats for Hari to float on the river and dolls for me to play with.

As Hari grew, his job was to ensure that we had fresh water every day in the house. Once he turned ten, he went to help Mama in the fields, and I went with them too. This made the sardar happy. Three working bodies were better than one.

I loved helping Hari in those days when he carried water. The buckets were heavy for a small boy, but I loved it because we went to the river with its flat rocks and grass. The river was far because our house was the farthest away. We didn't mind the walk, which was fun! The river reminded me of our old home. No Shanti to watch the clouds with, though, just memories of our stories and games. I loved this river equally as much because besides Hari and me, no one went there often. The place may have changed, but my heart still loved the same things even when they were different.

The men from our house went on outings on Sunday—the rest day. Even Dada Uncle left. But we didn't. I asked Mama once why we didn't go. She said women were only half as valuable as the men to the plantation owners, even if they made the men able. So, we couldn't leave the farm. Mr. Thompson said so. I could never understand why Mr. Thompson could tell us where to go. Did anyone tell him that my mama took a train and a ship with us to get here? I wondered if he knew how able my mama really was. Maybe that was what frightened him enough to keep us on the farm. One Sunday, I so wanted to go with the uncles, but Mama refused to let me go.

"Why can't I go? I just want to see the town! All we see is the sugarcane. I want to see all the people and the streets that the uncles talk about. Please, Mama! I promise I will do all the cleaning and do it better!"

"The town is not a place for a girl, and Mr. Thompson and the sardar will not let us go. You must stay here. A few more years, Uma, then we will be free."

There was no convincing Mama. A few more years felt like a lifetime to me. I felt like I couldn't breathe. The Port Natal air was fresh, but the sickly sweetness clogged my lungs. Why did I have to stay hidden? Hiding was my power. Hiding myself, hiding my feelings, sharing with no one. Not even Hari.

Uncle Madan and Uncle Mohan decided on that day that they didn't want to go out. They stayed with us and cooked for Mama and us—rice, dhal, and fish. We didn't usually eat anything but vegetables from the garden, so this was such a treat. After that, Mama started eating fish even if Nana wouldn't approve.

They took us fishing at the river earlier in the day. Neither Hari or I had ever fished before, and Hari couldn't even hold the stick with the line and hook.

"The worms are wriggling on the hook, Didi! They're alive! Let's put them back. Help me, please!" Hari's eyes were full of tears, and they ran freely down his cheeks. My sweet Hari baby had so much love in him that he couldn't stand to see the worms suffering.

"Don't worry. This is the worm's job. They are meant for us to catch fish," Uncle Mohan said.

Only after we caught the fish did Hari calm down. I didn't cry, though. I wasn't scared at all. The uncles made us help clean the fish. That was the worst part. Scales went everywhere. In my hair, in my mouth, and under our clothes!

Later we would become experts at catching and cleaning fish. At least it was something else to eat besides vegetables. It was also so much fun because there was someone else to be with besides Mama and Hari on Sundays. It became a regular thing, and often Mama would sleep on the Sundays that Uncle Madan and Uncle Mohan were with us. Once I even went to check if she was breathing! Uncle Madan said we must not disturb Mama because she was tired and worked hard. They looked at us with sad eyes when they spoke about Mama. I never understood that. Even on the days the uncles would go out, they would still bring a sweet for Hari and me. Uncle Madan told me about the shop they went to in Durban. He said a Muslim man from Hyderabad, Mr. Samad, owned the store. He was excited

THE STORY I TOLD MYSELF

that an Indian man could be a shop owner. I heard him telling Uncle Mohan.

"It would be wonderful to be in charge of your life. One day, I will be in charge of my own life once our work on the farm is over. I want to buy my own house and have a wife and children. I want to work in the town," Uncle Madan said.

Sometimes they brought a small toy from Durban. Uncle Madan and Uncle Mohan became the family we never had. They also told us that Uncle Gopal and Aunty Savitri were not far away. They lived on a farm in Stanger, the Blythedale Plantation. Uncle Mohan said they saw them in Durban at Mr. Samad's store. Our family was growing.

When Uncle Madan would say that he wanted to be in charge of his life, my mama would say, "Madan, you are in charge of your mind now. Make it strong now, so when you leave the farm, you can focus on building your house and family because you will know how to build your life."

Mama kept teaching Hari and me. She said she wanted us to know things, to read, to write. But Mama didn't know if our minds were strong. She didn't know that I was scared and sometimes hid deep in my mind to keep myself safe.

Megha Aunty was on Thompson's Farm too. She was first in the second house, but no one knew what to do with her because she just cried the whole day. Her belly was growing. The sardar told Mama that if Megha Aunty didn't start earning her keep soon, they would have to do something. Mama asked the sardar if she could stay with us, if only until the baby was born. We knew that Megha Aunty didn't want the baby. She told someone that the baby was a *rakshas* (demon baby), and she kept hitting her stomach. Everyone avoided her because we couldn't handle the tears all the time. It was so hard for Mama because not only did we have to share our rations with Megha Aunty (the owner wasn't going to give her rations if she wasn't working), but Mama was watching her in the evenings too.

Mama asked me to watch Megha Aunty in the day and to stop her from hitting herself all the time. But I wanted to go with Hari for walks to see the orange and purple flowers. I didn't want to stay in the house all the time.

Months had passed on the farm, and Hari and I came back home after one of our long trips. I knew that we still needed water, but Hari was too tired. We had been out for too long, and his baby legs were sore. Hari usually never complained, but we had so much fun running around, eating mangos, and watching the owner's wife. We stayed too long. The men and Mama would be back soon, and I had to heat the water for bathing. I told Hari to sit in the garden, and I hurried to the river. I had my spot for water. The sweetest water was where the rocks made a small whirlpool. That also reminded me of our grassy patch by the Neel River. Today, the water was the color of blood and sand mixed. The pool wasn't big, so I started looking for what made the water that color. The corner of the pool had a small parcel tucked under the rocks. At first, I thought it was just garbage, but then it looked more full. Maybe a dead animal? I was just about to pick it up and throw it away when I spotted a hand and face. It was a dead baby. I had seen dead before. Baba was dead when we left to go to the temple. But the baby looked like a doll. A boy doll. I didn't touch the baby and left it right there.

I went home quietly, talking to no one and without the water. So much changed right then. My body felt like ants were crawling all over, and my hands couldn't stay still. I went into the kitchen and started to cut vegetables for cooking.

"Uma, did Hari get the water? Is it ready? Uma?!" Mama had come home, and I didn't even realize she was standing in front of me or that she was speaking to me. Even though I knew dead before, I couldn't get the look of the baby boy's hands and legs out of my mind. Mama was busy starting to cook, so at first she didn't notice that I was stuck in my thoughts.

"Uma!" Mama turned sharply to scold me, and then she saw my face. "Uma?"

Mama wiped her hands on her clothes and turned my face toward hers. My neck hurt when she tilted my head, but the discomfort was easier than the pain inside my head.

"Uma, what's wrong, beti?" Mama felt the shivering in my body as she held my shoulders.

"Megha Aunty left her baby in the river. The baby is dead. I saw it," I said, looking at her with a tearless face. I had seen so much death in this short life.

"Hey Ram (oh God)! You all right, Uma?" Mama pulled my shoulders to her, her face scanning mine and her hands moving to cup my face in hers. Mama pushed my face into her chest and held me tightly for a few seconds. Then she asked me if I told Hari and Megha. The shaking had moved from my hands into my lips, and my words couldn't escape. I just shook my head to say no. My entire body felt like a leaf in the wind, shaking and falling wherever the wind took it, wherever a circumstance took it.

Mama gently took my hands in hers. "Take me to the spot where the baby is. I know it's hard, beti, but take me to the place. We must find the baby."

"I think the baby was a boy, Mama," I whispered.

"Take me to the baby boy, my little girl." Mama's voice was so sad that I had to look at her. Her voice was a soft lyrical lament, lost and scared, just like me, just like when we were at the temple. Her voice was low, and her face lost all its color. This wasn't the Mama from the boat or from the farm.

We went to the river hand in hand, quick stepped and eyes focused to seek out no one. Mama carried a white cloth. She had gone up to her room and tore a piece off her old sari. She never wore saris anymore, but she kept the two that she had. Now the sari would be a burial shroud for this baby. The water had cleared. The pool was no longer a mix of blood and sand. The baby had said his goodbye to the world even though he had just stepped into it. This place could be cruel to those who had no voice. Mama picked up the baby's body, gently wrapped him in the white sari, and stepped out of the water. We walked for a long time before she found a spot under an old palm tree. Many of the farms had rows of palm trees lining the entrances to the farm, and sometimes we would find a stray tree in the middle of the sugarcane. We buried the baby far away from the river and our house. We always burn the bodies when people died, but Mama said that no one must know about the baby. She knew the prayer to say. Her baba had taught her well. He had made sure his daughter was able to do anything, even say the priest's prayer at a funeral.

"Don't take water from the pool until I tell you again, Uma. The water needs to clean itself first."

I'll need to find another spot to fill the water now. More things to do.

"And don't tell anyone about the baby or Megha Aunty," Mama said. "Her mind is not right, and she might hurt herself if people ask too many questions."

"But won't everyone ask what happened?" Everyone knew Megha Aunty was going to have a baby. Wouldn't they ask what happened if Megha Aunty's stomach didn't look big anymore?

"Let me speak to Megha first, Uma. Did you see her at the house?"

I hadn't seen Megha Aunty that entire day. I didn't tell Mama that Hari and I were at the owner's house. I think she would be mad with me again if she knew. At least Mama wasn't mad with me now. So we kept another secret, Mama and me. We walked back to the house quickly because Mama still had to cook, and she didn't want anyone to know that something had happened.

When we arrived home, Megha Aunty was in the garden sitting with Hari. Mama saw her but didn't speak to her. She and I cooked first. The uncles laughed or napped as usual. Mama fed everyone, and Hari played on the veranda. But I didn't feel so normal. Every time we felt something was fun something bad happened, like the gods that had all bad things happen to them. I was too scared to be happy.

After supper was done, Mama and Megha Aunty went to Mama's room. Neither of them ever spoke about the baby, but I never forgot him. The next week Megha Aunty started working, and our rations improved. When Dada Uncle asked about the baby, Mama said that the baby died when it was born and that she had buried it far away. Death was common for us. It suited everyone to forget because Megha Aunty wasn't married when she got pregnant on the boat, and that brought back bad memories for everyone. And now she could work. Not talking about the baby was easier.

Everyone called Unni, the main house cook, *Khana Wala* (chef) Unni. We started to see him more often in our house. I didn't like him too much. He seemed to want to be better than everyone, especially the uncles and Dada Uncle. Dada Uncle never smiled on the good days, but he was even more grumpy when he saw Unni. Hari told me that he heard Dada Uncle telling Mama that Unni didn't think he was a coolie. But we all were. That was why it was strange to see him at our house. He didn't like us, so why was he here? He came in the evenings mostly, first he arrived after supper, and then he began arriving when we were eating. Since Unni didn't bring food, the uncles were upset when he arrived at supper. Once he came just as we started eating, and Dada Uncle and Mama told him that he couldn't eat with us.

Unni's face twisted and turned red. He balled his hand into a fist. "Your vegetables come from the seeds that I gave you! And you are stopping me from eating?!"

Dada Uncle said, "You gave us seeds and not rice. Bring rice and then you can eat with us."

Unni rushed forward to punch him, then Uncle Madan jumped up to hit Unni. Dada Uncle stopped them both.

"Stop. Unni, food is hard to get, and Megha has just started working on planting. Before that, we had to share our rations with her. There is not enough for us all. The children get no rations assigned to them, so we eat little. Adding one more mouth to feed is difficult for us all. If you bring rice every day or something at least, you can eat with us. Besides, you eat in the main house, so you have enough food there."

Unni didn't eat with us that night. He muttered to himself and scowled as he left, but he returned before dawn the next morning and gave Mama rice. Unni started to eat with us more frequently. Frequently became regularly, and regularly became all the time. I wasn't sure why he joined us when he could eat much better at the main house with his favorite lady, the owner's wife.

Once Unni started coming to our line house more often, Hari said, "Why is Megha Aunty washing morning and evening? I have to bring more water!"

These things made up Hari's day. More trips for water cut into house-house game playing time. Megha Aunty didn't pay much attention to anything, but she did seem interested in bathing (especially at night) and eating supper with everyone all of a sudden. Before the baby died, she kept to herself most of the time.

Megha Aunty never spoke about the baby. No one did. But she started slowly becoming part of life on the plantation. She went out to clean the cane rows, weed, and sometimes plant cane. No one knew what to say to Megha Aunty. Dada Uncle kept a close eye on her. Our house was safer than the other line houses. The uncles had Mama and me to cook and clean for them, so no one really complained. But I knew that in some of the other line houses the men would fight over the ladies. Dada Uncle was clear that no one fought in our house, and no one touched Megha Aunty, Mama, or me. Everyone listened to Dada Uncle. He was the grandfather of the house. He became my dada that day he helped with the latrine, even if he was a grumpy old man.

Bathing and communal eating took on a larger purpose, and slowly, Megha Aunty and Khana Wala Unni courted in the blistering heat of Port Natal, under the watchful gaze of two children, their mother, Dada, and all the other house uncles. Courting was hard on the plantation. Most of the time, single women were instruments used to punish or reward the male workers.

You ran away? No woman for you! You stay lonely tonight. You worked well? You snitched on your fellow coolies? You could have a woman tonight or buy a woman for cheap to cook and warm your bed. No loneliness for you. They said this even if the woman didn't want to do those things.

The English didn't really want women on the plantations. They were scared we would have babies and then there would be more Brown people than White ones in Natal. *Imagine the horror of Brown people taking over!* But even if they didn't want Brown women, they knew how to use us. I never saw this, but I heard the aunties from the other line houses say that they were lucky that Mr. Thompson didn't like Brown women.

Some owners thought being the house servant meant being their bed servant too. And most of the madams turned a blind eye. The aunties told of the story of Velliamma. She was a house servant on a farm down the South Coast near a place called Bazley. Velliamma told the police that the owner had raped her. No one believed her, especially when her owner said that all Brown women were too ugly to want to bed. Why would he want her? The police and the courts believed him. He was innocent. She overpowered and seduced him.

He was powerless. He was the master, and she was the slave. That was the story they made up. The sardars joined in by using single women as punishment or rewards to keep the coolies in line.

As much as no one liked Unni, everyone liked Megha Aunty. Mama watched her every day, especially when Unni came to visit. Mama had taken Megha Aunty under her wing, watching over her from the day we brought her into our house. Mama said that maybe Megha Aunty's mind might get better if she married and had more children. I didn't know. She seemed sick and broken to me. But Mama was too scared that someone else we knew might die. She wanted to be the person that glued all the broken souls back together.

The sugarcane was the backdrop to their romance. Evening meals became long walks with Dada as the chaperone. That was funny! All the uncles would watch Dada walk behind the couple, a fair distance away, not close enough to hear what they were saying, but close enough to watch what they were doing. Dada and Mama were not going to have another baby around. Dada got more exercise than he needed with those two! The walks were long and meandering through the gardens of green with Unni talking about the main house and how good a cook he was. How could Megha Aunty stand it? But apparently, she liked being the quiet one and letting him do all the talking. After some months, Dada stopped going with them. They would disappear for at least an hour after dinner on most nights. No matter how good a cook Unni was, he never brought any of the food from the main house. That was a line he never crossed. Unni had loyalties.

The only time I saw the men fight was when they drank cane and Unni joined them. Cane was the drink that the men made from the sugarcane juice. I didn't know what cane tasted like, but Dada made a face when the other uncles spoke about it. He said in other parts of the world, they made the sugarcane juice into rum. Here we just drank the raw liquor that burned the day away, as it made the men loose with their tongues, hands, and lips. He said coolies drank cane, and owners drank rum. That was the difference between us.

As the evenings got colder, our uncles would make a fire in an old drum, a *bowla*. Everyone would sit around the bowla, and the men would drink and talk. The women would warm themselves. Mama and Megha Aunty didn't drink cane. But I know that the aunties from the other line houses did. Hari loved to dance to the songs that were sung. Unni would sing songs from the place he grew up in, somewhere close to a place called Hyderabad. Dada was from a place called Madras. I thought I heard this name, but I didn't know for sure because he didn't sing. He spoke differently, and when he was back at the line house, he wrapped his waist and legs in a long cloth, almost like a sari, around his waist. His shirt went over it. Mama said it reminded him of how he dressed back home in his village. Dada didn't drink the cane. But he watched over everyone when they did. I liked to sit around the bowla. It felt like a family with uncles and aunties and grandfathers.

When Unni drank cane, Megha Aunty would scream at him. Mama said that it was because on the ship the men used to drink the cheap alcohol that the English used to give them. The man that raped Megha Aunty was drunk when it happened, and she was scared of drunk men now. Megha Aunty sat around the bowla to watch over everyone and make sure they didn't get too drunk. I don't think she did a good job of stopping the uncles. Sometimes they would get drunk, and they were funny. Mama said that not all people were funny when they were drunk. Some people were scary. Unni drank, not all the time, but enough to scare Megha Aunty sometimes.

The sugarcane had a strange attraction, though. It made some people rich. It made some people tired. It made some people sick, and it made some people drunk. The cane juice was fermented into Dada's hated liquor. Juice that could make a man into a lion; it was that strong! Cane made people forget themselves. It made men forget their wives and children. Even though it started slowly, it made Unni unbearable at times.

Everyone was so excited when Unni and Megha Aunty said they wanted to get married. The uncles got drunk. Uncle Mohan put a sari over his head, and Uncle Madan acted like Unni. Even Dada's face looked a little less grumpy. Unni didn't drink that day. He just sat with Megha Aunty holding her hand. I could see that Mama and Dada were happy, yet both looked worried.

"It costs five pounds for a legal marriage license," Mama said. "No one will allow you to marry without it. And doing a wedding without the license will just mean that the plantation owner can separate you both. They can sell or move you or Megha and no one can stop them. Even a wedding in front of *Ishwar* (God) is not enough for these Englishmen."

"How can you afford the license?" Dada was looking at how to make our lives easier, smoother, and avoid trouble. Sometimes that meant making us all think about uncomfortable, sad things. But you can't think about hard things. Sometimes you just have to believe in good things.

Megha Aunty cried a long time that day. "I will ask the madam. She will help me. I am sure of it," she said.

I wondered why the owner's wife would help Unni and Megha Aunty get married. But then she was nice to Hari and me, so maybe she is a good lady.

Unni got a loan of five pounds from the owner's wife. This was more than he made in a year on the farm. What Unni didn't tell Megha Aunty immediately was that it meant they had to stay on the farm for another five years after this indenture period was over. Unni would never repay the loan, so he and Megha Aunty would have to be almost slaves again to marry legally. I thought that Megha Aunty would be angrier, but she said, "Better to be married and living with the man I love like a slave, than to be bought and sold at an owner's fancy."

While the owner's wife had gotten the money for Unni, the cost to her was a lot. Mr. Thompson had taken his whip to the madam to keep her in line so that she knew that he was in charge, and yet she still gave Unni the loan. The same lady that gave us seeds threatened to report Mr. Thompson to the colonial protectorate if he didn't agree. The colonial protectorate was in charge of keeping the coolies safe, but no one really knew what they did. Dada said Mr. Thompson was already in trouble with the colonial protectorate because a coolie had died because he stopped giving rations when the worker was sick. The worker had died from starvation and dehydration. He didn't need more trouble. Anyway, his sardar made sure now that none of the injustices got so bad that people died. Just bad enough so that coolies wouldn't get out of line or stop working. He had Unni and Megha Aunty's labor for another five years and got a chance to whip his wife and show his strength. A win on all fronts for him. The madam didn't come outside for a few weeks. Hari and I missed her waves from the veranda.

No one knew how to do this marriage. Where would they do the legal English marriage? Also, they had no priest, no temple, and no place where Ishwar could witness their commitment. All eyes went to two people. Everyone knew that Mama and Dada could do almost anything. We all knew that these two people would take care of everyone.

Dada had a good friend in the first line house. When Dada wasn't walking in the evenings behind Unni and Megha Aunty, he would visit his friend, Sadasivan. He must have been from the same place as Dada Uncle because they spoke a language I didn't understand. Sadasivan was the man who reported the crop volume to the magistrate when the harvest was done. Uncle Sada (Dada called him Sada) had worked on the plantation forever. He had come with one of the first lots of coolies in the first crossings of the Kaala Paani around 1860. But he never left. His debt was too big. He owed too much money to Mr. Thompson. He may have told Dada why his debt was so much, but Dada never told us. Uncle Sada was the cautionary tale that we all watched from the sidelines. We must be careful, or we will never leave this plantation.

Dada asked Uncle Sada to take Megha Aunty and Unni with him when he went to the magistrate's office. He agreed, but only if Mama shared the vegetables with them. Mama agreed quickly. She didn't mind sharing. Mama and Dada could make anything happen. But the sardar had to agree, too, because that meant on that day Unni and Megha Aunty wouldn't work. The sardar was a cruel man. He insisted that Unni pay one pound to go. That was a lot on top of the five pounds to register for the license. They could only go on a working day because the office was closed on Sunday.

Uncle Sada was worried. "Unni, are you sure that you want to get married? The debt is getting bigger and bigger."

"Megha and I love each other. We are getting married. Nothing will stop me from marrying my Megha."

"Love is not enough. Debt is bigger than love. You will find this out as the years pass," Uncle Sada said.

Everyone was so caught up in the wedding preparations that Uncle Sada's lone, quiet, resigned voice got lost in the revelry. He knew what debt meant. Dada held Uncle Sada's hand in his and shook his head, telling him not to bother.

Megha Aunty and Unni made it to the magistrate's office. They had a license, a piece of paper that meant nothing for the people getting married, that only the owner could read. I was happy for them, but I was never getting married, so I didn't care.

Mama, the uncles, Dada, and Megha Aunty planned the wedding. There was no priest to pray or temple for the ceremony, so Mama went to the sardar and asked him to speak to Mr. Thompson about a priest from Durban coming to the farm. Mr. Thompson said no, or at least that was what the sardar said. Mama and the sardar had a strange relationship. She was never afraid of him, and the sardar knew this. Sometimes, you could see that he hated Mama but never said anything. When she went to visit the sardar, sometimes she would be gone for a long time, so Dada and the uncles would play lots of games with us to pass the time.

When Unni and Megha Aunty heard no priest would come, they asked Mama to read the Ramayana at least.

"Shivali Didi, please read the Ramayana for us. How can I have a wedding without any blessing?" Megha Auntie said.

Mama, Megha Aunty, and I were sitting in the setting sun on Saturday evening. It was warmer now; the winter had passed, and spring rains were common in the evenings. Nature was washing Megha Aunty's slate clean to start a new life with Unni, trying to make right the rape on the ship, the pregnancy, and the death. Two women and a girl, trying to plan how Megha Aunty would look on her day, just like any wedding back home.

"I must be cleansed. I can't start my life with Unni without Ishwar's blessings," she said.

Mama was nervous to do this; I could see that. But maybe it would be just like when she read for Shanti and me at the Neel River. The story of Ram and Sita marrying was the most beautiful! Unni wasn't Ram. He didn't win Sita's hand in marriage in any contest. But he won her heart and made it peaceful again. At least a little bit. At least for now.

Mama was nervous, but she was excited to read the Ramayana with lots of people. I realized that about my mother. Even though she hid a lot of herself, she still liked to make others feel good. She saw the pain of leaving their villages in everyone's faces, and reading a piece of home made everyone feel like this was home now.

Since we had no temple, all the uncles decided that they would build a small temple for Ram and Sita in a patch of ground in the middle of the cane fields. It would serve the wedding but also it would be a place we could all pray afterwards. But they still needed permission to build the temple. This caused so much worry for days until my mama walked up to Mr. Thompson one day in the field while she was holding the sickle in her hand.

"Mr. Thompson, we want to build a temple for us to pray. We are building it just beyond the first field. The water doesn't flow too well there so it's dry, and the ground is too hard for the cane. But it's just right for building a small *mandir* (temple). The coolies will be happy if we can pray to our God. You will have less fighting, and they will feel like this is home. They won't want to leave," Mama said in Hindi because Mr. Thompson understood Hindi.

I thought my mama in her dhoti and coat, with her big eyes and scary face, made Mr. Thompson agree out of fear. Mr. Thompson may have hit his wife, but he couldn't raise a hand to this fierce woman.

Building the mandir gave all the uncles an extra sense of purpose. The men from the other line houses came to help. Mama looked at them and shook her head. "So many men to build this small mandir. I could use help to cook and clean, but no one really wants to do that," she said under her breath.

Mama was no fool. She knew that it helped to keep everyone busy so that they didn't drink cane from boredom. It was so small, this temple. Just a tiny square structure that could hold two stone statues. Our statues were so rough, I wasn't sure the God of the Ramayana could be in the statues, but they dressed them in saris and sari cloth, so we made these our Gods. They also built a small court-yard in front of the statues. It had a grass roof and bamboo poles that kept the roof up. This was where the wedding would be. Mama planned to sit in front of the statues to read. Even though we didn't talk at all about the temple where Hari and I sat near the bull, this reminded me of that temple, that day. It had been a long time since I thought of that temple. The bull, the dust, and Mama.

All the line houses came to the wedding. Megha Aunty wore a sari that she already had, and Mama placed pink and white flowers in her hair. The pride of a Hindu woman was her jewelry. It was the only wealth that a woman had of her own. Usually, her parents would give her *kanganas* (bangles) when she got married. But there were no parents or kanganas to give. Hari kept on asking for laddoo and *jalebi* (sweets). He said that Sakshi's sister Madhu had these at her wedding. We didn't have sweets, but we had fun! The food was similar to what we ate every day, rice, dhal, and vegetables. Mama said we should pretend that we were eating *biryani*, the food of kings, but dhal and rice wasn't biryani, even if Mama said it was.

Mama read from the Ramayana. She told the story of Lord Ram and Queen Sita's wedding, of Lord Ram's love for his Queen Sita and how he won her love. Unni and Megha Aunty came from different villages with different rituals. No one knew exactly what to do for each village, so the wedding became a mix of many rituals. Unni put sindoor in the middle parting of Megha Aunty's hair. His arm gently came around the back of her face as he put a dot of the same powder on her forehead with the ring finger of his right hand. Her kanganas were made from flowers, and a toe ring that Unni placed on her second toe was made from a beautifully woven piece of wire. Later, he would replace it with a cheaper gold. But, for now, it would do. Unni wore a cloth like Dada around his waist with a clean, crisp, white shirt that the madam gave him. Everyone cried, except me. I loved the wedding, but I didn't cry. Megha Aunty and Unni moved in together into the small cottage next to the main house, and Megha Aunty started cleaning the owner's house. This was the work of many Indian women trying to keep their families alive. It became the next years of Unni and Megha Aunty's life. She was lucky Mr. Thompson didn't like Brown women.

Sometimes Uncle Zweli would come to visit us. He lived next to the farm, although far away from us. He worked for a day wage, not on contract on the farm. We really liked Uncle Zweli. In the beginning we didn't understand him at all, but over time, we learned a few words of Zulu and he learned a few words of Hindi. We were all learning some English. Uncle Zweli would make small animals out of wood, and we would play with them together. Hari and Uncle Zweli became good friends. Friends that would look for each other. But the sardar didn't like that. He would get angry with us and Uncle Zweli, but he would just laugh and still come to visit.

One day, Uncle Zweli stopped coming and we didn't see him around the farm anymore. Hari and I waited and waited for him. For so long. It was a while before the uncles told Mama that the sardar didn't like the Brown and Black people to be friends, so he had moved Uncle Zweli to another farm. That was how the farm worked. All the colors had to stay separate, White, Black, and Brown. Mixing wasn't allowed. *Why do we keep on losing people?* Hari was sad for a long time. Toil and sweat made themselves permanent companions for five years. When I turned thirteen, we entered another five years of slavery.

Chapter 11

Uma's Sweet Mango Nectar

1900

Hari loved white guavas. He didn't stop talking about how he hated the red ones. I couldn't stop laughing when he scrunched up his face, made a furrow in between his eyebrows, and balled his fist in anger at anything red, even flowers! I knew, though, that his childish hate was real and had so much pain at its center. Hari hated anything that even looked like blood. I loved my Hari, and I would not let any blood come near him again! But I couldn't stop all the red in the world. That was for sure.

I had come to love mangoes, especially the oblong, orange ones that tasted like sunshine—Bombay mangos. *I wondered why they were called that.* The flesh was sweet and not stringy like some of the others. It was quite firm. And they looked like some of the green pods that hung from the trees that grew here. But my favorites were the round deep reddish green mangos that grew on the huge green tree in the yard of the plantation main house. That tree spread itself so wide that nothing grew underneath. Its mangos were stringy, and they got stuck in your teeth when you bit into them. You'd have mango strings in your teeth for almost the entire summer! They were the sweetest mangos and were extra juicy. The smell! Oh, the smell! It was heady and intoxicating. It made you want to devour the mango right that second! The juice created a sticky palate that ran over your chin and tickled your nose, yet at the same time made you want to go slow, so you could savor the momentary taste of heaven. *Oh my, those mangos smelled like my Richard.*

The first few years of going to the main house were simply to see other children, wave to the madam, and watch them from behind the low, white fence. We rarely interacted with anyone, except Richard. Richard would offer mangos and want to talk. Hari spoke to Richard more than me in the beginning. For a good number of years, I was too wary of people and would just look on curiously, take mangos, and watch Richard. Most of the time, Richard went to Johannesburg. He worked there in his father's business selling sugar to the rest of the country. I met Richard twice. First when he met Hari and I—just two children peeking voyeuristically into people's gardens. Then again when two potential soulmates met: me, a fiercely independent and lost sixteen-year-old girl coming into her womanhood, and Richard, a young person becoming a man he could be proud of—a principled man of twenty-four who was learning what it meant to be a White man that may love a Brown girl.

I hated the Sundays when everyone went to the town, and we had to stay on the farm. It felt like I couldn't breathe. When that happened, I would walk. Walk for hours and hours. Walking made me feel free, even in my green wavy cage. Hari and I would walk to ease boredom, and I would walk alone to scream in peace and solitude. At first, they had to be quick walks along the dirt roads when Mama was sleeping. She wasn't happy if she woke up and I wasn't there. She also wasn't happy if Hari was alone. As I got older and Mama started trusting the place more, she let me be on my own on Sundays after lunch as long as I returned before sunset.

The uncles knew I needed to be alone, and they would watch Hari. As Hari grew, he played more on his own. Those walks were also the only times I was free of any responsibility of Hari, of cleaning, of cooking, of anything. I could just be Uma. The walks became less about following the roads and more about pushing myself to see how far I could go. What new I could find. How lost I could get. This place was quite deceiving. Green cane as far as the eye could see felt boundless, but the reality was that green could be the sweet poison that kept you trapped. Maybe I was trying to reach the edge of infinity. I cherished the scrapes and bruises that came with trying to find that edge. At least I was alive.

On one of those Sundays, I found my end, my own place. The river where we got water was pretty, but there were people there. You couldn't be alone. Someone was always getting water to drink and wash, or someone was washing clothes, and I had the bad memory of finding Megha Aunty's baby. I needed to be alone without anybody's life happening around me. I found my own special spot, and it was ordinary. No green grass patch, or big tree, or wide flat stones. Just a quiet spring with overgrown grass and weeds. A few wildflowers, the small yellow ones, but nothing like the orange and purple birds-of-paradise or the blue flowers. The place was quiet, it was far, and it was mine alone. No Hari or Mama either. I wish I thought about important things there. I wish I made plans there. But all I did was lie flat on my back, close my eyes, and breathe in the scent of the grass. I'd close my eyes and hear the murmurs of the water trying to calm my heart. My breath and the water created their own song. I thought of the things I loved and how they wove into my song, and I felt free, like the birds I watched soaring so easily way above me.

"I didn't think anyone walked so far out into the farm," Richard said.

Hearing his voice startled me. I was so used to the silence that had come to be my companion here that I didn't even register him walking closer. In my rush to stand up, I fell deeper into the muddy ground around the spring. He grabbed my hand to steady me, but I pulled back. I didn't want anyone to touch me, especially those who looked like butter. Doing that made me slip again, and this time I landed fully on my back.

"I'd better stay away, or soon you might fall into the spring," he said, his eyes crinkling with concern and his wide smile showing square, white teeth.

I just wanted to stand up with as much dignity as I could muster in such an undignified situation. It was bad enough that everyone knew us as coolies; Richard shouldn't think I was clumsy as well. I didn't want him looking at me with pity or disgust.

How did I want him to look at me? The thought shocked me. I couldn't answer the question at that moment. I got up and walked away without a word or another look at that bearded man.

"My name is Richard, by the way," he called after me.

I knew that! Did he think I was stupid? I hadn't spent years looking into his garden and not know his name. The next time we met I didn't just want to be the girl looking into the garden.

I kept walking. I wasn't going to talk to this man with mud all over me. I didn't know why I wanted to look nice when I spoke to him. My heart felt weird the entire week after that. It danced in my chest, yet in equal measure squeezed hard. After a couple of days, Hari asked me if everything was fine.

"Didi, why are you so quiet?"

"I'm usually quiet," I said.

"You're quieter than usual. Are you sick?"

"No, baby. I'm not sick." I laughed and hugged Hari tightly. He worried about me. He shouldn't. I didn't understand what I felt. I wanted to see Richard again, but I was afraid. The week couldn't pass quickly enough, and on Sunday after lunch, I set out to my spot secretly hoping that Richard would be there to see me again.

He was already there when I arrived, and he looked comfortable on the grass, as though he had been there for some time.

"Well, hello there. I was hoping you would come here today. I didn't know for sure. But I hoped," Richard said.

His voice was as tentative as mine. His heavy browed eyes searched mine for something. Agreement? Acceptance? Acknowledgement? I wasn't sure. He extended his hand for me to sit near him. I stood for a minute, contemplating if I should. What was I thinking coming here, knowing that I was hoping to see this beautiful man. What if I left now? Would that be better? But wasn't this what I wanted? I sat near Richard but didn't take his hand. That was a step too far at this point. We sat for a while, not speaking, just sitting in silence.

"My name is Uma." My voice didn't have the motherly feel of when I spoke to Hari, or the work-like efficiency of my conversations with Mama. It sounded grown up, like a woman. Richard looked at me and smiled. We sat in silence for a while longer before he broke the quiet.

"You probably don't see me all the time here on the farm. I live here and in Johannesburg, which is a big town. There are so many people there compared to here. It feels crowded. But father's business needed me to be there," he said.

Richard told me about the streets and the horses and carts, the people, his friends, and about how he missed home and hoped one day to come back here for good. He took the train when he traveled to Johannesburg. The last time I was on a train was one I tried so hard to forget. I hid it deep within my mind. Only Hari knew that place. We made it together.

Richard told me about his brother and sisters. They were younger than him. His brother was going to school in London, and two of his sisters were engaged to be married. They were not much older than me. One of his sisters, Eloise, was marrying a boy from a large farm inland called Dalton. His other sister Penelope was engaged to a boy in England.

"Both these matches will make the family fortunes stronger, and that makes Father satisfied, I think. I just want them both to be happy. England is far away," he said as he looked at the river.

I heard sadness and longing in his voice. It was deep and melancholy. We sat for a while longer, and then I got up.

"Thank you for telling me about your life," I said quietly. "Will I see you next week? I have to leave now." I didn't know why I asked him that. All I knew was that this was no longer just my spot. It was our spot.

"I have to go back on Tuesday and will be away for some weeks." Richard sounded sad when he told me. I was so used to people leaving I thought I would be perfectly fine. But this was different. I didn't want Richard to go.

"I'll miss seeing you, Richard." I loved the sound of his name in my mouth. It tasted like peace.

Richard took my hand gently, turned it over, and kissed the inside of my palm. "Keep this kiss safe for me until I return."

I walked back home, the melody in my heart singing a little more to its melancholic tune. The next weeks passed with me counting minutes and seconds, and this became our rhythm.

Sugarcane life passed exactly in the same way as the last eight years. I spent the morning helping Dada make the fires, worked in the fields, and worked in the house in the evenings. My uncles played games with Hari, and I lived my secret life. Only this time, my hidden life was a happy one—and not just hiding all that we had done.

The one ripple in this continuity were the moments with Richard every Sunday. He took my hand the second Sunday after his return, and I let him. We sat together, close enough so that our shoulders touched. I had held Hari's hand, but this was different. Richard's hand was rather large, with clean, square nails, and my hand looked so tiny in his. It looked exactly how my heart felt—safe and secure. I liked my hand in his. His hand looked like smooth butter, and mine looked like burned butter, like the bits left behind when you make the ghee.

I told Richard about what life on the farm was like, about Shanti and Hari in Ishapur. But I didn't tell him about Baba or the temple. That was not for telling outsiders. As the weeks passed, our conversations deepened, and we spoke about what indenture was like for people like me and for people like him. I could tell Richard was uncomfortable with these conversations.

"We are little more than slaves, Richard. Our lives are not our own," I said.

His blue eyes became dark, and his brow knitted as he listened. His hands clasped almost in prayer as he leaned forward and rocked slightly back and forth. This was Richard's listening stance. He never stopped asking about life for an Indian, my life, my mama and Hari, even when he was uncomfortable.

"Were you and Hari scared in the holding yard before you left India?" he said, his eyes taking on an even darker look.

"Our fear was out of losing Mama more than of the people. She was our only family, the only person we knew," I said.

Aunty Tara was a topic that took a long time to come up. When it did, I couldn't stop the words or the tears. "I loved Aunty Tara. She was the only person that saw me as Uma and talked to me. With Mama and Hari, we were and are just surviving. Just working and surviving so that we could see tomorrow. She was my only friend in the holding yard, and now she's gone. How can people hurt others so much, Richard? She was such a lovely person, and he hurt her so much. I miss her."

Richard held me tight. He was still rocking back and forth, but his prayer hands now held me. I was his prayer in that moment. We didn't speak much after that. Just normal chitchat as we sat together in our discomfort, our tears, and our budding love.

The next Sunday, Richard had a bag in his hand. As I sat, he opened the bag and pulled out a juicy, ripe mango. My eyes widened with the thrill of anticipation.

"I know you like mangos, Uma, so I picked these from our tree. These are the juiciest ones."

"Do you have one for yourself too?" I asked him without hesitating. Eating mangos with Richard would be so much fun.

"I do, but. . ." He paused. "Maybe we could share one mango together?" His words were a whisper, as if almost expecting a no.

I nodded yes even though I was disappointed and wanted my own mango. The surprise of sharing a mango with this man made me feel oddly excited. My hands longed to feel his hands, and the thought of my lips touching the same spot as his made my heart race, my palms sweat, and my lips dry. I watched him wipe the mango tenderly on his crisp white shirt. Rubbing it on one side, examining it, and then the other side.

"It is just right for eating, Uma. It's perfect! Perfect, like you."

Most times I felt comfortable with Richard, but this time I knew he was the one who could make my whole body shiver. That made me unsure of myself with him. I knew this man was capable of keeping me safe and making me take leaps all at the same time.

"Let me take a bite first. I want to make sure that the mango is ripe and there are no worms," he said.

I watched him bite into the mango. It wasn't a big bite, but large enough that orange-colored juice slowly trickled into his beard, mingling with the dark hair and losing itself in his sweetness. My hand had a will of its own as I reached out to wipe the juice. My fingers became sticky. I took a bite in the same spot that Richard had placed his lips. The flesh was so firm but still tender enough for it to give way to the force of my teeth. It tasted like sunshine and *hurdee* (turmeric). The mango was warmed by the day and Richard's hands. This made it even juicier, and a rush of juice rolled down my chin. I wiped it off. The juice from Richard's chin and mine was now intertwined and undifferentiable. Shyly, I licked my fingers, tasting the precious golden orange nectar. This was the taste of Richard and me.

When he took my fingers in his, I let him. When he gently tasted the nectar, I let him. When he reached to draw me to him, I leaned into him. Our lips gently touched at first, like greeting a soul that you knew was there but out of reach. Joy bridged the gap of anticipation and flourished in that moment. The gentle touch molded into a dance of lips and of need. That need became more urgent as our lips held onto the bridge we created for our souls, for our bodies, for our minds. As our kiss deepened, I lost myself completely. I lost all sense and awareness of what was around me. Richard may have reached for me first, but my tongue was the first to penetrate our lips. And he welcomed me.

In that most precious moment, a Brown girl-woman and a White man held onto each other, sealing their love with the tenderest, sweetest kiss. The only witnesses to this blossoming love were the mangos and the cane, orange and green as far as the eye could see.

That evening, when I went back to the line house, my steps were a little lighter, my smile just a little bit brighter, but my heart was just air. Dada asked me if I was all right.

"Uma Beti, is everything right with you? Your eyes are shining." Odd for Dada to ask anything because all he did was scowl, even at me, although not so much anymore.

"I'm fine. Nothing is wrong. Just happy with everyone." I don't think he believed me. He just looked at me, a little more sad than usual. This time, though, he came toward me and gave me a hug. The kiss on my forehead was what broke me. I hugged him back tightly. Even if Dada didn't know about Richard today, I would tell him soon. I would never forget how he had helped me with the toilets. This man loved me too.

Sunday rituals now included mangos whenever they were in season. I also learned about a new fruit, litchees. So sweet, so juicy! What was it about Port Natal that made everything so sweet? Sugarcane, mangos, and litchees. And Richard. Our rituals also included kissing (one of my favorite parts!), learning about each other and our worlds, asking questions of each other, and learning about our lives and our dreams.

"Do you not want more? More than working on a farm?" he asked.

"What is more, Richard? Like what? Tell me." I didn't whisper because I was a little bit angry. He was asking me if I didn't want more like this life was a choice.

"Maybe a house of your own, a life where you can do something for yourself. Maybe something that is not about working on a farm."

"We think about *more* all the time, Richard. The *more* of not being on the farm. The *more* of freedom from almost slavery."

Richard saw the fire in my eyes and the darkening of my face as I flushed with anger. He saw a tongue that held itself back all the time now reaching out to suck up all the ignorance around it.

"Everyone thinks of what life could be. Uncle Madan wants to be a master of his own life. Uncle Gopal and Aunty Savitri want to live their lives as they want to. Hari, Mama, and I don't want to live here for another five years, but what can we do in this moment?" I crossed my arms in anger.

Richard was asking the question that I asked of myself. But he was asking it as if I had a choice. I was asking questions about the choice that I would make once this indenture was all over. How would he know that we needed to survive first? The days were too long, hard, and dirty to think about what we wanted. All we could think about was ending this cycle of slavery and poverty. My rage made me vicious in my responses.

"Do your sisters dream of more? A life where they can do something of their own? Or is it perfectly acceptable for them to live the lives your father chooses for them?" Nothing could stop my need to hurt Richard with my questions. "Are you as their brother going to stand by and watch them being traded for more wealth? Your family has so much money, Richard, more than I can even imagine! Think about how it is for us coolie women. We are the punishment and reward for bad or good behavior on the farm. We have no choice in our lives, and if we dare ask for more, rape and beatings or death is our reward. So don't ask me about if I want more!"

Richard looked sadly at me. "I am sorry, Uma. I didn't mean to hurt you."

His softness took all the fight out of me. He took my chin in his hand and turned my face toward him. He knelt in front of me, my hands in his free one.

"My sweet girl, I love you. I love you with everything that I am. I ask because I want more. I want a life with you. I want to marry you and have a family with you. I see you with Hari, and I hear you with him and know you will be the best mother to our children. I want the Uma that is scared but still does what she thinks is right. I want the Uma that is fierce and caring. I want the Uma that thinks deeply. I want to marry you, my Uma. I love everything I am with you and hate everything that exists without you."

Seeing Richard lay his heart at my feet broke my anger. Everything I said was true and right. All of it must still be spoken about, but in this moment, Richard's question and my answer were so far apart because I couldn't even contemplate a life with him.

"Why would you want to marry me? You can't marry me. I am little more than a slave," I said.

"Let me tell you what I see. My dearest, I know your heart is hurt, but when you smile, the whole world smiles with you. You brighten not just the day; you take the storm away with your courage and fierceness. The clouds all move away, and the blue sky shares its brightest colors with us. I see the most beautiful brown eyes filled with so much pain and yet are still able to bring light to all around you. I see the loveliest shape of a face that looks like the curve of a waterfall where dark hair cascades like silk. I see a mind that is curious and a soul that is questioning, and I want to be a part of your journey. If you see yourself through my eyes, Uma, you will not ask why I want to marry you. You should ask if I am worthy of you."

Sadness filled me. Did I even dare to think about a life with him? I didn't think Richard understood that there was no life with me, but I knew that. Knowledge of something doesn't prevent you from diving headfirst into it. This was a truth that the world experiences. I loved Richard, and for the first time, I acknowledged this to myself. He made my heart beat stronger.

"Richard, there is so much you don't know about me, about us. You will not like me when you know. Best you decide if you love me after I tell you." Those secrets buried for years were knocking at my future's door. The problem was if I kept them locked, they troubled no one but also held me hostage. If I opened the door, they could infect everyone around me. Richard could hate me.

"You are right," he said. "Sometimes when we know each other, we may change how we feel. But now that we both know there is more to tell, we must. In my mind, nothing you can tell me will make me hate you. But you need to tell me for us to build a life."

Richard was still talking about building a life!

"We left Ishapur because my mama killed Baba, and I gave her the knife to do it," I blurted out.

Richard was silent as I told him about Baba and his fists and all the blood. I told him how Mama had almost died. I told him about Hari and how Baba hit a small baby boy. I didn't cry while telling him. There was nothing to cry about. It was done. Each action had a set number of tears, and all of mine had fallen for those already. But my tears for Richard had not even started.

"I'm the one that made my mama kill her husband. She's a widow today because of me, and I don't regret it at all. That man would have killed us all. We left India and crossed the Kaala Paani to escape him. I know she still has the knife with her. I keep the memory of that knife alive because it reminds me that no one gets to hurt us that much."

"No one gets to hurt you ever again, Uma. I'll make sure of that. My darling girl, it's impossible for me to think about what you went through, what Hari and your mother endured."

Richard held me tightly, and then gently kissed my eyes and my hands. "These eyes have seen too much, and these hands have had to do too much. Now let them rest from the pain and let them experience love," he said.

Did he not get it? I was tainted with blood. I said so to him, and he just hugged me closer.

"The blood of the past is not our life today. I love you, Uma."

I nestled in his arms, but I knew that this wasn't a future on which I could depend. Richard was a White plantation owner's son, and I was a coolie working on their farm. I knew what coolie women were used for by White farmers. And it wasn't to be a wife. But being in Richard's arms was comforting for now, so I buried myself deeper. Maybe even if it was just for these few moments, maybe a few days, or even a few months, I could forget that this couldn't be. I thought I could live a lifetime with Richard while it lasted, so I let him live with his false beliefs. He made me feel good for now, and it made me love him even more. He thought that love beat everything. Let him believe until he can't. I would always love him. Fiercely, both when I'm with him now and from afar when the day comes that the world will no longer allow us to be together.

The days passed fluidly in such false beliefs. These bucolic days meant escape from a harsh reality that awaited us, and we sucked it up. I indulged Richard in his fantasy of a life we could create.

"Tell me again about the house that we would live in," he said. This man, caught up in this love bubble, asked the same question whenever we met. Today, he was lying flat on his back, eyes closed. I lay in the arch of his arm, almost hidden. His heartbeat was strong. My hand slowly rose and fell to its beat.

"Remember, it's less about the house and more about the garden," I said with a laugh. Richard knew of my love for flowers. "Our house will have the most beautiful gardens, filled with orange and purple flowers. The birds-of-paradise must grow in our yard. It will be lovely to have a little river, not too big, just a small brook that runs past the house. If there were large flat stones that we could lie on and watch the sky, that would be perfect!"

Richard smiled at me.

I continued. "I love the large mango tree in your garden. I would love us to have one of those, with a large flat swing that we could swing on."

Maybe I indulged the fantasy because, secretly, I was hoping that it would come true. I had a hope buried so deep that maybe I could be happy forever and not just for now. I hoped that I could love my Richard with the love he gave me, unconditional and unwavering. I knew how I loved this man so brightly, like the hottest flame that knows its end is near when its oxygen runs out, when it can't breathe anymore. So I indulged the fantasy, lighting the flame of hope and extinguishing it almost immediately. Over time, I put out the flame less frequently, until one day, a tiny gift of hope took a permanent hold in my heart. I was still thinking about the garden when I got home. The sun had not set yet. I didn't need to rush. Mama only got angry if I came after sunset. I walked slower just to keep the feeling of Richard for a bit longer.

"Where have you been!" Mama screamed at me when she saw

me. "We have been looking for you for hours!" I wasn't sure what was happening. Mama's eyes were swollen, and her broken healed nose was red, as red could be on a darkened brown skin. She shook me so hard my teeth chattered. Uncle Mohan grabbed me before Mama could shake the life out of me.

"Leave her, we know she goes for a walk," he said.

I turned to look at Uncle Mohan, and I saw Hari sitting in the corner near the kitchen. He was fourteen now and growing into a man, but still a boy. He was crying. His face was flush with tears.

"Hari, what happened?" I pushed Uncle Mohan aside as I ran to Hari. "Why are you crying? Tell me!"

Between sobs, Hari said, "Dada was trying to light the fire again for supper." Hari started to cry again. This time the sobs racked his body, and he couldn't speak. I thought if no one was going to tell me what was happening, I would look for Dada myself. As that thought formed, an unspeakable terror took hold in me. My chest tightened, and I felt my heart pound with fear. My palms were as icy as the sweat on my forehead on this uncomfortably hot Natal day. I knew my dada was no more without anyone saying a word, but I needed someone to say the words into existence.

"Hari baby, tell me what is happening!" I said.

"While Dada was trying to make the fire, he fell over. He was holding his chest. Madan grabbed him as he fell, but he took his last breaths in Madan's arms. Dada died about an hour ago." Mama spoke the terror into reality.

The iciness on my palms and forehead exploded. Even though death was my constant companion from when I was small, I couldn't accept that my dada could leave me.

"No!" I screamed at Mama. "No! People are always dying! No! No! No! Dada loves me, and he wouldn't leave me!"

Mama came to hug me, but I pushed her aside. I didn't want Mama. I needed Hari. And I needed Richard, but that would have to wait for now. Hari and I held each other for the longest time. This was my memory: Mama telling us bad news, and Hari and I holding each other to ease our pain. I knew where my safety lay.

"Who is going to save me when you scold me all the time?" I said.

Mama stood still as my accusing eyes tore into her. There was no screaming at Mama. Just a cold tone letting her know that Dada was her counterbalance in my life. The man who had no smile. I knew that I was being unfair to Mama. She was the one that kept us all together. She kept us alive. But in that moment, all I could think of was the only grandfather I knew was gone, and now I would have to face Mama alone every day.

In keeping us all together, Mama had become a force, a source of power capable of extreme love focused without respite on the work of keeping us all alive. Except the work had changed, we no longer needed to be kept alive; we could do that ourselves, but my mama didn't know that. She stared at me silently, her eyes registering my words. The thing with my mama, though, she would be our force forever. She slowly hugged me and Hari, even though I had said bad things to her.

Dada was everyone's grandfather, not only our line house, but all the houses. When the news spread, everyone came to our house. Dada was loved and feared by all, but mostly loved.

The heat of Natal meant we had to do Dada's funeral quickly. The bodies decayed rapidly in this climate. If coolie lives had no value in life, their bodies certainly had none in death. There was no place to store Brown bodies while we waited for a funeral, so it had to be done quickly. The sardar and a few men came to the house to discuss the arrangements. Mama and the uncles spoke to him. The sardar looked both slightly fearful of Mama and controlling of her at the same time. It was decided that Dada would be cremated in the place that the coolies were burned. It was close to another farm, in a place called Verulam.

That was decided, but the real fight was about when the funeral would happen. The sardar wanted to wait until next week Sunday so that no working hours would be lost. But that wasn't possible for two reasons. Firstly, Dada's body would decay in this heat with no place to keep it, and it would be dangerous for everyone. Even the sardar couldn't argue with that, although he tried hard to say we should keep the body covered in the farm for the week. I don't think even Mr. Thompson would agree to that. He even suggested that Dada be buried, and that got everyone angry. We don't bury! How would the soul gain peace? No, that wasn't possible. Even the sardar knew that was wrong as he said it. He wanted his own body to be cremated. Secondly, funeral rituals start from the day of death and have a defined period in which they must be carried out. Completing these rituals whenever it pleased the sardar meant that Dada's soul would not have peace.

"Do you want Dada Uncle's soul to be around for all that time?" Uncle Madan was furious. "If we don't cremate him within the next two days, I'm sure he will haunt you. His soul will roam with nowhere to go."

The thought of keeping Dada's soul around for a week was too frightening for the sardar. "Let me speak to Mr. Thompson. We certainly can't lose a full day's work. And know that even if he agrees for you to go for the funeral, you won't be paid," he said.

Everything had a price on the plantation, and those who did the farm work paid the highest prices, with their wages, with their lives, and even with their souls. Sadly, everyone knew this and made peace with not being paid the day of Dada's funeral. At least Dada had the courtesy to die on a Sunday so that we didn't lose more pay.

When the sardar left, Mama, the uncles in the house, and Unni spoke about what they needed to do. Dada was from near Chennai, but no one knew any rituals from there. Mama tried to find Uncle Sada, but no one could tell her where he was. That was strange. Uncle

Sada and Dada were friends. The group decided to follow some of what Mama knew and what Unni could tell us. Some of the other uncles and aunties also shared what they did at funerals from their villages. But no one knew exactly what to do for Dada. A simple solution was to take the unique village funerals and make them into something we could do here in Natal, but one that our families back in India would barely recognize. But then, we were not in India. The essence stayed the same, though. Unni had spoken to the lady from the main house, and he would bring flowers for us from the gardens.

They decided that the cremation would be on Monday, but that everyone couldn't go because everyone couldn't lose wages. Only our line house would go, and just Madan, Mohan, and two other men from our house. Unni would go as well. Mama and Megha Aunty would stay behind because women didn't go to cremations. No one even thought to ask me if I wanted to go.

"I want Hari to go," Mama said. "He is their grandfather, and Hari should be there."

Again, no one asked me. He was my grandfather too. I didn't say anything. I knew what the answer would be.

"What about Uncle Sada, Mama? Shouldn't he go too? He was Dada's best friend. How could we forget about him?"

"Everyone has tried to find him. The men from his house told Madan that when Uncle Sada heard about Dada, he walked deep into the sugarcane, and they haven't seen him since." Mama turned to look at the green expanse in front of us, as if searching for Uncle Sada. "I hope that he comes back in time for the funeral."

"I hope so too," I whispered. Dada left so much behind in India. At least he found us here, and he found Uncle Sada.

Hari and I sat with Dada. We knew what we lost, and it wasn't rations or a day's wages. Mama was the only family we knew. Our family slowly became the uncles, Megha Aunty, Unni, and Dada. He was the person who saw us even through his scowl and angry face. Hari and I sat in silence, each holding our own feelings while holding each other's hands. As the plans became more solid, more people poured into our house, and we prepared to spend the night in vigil with Dada. The lamp for the soul was lit. Everyone sat together, giving Dada's soul a peaceful passage into its next life.

The nature and tone of the voices outside changed. I could hear the sardar again, and this time a few English voices. Hari and I went to see what was happening. Mr. Thompson had come to pay his respects and agreed to allowing some men to go to the cremation in Verulam tomorrow. Behind him was Richard. I wanted to run to him and let him hold me tight. Richard's eyes searched for me too. We both knew that we could share the air only right in this moment. We couldn't even share a gaze with each other for longer than a few seconds. Prying eyes would cause too much chaos. My heart almost burst when I saw him. He knew that I would be hurting, and he came just so that he could see me and I him. No words or contact needed to be exchanged. Richard sent me a silent promise to meet on Sunday again. That was all that I needed.

The sunrise brought a deeper heartache and a new mourner. Uncle Sada crouched outside the yard, waiting for Dada. No one asked him where he had disappeared too yesterday. Four men brought Dada outside, and everyone placed a flower on Dada as they said their goodbyes. Uncle Sada slowly approached his best friend. We watched him trace Dada's face, put flowers on his chest, and touch his feet. He placed his head on Dada's feet, kissed them, and left. He didn't say anything to anyone.

The uncles, Hari, and Unni left early in the morning for the journey to Verulam. They would take the better part of an entire day to get there, do the final cremation rituals, and return. Hari scattered Dada's ashes in a river along the route back home. Mr. Thompson would not allow us to scatter them anywhere on the plantation. Hari's head was shaved, and he was the person that carried out the

role of primary vigil-holder by keeping the soul's lamp lit throughout the sixteen-day grieving period. That was Dada's tradition. Our
grieving also had a process for the first ten days. We woke up to a new
rhythm. Uncle Mohan now lit the fire in the mornings. Work continued as normal. Neither the plantation nor the sugarcane grieved for
the loss of a father until the evening when the home grieved. Mama,
Megha Aunty, and I would cook the blandest food (like what we
ate everyday anyway), and after supper, we would settle to listen to
Mama read from the Ramayana.

I was especially interested in the story about how taking the
name of Lord Rama with your last breath would give a soul salvation. I hoped Dada took Lord Rama's name. On the first night, after
eating and listening to the Ramayana, Unni shared a story about
how Dada made his and Megha Aunty's wedding possible. We all
knew the story, but it was good to listen and remember. Unni and
Megha Aunty came every day for those days. They were family.
Everyone told a story of Dada during that time, including me. Stories
of him helping them, stories of him scolding them. I told them the
story of cleaning the toilets. Mama lowered her eyes, but I looked
straight at her.

Each day moved slowly as I waited for the following Sunday
to arrive. Mama had so many chores for me on Sunday: prepare
for the ceremony, clean the house, cook lunch for everyone who
could spend time with us. Mama also was preparing for a longer
Ramayana session that day. There was so much to do, but I wanted to
see Richard. By lunchtime, the house filled with everyone from the
line houses. This was the only time they could come without losing
wages. They brought some rice, dhal, and vegetables so that we had
enough for the week after.

When Mama started reading, I knew the start would take about
an hour, almost an hour and a half. No one would miss me with
so many people there. As I left, I checked on Hari. He was always

looking for me, and the uncles were too busy with the ceremony to distract him. My quiet exit became a run as I made my way to our spot. When I saw Richard, I couldn't move. My feet were rooted to the ground. Richard came to me, picked me up, cradled me in his arms, and held onto my grief-broken body. The sobs rattled me, and I heaved and gasped as I cried for Dada with the man I loved. Once the sobs passed, I told Richard about this darling man who showed me his love through his care for me instead of words or smiles, and of his best friend who kissed Dada's feet. I spoke of Dada until it was time to leave.

Richard held my face in his hands and said, "My darling girl, I wish I could take all your grief away. Even though I can't, let me hold it for you for a little while so that your heart can heal."

I let Richard be the keeper of my pain from that day. Most importantly, Richard was the keeper of my heart.

Dada's death changed us all, but in some ways, we found new rhythms in our lives. The time came when we were finally at the last hurdle of indenture. I was eighteen when our indenture was over. When ten years of working someone else's cane ended, Mama was given a choice. We could go home if we wanted, or we could get a small parcel of land. Mama didn't ask Hari and me if we wanted to go home. She knew we didn't want to leave. Our choice was to be free here. In this new land. In our new home. Hari, Mama, and I grew up here, and these people were our people now. India and our village didn't feel like home anymore. I still had memories of Shanti, but I had forgotten what her face looked like. I remembered the Neel River, but it was more the feeling of being free that I remembered. The feeling of carrying no burden. Carrying no secrets.

The days around the end of our indenture were scary for us.

Mama worried about how we would live. Hari was worried about losing all his friends. I had my own worries and my own hopes. The day that our indenture ended was the first day we were free to live a life in hope and not fear on a small piece of land that was ours. We built our home with its garden and bird-of-paradise flowers where the pieces of paper fluttered in the wind like prayer flags. The village was called Hillary, and many of the people who came with us made a home there. There were lots of new people, too, but it was good to have people of your own.

Mama started wearing a big black dot. Her face, though healed a long time ago, wasn't as beautiful as before we left Ishapur, although I couldn't remember clearly what she looked like then. Years of struggle created a new face for Mama. She still cut her hair, but no one outside of Hari and I saw it. She started wearing a turban the day after we were free. She still wore a coat—it was a new one now—and her dhoti was white, not dusty and sweaty. Now she read the Ramayana for everyone every Sunday under the large syringa tree. The tree was full of leaves, and the air underneath was cool most of the time. The aunties especially loved to listen to her. Megha Aunty brought many of her friends to hear Mama.

Uncle Gopal and Aunty Savitri looked for us when their indenture was over. They didn't have children of their own, and they desperately wanted children to love. They loved us. The village and its children became theirs. Many of the village men didn't like Mama. They didn't like that she could read. They didn't like that their wives came to listen to a woman reading. I heard them say that Mama didn't know her place. When Megha Aunty told Mama that Unni had hit her, Mama told her to stay with us for a while.

"The cane makes him so angry! He only wants to fight! And when he drinks, he accuses me of sleeping with Mr. Thompson," Megha Aunty said.

She came to stay with us in our two-bedroom house with her

two babies, Shanbagavelli and Nithya. When Mama went to get our water from the tap down the road, Unni came to fight with her. People still talk of the day. The uncles had never seen such an angry woman. She made Unni get on his knees and beg her forgiveness. I don't know what Mama said, but Megha Aunty went home the next day. Not all the men were happy, though, and I heard them grumbling about a woman "acting like she is a man." Mama was fierce, and they feared her. She still scared me. I loved my mama, but I wasn't sure I liked her anymore.

My solace was Richard, but in this new world, we had to find a new way to meet. I was sad to leave our spot. It was the place we fell in love with each other. It was the place that Richard won me over to believing this Brown girl could make a life with this White man. It was the place where I started seeing a world that could maybe not be so full of pain and secrets. Sweet Richard was determined that we would find a new way.

Mr. Thompson had become powerful with his plantations and businesses. Richard stopped going to Johannesburg and spent more time at the terminals in Durban where the sugar was shipped out to England and other places. The sugar business was growing, and Durban was becoming a sugar port for the world. Richard came to the terminal every day now.

Once we no longer worked on the farm, we had to earn a new living. We had a choice to work on the farm as paid workers and not indentured laborers, but neither Mama, Hari, nor I wanted to do that. Sugar was what brought us here, but it was also our prison for the last ten years. We would not go back to prison.

As more people like Mr. Thompson became richer and richer, they wanted bigger houses, bigger buildings, and the demand for stone increased. Quarries to extract stone became common, and stone became a lucrative business. Such a quarry opened near us. There were few things we were good at after working on a farm for ten years, but digging, carrying, and doing backbreaking work was our strength. My job was to carry the smaller stones in a basket to the stone piles.

I looked even filthier than when I was on the farm, but at least now, I was making my own money. Richard would often meet me at the quarry, and some days when I finished work, we would go together into the town. We had to be discreet. I would meet him at the end of the street. He would complain that I shouldn't be doing this work, but that was easy to say when you lived in the main house that the stone I quarried was used to build. He would come in his car with clean clothes for me. Richard's father was so rich that he was one of the first men to import a car. Richard told me that the very first car arrived in South Africa for President Paul Kruger just a few years before, and his father brought not one, but two soon after that. I was nervous to get into the car. What if people saw us? But I also wanted to be with the man I loved.

"Let's run away together," Richard said. "I'm staying here only because of you. Why do you want to work in this quarry?"

He wanted us to get married, have children, and live happily ever after. I wanted that fantasy, too, but that wasn't the world we lived in. Richard and I lived in parallel worlds that coexisted but never met. Why did he not understand that Mama and Hari would have no face in their world if I left? People would spit on them, and they would be forever shamed by my actions. No, that wasn't something I could do.

"I love you. But I can't leave Mama and Hari," I said.

"I'm not asking you to leave anyone, Uma! The four of us can go away far from this. We can build a life together. Maybe we can go to Cape Town. No one will know us there at all. I want you to be happy, and I know having your mother and Hari with you is important. We could have a house for them and one for us. Or they could live with us. It doesn't matter to me. What matters is that I'm with you and that you're happy."

I laughed at him, and I could see his anger building.

"Have you met my mama? Do you know my mama? She will never go anywhere with you or anyone. Mama has built her community and her life single-handedly, and nothing will take that away from her. Not even my happiness."

"What does that mean for us, Uma? Will we ever get a chance to be happy? Will I fetch you like a thief for the rest of my life? You talk about Brown girl and White man, but I only think about the woman I love."

"It's your station in life, your wealth, your privilege that allows you to even talk to me about not seeing our differences! It's the ease with which everything comes to you and that you don't see that I can't leave without Mama and Hari, and they won't leave because this is their life that they worked so hard for. It was easy for your sisters to be married. They went from wealth to wealth without a day of work. That's not the life my family lives."

"I think you should stop right now," he said, shaking with anger. His blue eyes darkened, and his dark brows seemed even more hooded as his face reddened. Richard's body tensed, his fists balled, and in that moment, I tensed and shrunk. I pulled back and crossed my arms over my face. An old instinct for protection came back. Balled fists, dark eyes, and angry faces meant that I should prepare for blows to my body. The silence that followed felt like an eternity.

"Uma, what's wrong? Why are you hiding yourself from me?" Richard crossed the chasm that had developed from our fight in a second, and he pulled me into his arms. His voice was urgent and soft, full of concern and worry. "I'm not going to hurt you. I will let no one hurt you."

I melted into Richard, and all my fears poured out through my tears. Richard was crying as well. It wasn't a cleansing or a renewal. It was a sad acknowledgment from both of us that love may not be enough for us. That no matter how hard you loved, how fiercely you loved, some things were more important, like the life and sacrifice that was made for you to live. The moment felt like a nod to the end that would come, just not now.

As Richard's mouth found mine, I made a choice to be happy and let go in this moment. I didn't know how many moments like this I would have with the man that held my heart. A man that played guardian for my soul even when he knew that he wouldn't have me for our lifetime. I let go and surrendered to the love that was us.

We were at the terminal one Friday watching the sugar being weighed and loaded onto the ships. Usually Friday to Sunday were loading days so that the ships could leave with their golden cargo by Monday. Fridays were usually quieter as most of the sugar came in on Saturday. Richard being Richard was stealing kisses again, laughing as I stole my own kisses back. It was breezy and cooler, most usual for that time of year, which usually meant a hot and humid period to come.

"My, my! What have we here? Does your mother know that you parade yourself around with White men?" a voice giggled with a delicious discovery. It was the old sardar. The sardar was in charge now of loading ships for all Mr. Thompson's sugar from all the plantations.

The sardar turned to Richard and said, "And does your father know that you're messing around with brown sugar?" He laughed. "I'm sure he'll be fine for you to sow your oats. Have your fun, boy."

"What's wrong with you?! You forget I'm your boss!" Richard said.

"No, boy, your father is my boss, and he doesn't like Brown flesh. So don't forget that! As for you, your mother is acting like she is better than everyone. Maybe everyone should know how her daughter is wild and sleeping with a *gora* (White man) while she is reading the Ramayana so piously!"

The sardar walked away before Richard or I could respond.

"What are we going to do? This man is the most horrible man, and everyone hates him, but he can create trouble," I said.

"Maybe we should tell your mother and Hari now before he does. Let them know that we want to marry and live together with them. Not here. I can tell Father that I'm leaving. He has his other son to run his business."

To think I even considered what Richard was asking was a testament to how much I loved him. I wanted to believe in the world that Richard created, but I knew that was a false world. A worry was forming. I hadn't bled this month, and Aunty Savitri saw me vomiting yesterday morning and this morning. I still went to work, so I didn't think she suspected anything yet. I didn't even know if there was anything to suspect.

"Let's first see what the sardar does. Maybe he's too scared to say anything to your father," I said. "I know he fears Mama. We can think about what we need to do."

Richard wanted to tell the whole world right then, and I wanted to wait. This moment was like every moment in our relationship. Our parallel paths were still strong, sometimes breaking all the rules of science and custom and making magic just for a few moments.

Richard sighed warily, with the tiredness of waiting. "Let's wait for a few days to see what happens if that's what you want, but I'm telling my father in the next two weeks. I want him to know the woman I love and will marry. You underestimate this fiercely powerful woman that is your mama. I think she'll understand, and she'll want you to be happy."

Dear, naïve Richard. You don't know my mama. I love her and she loves me, but I don't like her all the time.

Chapter 12

Shivali's Whispered Songs

Uma didn't like me. I loved her more than enough for that not to matter. If love happened only when the other person loved you back, then I had only known love once in my life. And it wasn't love for the man I married. To him, I was the walking womb his parents found for him to ensure his soul would pass on through the birth of his son. That was one of the two jobs that wives had—to bear sons, not daughters, just sons, that would provide passage for their souls to be reborn in this world through their children. The second job was to serve, without question, the husband, and his entire family. Your worth as a woman was measured against these two jobs. Failure to have children or to have only daughters was your fault alone. The fault was never the man's because God had blessed him with sperm that did its job. The weakling in the chain of life, death, and rebirth was the woman.

The night of the day we took our vows was the death of me. Or maybe the beginning of death for him. I was scared of what it meant to be a wife to this older man. He was twenty-nine years old. I was fifteen. His mother and father came to meet me before the wedding to ensure that I wasn't deformed and that none of my family was. They wanted sons, and they didn't want deformed grandchildren.

They also wanted to see how many girl children my family had. Luckily for them, it was just me and my two brothers. That ratio was acceptable. My family produced two sons to transport souls and one womb to secure their birth. The womb had to be virgin, unscarred, and free from any possibility of defective children. They were Brahmins. They wanted Brahmin wombs, and my brother was keen to rid our family of the burden of an unmarried daughter.

After Baba died, Indra Bhaiya (my elder brother) waited only for forty days after the funeral. He sent word out that there was a virgin Brahmin girl ready to marry with a dowry of gold and cows. That brought this family to our house. All their needs could be met. The only mark on our family and the offer was that I could read and write.

"That's not a problem, Ma-ji," Indra Bhaiya said to my potential mother-in-law. "My father liked to teach her, but he's dead now and I don't believe in wasting time teaching girls. She will be married, have children, and serve her in-laws now. And if she's disobedient, just hit her. She can cook, my mata-ji taught her, so she should serve your family well."

My mother-in-law was a large, fair-skinned, red-lipped woman. She was heavily laden with jewelry and wearing a bright red sari. She wanted my brother to know how influential they were and how much money they had. Her life was one of service to her in-laws, and she had produced three sons. She had done a good job and fulfilled her duties as a wife. It was now her turn to demand. Her husband sat there just drinking chai and eating snacks. He left the negotiation to her.

"What about dowry? What will you send her with?" she said.

"We're a Brahmin family. Gold and cows are our dowry. I'm sure you'll find this more than generous. Also, Ma-ji, we won't interfere in your affairs after the marriage. Once she leaves our house, she's no longer our family," my brother said.

"We'll decide if it's enough when we get it. My son is in great demand. You're lucky that we're even considering your family. If the dowry is not enough to meet our standing in our society, we'll turn the groom's party back and you'll be disgraced. There are enough girls ready to marry my son."

Indra Bhaiya smiled, "I'm sure you'll be more than satisfied. This is our honor." His face held no contempt for her ask. He was certain he was better than her.

I was standing behind the door while my life was being traded. Womb, cows, and gold for society's acceptance of my family. No one asked me if I wanted to marry, or if I wanted to marry him. I hadn't even seen him. His mother scared me so much. Her red lips and orange teeth were stained by the *paan* (betel leaf) that she chewed. That made me even more fearful of what was in store for me.

That he was almost twice my age didn't matter. Indra Bhaiya didn't care. My mother didn't have a say in this at all. She just listened to Indra Bhaiya. She transferred her subservience from her husband to her son. She knew nothing but how to be a servant of the men in her home. My younger brother, Kishan, was still playing with sticks and stones with his friends. At twelve, he cared about other more childlike adventures, as he should have, or maybe he didn't understand what was happening. Either way, the outcome was the same. I was alone and watching from the sidelines as my life was bartered. When alone, I sang Ramayana verses to calm my frightened heart, but my prayer wasn't to a god that I didn't know, or who allowed this situation to happen. My prayer was to my father, my baba, the man that taught me to think and to hope.

"Baba, help me please. These people are scaring me, and I'm afraid for what they might do to me," I prayed.

We all heard stories of the ladies that had "accidental kitchen fires" when they didn't have children after two years. That was considered generous. Sometimes after just one year, a teenage bride would have an unfortunate death, and her husband would find a wife within the next month. Then there were those who had daughters and produced no sons. That was a special kind of torture. The first daughter was maybe left to live, a token of acceptance because at least society and family knew you could have children. But the second, third, or even fourth (if you were still alive by then) were drowned, or similar. You were still expected to produce sons immediately after your child's death. And then if you couldn't, you welcomed the "accident" to be rid of the fear and pain. Pain peeked at every corner, and both men and women were equal gatekeepers of the torture.

I prayed to Baba to please keep me safe with this man, to watch over me and my children when they came. Maybe even though his mother was scary, he might be kind? Maybe I would be lucky again, and he would be like my baba. Maybe he would love me. The love I had known in my life was from my own baba. He loved me enough to teach me to read and write. He loved me more than enough to ensure that I had an equal place by his side. Indra Bhaiya didn't like that. He and Baba fought about Baba teaching me and Kishan at the same time. Kishan didn't fight Baba. He did as Baba asked and then was ready to go play.

Indra Bhaiya loved his place as the Brahmin in our village. He liked that people came to our house to talk to Baba and ask for guidance. He liked being in charge of everything and everyone. Indra Bhaiya was much older than me, he was twenty-four years old. My mother had two children between him and me. Two boys—one boy child who died at birth and another who lived for a year before he died from diarrhea. My mother was desperate to replace the sons, and then I arrived. I know that my mother resented having this girl child, even though she had Indra Bhaiya. My life and the death of her two sons represented her failure as a wife. When Kishan arrived, I wonder if she felt relief and release from her fears? What my mother didn't give me, Baba did. The safety and peace of being loved. Baba did that. And then he died and left me with all these people who were so eager to get me out of their house. Prachi Bhabi, my brother's wife, was the only one who knew how I was feeling. But she would never say anything. Indra Bhaiya wouldn't tolerate that in any way. He was honest when he said that he would never interfere in how this new family would treat me because he didn't tolerate anyone interfering in how he treated his wife. She already had two children, a boy and a girl. For now, she was safe, until the pressure to have more sons mounted.

I didn't see my husband's face until the wedding night. Custom was for the bride to be fully covered. No one saw my face, and I saw no one. *If I'm not seen, do I even exist?* When the groom's party arrived at our house, my brother welcomed them with a tour of the ten cows that he was sending with me. He told them of the gold neck-lace that I was wearing, and that was now theirs. The party didn't turn back, they were satisfied. Indra Bhaiya's honor was intact. His burdens were now relieved. I was married off to an unknown man never to be seen again. What joy that night would have brought to my bhaiya. There would have been full on celebrating of the relief of their burden.

That night brought me no joy. My husband's family decorated the marital bed with flowers and led me to it. They were saying things I didn't understand about what was about to happen and how I would feel in the morning. The morning was particularly prominent in the discussion. His aunt told me that they would be coming for the sheets in the morning. They were a Brahmin family, and all the girls must be virgins. Blood on the sheets would be their proof.

"Tonight, you will become a woman. Your husband will mark you to make you a woman, so you must bathe and wash your hair before you see anyone. If anyone sees you before you bathe, especially the young girls, this will bring bad luck to our family."

I wanted to laugh at this, but his aunt was serious. Her face looked like she may have experienced bad luck herself! Baba had taught me not to believe in such things as good or bad luck. Baba said we made our luck. But he wasn't here, and these people believed this. She believed in it. She wasn't unkind, just telling me what this family wanted. The family bathroom was across the yard.

"How will I cross the yard to get to the bathroom with no one seeing me?" I asked.

"If you get up before the sun comes up, no one will see you. The boys have drunk a lot tonight, including my husband. They're celebrating this marriage, especially after how the last one ended. They'll only wake up much later, and no one is working the fields today," she said.

Brahmin families drink? Mine didn't.

He was married before. I didn't know that. I wondered if Indra Bhaiya knew. He was much older than me, so it was plausible that he was married before. I asked his aunt.

"Shame, his first wife was so pretty. A small, tiny girl from a village a day's ride away," she said. "They had been married for five years. She fell into the old well and drowned. No one used that well and we all wondered what she was doing so far away from the house. They found her body a week later. That was almost four months ago now. Lucky, there were no children in the marriage. No children that are now motherless. You don't have to take care of anybody else's children, Shivali."

That was the first time that someone used my name today, and it was in the same conversation to tell me that my husband had a wife who died in a suspicious accident.

"Baba, please stay with me. I'm so scared," I prayed, as the well-meaning aunt left me alone to face this man I had never seen.

I sat in the middle of the bed, head covered, waiting for him. The room was small, not too much bigger than the hallway at home. A glass of milk sat on the counter, laced with who knew what so that he would be relaxed to perform his duties for the night. It was the dust I remembered the most. The dust that hung over villages gathered in groups on the floor. The dust and I had a special relationship. Dust was the witness to the start and end of my marriage. On my wedding night, the dust gathered and whispered in the corners. The day I killed him, the dust welcomed the end of my marriage as my half-moon bangles lay strewn across the floor.

The door opened quietly, and my husband entered the bedroom. I was expecting him to be drunk. His aunt had said that he would be celebrating. But the man that entered the room was in his senses and deliberate. He went for the milk glass and drained every drop before he came to stand at the edge of the bed.

"Lift up your veil. I want to see your face." His voice had an edge of steel to it. The words he uttered had menace and fear as companions.

I lifted the covering, and I looked at him.

"I asked you to lift your veil, not to look at me. You haven't earned that right yet." The blade edge of his anger sharpened his words. I dropped my eyes.

"Baba, please, please take care of me. Don't let him hurt me." These words formed their own mantra in my mind.

"Fair face, nice features. Pretty like Mohali. Hopefully not barren like Mohali. You wouldn't want to find yourself in the bottom of a well."

"Mohali was your first wife?" I asked. I clearly had not learned my lesson. The back of his hand across my cheek was my reward.

"You have not earned the right to talk to me. Do you understand?"

My hand raced to my face, and I was too busy feeling the pain to realize the question was waiting for an answer.

"I said, do you understand?"

My hair was pulled back in one stroke, and I looked directly into his eyes. The eyes of the beast. Red and calm. I nodded in acceptance. And my hair was released from his grip.

"Mohali was defective. No sons. So, no more Mohali. Just so you know what your job is and what may happen if you fail." All of this was delivered like he was talking to a child, telling a story that people wanted to listen to.

That night passed with fear and so much pain, unbelievable physical pain, a kind I had not experienced before. I became a woman apparently, but I felt like a scared child. And he lied. My job wasn't just to give birth to sons; my job was also to be his place to release his anger.

When I was pregnant with my first child, there was excitement and celebration. I was pregnant so quickly, and they were going to bring another son into the world. No one even considered that it might be a girl. When my daughter was born, everyone mourned but me. Some relatives flung themselves on the floor in despair. No one spoke to me, and his mother told me that they would get rid of her immediately. My Uma was born fighting, though. She breathed fight into me too. I refused to let them take her. I told his mother—why she agreed, I don't know—that the next child would be a son, and if it were not, she could kill them both. I knew that I would leave before that happened. They didn't even care what I named this beautiful girl child. In all the mythical stories of Shiva, Sati sacrificed herself and was reborn as Uma. I named my daughter Uma. She was the one that never gives up, the one that pushes on. She was my Uma, my beautiful, relentless daughter.

When Hari was born, it was like the first child was born. They all forgot that we had a child, Uma. But I didn't. Little girls should not have to feel that other women, especially their mothers, don't want them. Uma would never feel that she wasn't wanted. I loved my Uma, even though she may not have loved me all the time. Baba may have taught me the Ramayana, but he gave me something much more. He gave me the feeling of being wanted, and no one could take that away. Hari and Uma would know they were loved and wanted.

I knew why Uma felt so distant. There was nothing I could do about it. How did I explain to her that you couldn't build a life with just modesty and dignity. My modesty left me the day he thought it was fine to threaten me with his first wife's death. My dignity came from my children leading a safe, good life. On the plantation, while the men in our line house were kind to us, not all the men and women from the other line houses were. On the kindest side they would say nothing. The meanest would say to the children, "Your mother is the sardar's mistress. She sells herself to him. She is nothing more than a prostitute." The children at first didn't understand this, but as they grew and understanding deepened, I saw their eyes change when they looked at me—especially Uma. Hari may have not fully understood, but he heard the words.

Dada shielded them a lot from cruelty and poison, but he couldn't all the time. Dada was their fiercest protector. I missed him so much. Often after everyone had gone to sleep, I would sit outside on the stairs, staring into the darkness. Even though I knew the sugarcane was stretching sharply green for miles, all I could see was pitch black in front of me, behind me, to the side of me, and in me. Then some days, I would walk back from his house to the edge of the sugarcane. The sardar extracted his full price for putting Hari, Uma, and me on the cart the day we arrived. I wondered if it would have been better to just wait at the dock or if this was a better life. Dada was the one who waited for me. Chai was ready before the fires were put out for the night. Dada never asked me where I came from. This was left unspoken but understood. Where my father was no more, Dada stood in his place. For me, for them.

Uma knew I couldn't bind myself to them. Time had whispered too many loving lonely words in my ears. Songs written with sickles in the heat of cane fields. Songs fired in the kitchens of the sugarcane workers. Songs steeled on beds of the sardars, and songs transformed through the reading of the Ramayana. I silently laughed as the flies on the sardar's ceiling played hide-and-seek with my pride. Pride vaults could only be emptied if they were filled. I had no vault. I had no pride. I knew the flies as intimately as I knew the words of the stories I read. One only became good at something if you repeated it enough times. I watched the flies often, without pride or dignity. Only the promise of freedom kept me alive. I thought when our indenture was over, freedom would fill my vault. But instead, emptiness stayed. Freedom just kissed my face and left my soul as lonely as ever.

Mohan and Madan were the most protective of the children. You could be forgiven for thinking they were the children's elder brothers. They never questioned me, but they took care of the children. Now, we were all older. Uma was almost nineteen. She worked in the quarry and contributed to the home we had built in Hillary. Uma had never asked me about the sardar and the farm, but I knew that she knew. She didn't like me much, but I loved her.

My darling beautiful Uma. My sweet, sweet baby girl, who saw too many adult things in her short life. She had never spoken about her father or the temple or the train. All of it stayed hidden, the knot wrapped too tight to open. She showed emotion only to Hari. She had never left Hari's side. How often had I watched her tend to Hari when they were little, taking on the role of mother to him while I built our life. She was a mother to Hari even now when he was seventeen years old. Sometimes when I watched them together, I felt like they didn't belong to me. While only two years separated them in age, the tragedy of experience and a lifetime of pain and fear made two years feel like twenty. Uma was Hari's mother. I just gave birth to him. Hari was a man. And a child. He bought white guavas for Uma. I saw them. Hari was the only living being that Uma shared any bond with.

This separation from me came gradually, and I didn't even know when it happened. I just remember the day I realized that I wasn't a part of their twosome. Like most Sundays on the sugarcane plantation, everyone went off to the towns that surrounded us. In the beginning, I used to be so tired all the time. Sundays were the days to catch up on rest so that my body could function for the rest of the week. I needed to recover from nights with the sardar and Sunday was his family time. I needed to recover from working the sugarcane the whole week, from cooking for my line house, and from being a mother to two small, frightened children, at least in the early years. This went on for years, but that changed over time.

Uma and Hari took on more as they grew, giving me the chance to heal my body and my mind. Uma wanted to go with Madan and Mohan or any of the other good men, but I wouldn't hear of it. I was too scared to let her go out on her own, and besides I needed her to take care of Hari while I rested. Madan and Mohan would watch over them when they didn't go out. But even they had to get out of the farm at some point. One Sunday, I realized I had been on my own for the last three Sundays. Uma and Hari didn't want to be with me. They were in and around the farm on their own. I was alone. It was fine for the first two Sundays, after a while it stopped being comforting and became lonely. No one wanted to be with me on the one day we had to rest.

Everyone had created new lives without me. That felt like the path of my life. I had been attending to our survival. The one leading my family to safer pastures. Our safer pastures had been swathes of blue as we crossed the Kaala Paani and oceans of green of the sugar-cane fields. Safer but not without danger, yet I had protected them. And still then, the world that Uma and Hari created existed for them only, and to be a part of it, you must be invited in. I had never received that invitation. I was still their mother, and they loved me, but their world didn't need me anymore. The subtle and pointed rejection sat like stone around parts of my heart. I felt the pain deepening every time I saw them together. Each step we had taken had been to survive, and yet every step had slowly killed our bond. Where we were three of us before, now two was enough for them.

Even though I felt the distance, I made my heart strong, like a stone that didn't break even with the hardest force. The scared, vulnerable Shivali was invisible to everyone, and even my own children didn't see me anymore. Everyone knew that you existed and saw you for what you did, but no one saw you for who you were. I had come to like who I was today, in parts. I allowed no one to trespass on my heart. I liked the parts that would not allow anyone to tell me how to live, when to cover my head, when to speak, or when to read. I struggled with the parts that were lonely, that had known little love and compassion.

Joy had not been my dear friend. If anything, joy had been that infrequent guest who visited only to taunt me and to give me a glimpse into what I didn't have. That part I didn't like. My mind and body healed in this land of Port Natal, but my spirit sometimes struggled to rise and mend its shattered remains. Who knew Shivali as joyful? No one around me could say that they knew me as happy. The only people who knew me as joyous and playful were dead or long gone. Did that mean that a happy Shivali never existed? Maybe it did, and maybe it didn't matter anymore. This adult, strong fierce Shivali was all that there was. My baba died, and he took his child Shivali with him.

Thinking of the me that was lost forever was hard, so I focused on the parts that I liked. After we left the plantation, more people asked me to read the Ramayana for them. I liked reading the Ramayana. It gave me solace and purpose, and the shadows of the Shiva's temple had been my companions. I loved the stories and the rhythm of them. Baba taught me to appreciate the poetry and construction of the verses. He opened my mind to appreciate the multiple layers of understanding that the Ramayana presented to the reader and the listener. The thing was I didn't believe in God. I didn't believe in a power that would save me from this world. Why didn't God save me from my husband back then? No, I believed in the power of this world and all in it. I believed in the power of owning your destiny, just like Sita owned hers in the Ramayana. But for these people, listening to the Ramayana kept them linked to India they said.

"Didi, I miss everything about my village. Mostly, I miss my mandir and doing my prayers. Listening to you read us the story of Ram makes me feel like I'm home, even for a little while." This was a common comment that people of Hillary shared with me. Listening to me read the Ramayana made them feel a little less lost.

"Sometimes I wish I could just go home, but there is nothing there for me. No one will even remember me I think." This was another sorrowful cry that I heard often. This feeling of loss changed over time. After a while, it went away, but in the early days, we still longed for the land of our birth.

My love for Uma and Hari was everlasting, but my separation from them was devastating. No breeze could wash away the feeling of being so isolated, even when surrounded by people. It seemed like my only companions were my turban and my dhoti. They readied me for the day. They watched over me and gave me solace when desolation walked as my companion. My body held the ringing of too many songs. Everybody—Baba, Indra Bhaiya, my husband, the sardar, Uma, Hari—everyone had written a part of the song. But they only saw their piece of the story. No one saw the whole melody. The whole only had sound for me.

I taught Hari and Uma to read the Ramayana. They were able not just to work in the sugarcane fields. Maybe they could teach the generations to come. I knew that generation would only be Hari's, though. Uma would never marry. She said so many times.

Some of the men didn't like me reading the Ramayana. Often, I would hear mumblings in the background. No one would dare confront me. But they would stand whispering in the shadows. Why didn't they read then? But of course, no one would, because no one could. They were stuck with me until someone could teach them. The women were not shy to share with me the fights and drama once we were done. Uma normally made chai for everyone, and we sat and talked. Hari took chai to the men who often sat on the edge of the group. Some women braved their husbands when they came to hear the story being sung. Some of the men were angry, but the majority liked to listen. Many came because they felt the song in their hearts, regardless of the person who sang it.

What a song it was. Under the syringa tree, in the village of Hillary, in the cool of the morning, people listened with curious minds. The grace of the words tantalized the ears. The mystical melody caressed the faces of those around me, working its magic, changing the souls of generations to come. Who would have thought that the fear of crossing the Kaala Paani would transform into the joy of a new bond? This pact with Port Natal was solemnized by the cool ocean breeze and inked with the sweat of hard work.

While the syringa tree's leaves provided a large pool of cool shade, the ground was hard like the rock of the quarry it sat upon. This area given to each one of us as part of our contract was hard and sat on the fringes of lushness. But this community didn't mind. Brown, dusty land that belonged to all of us was more comforting than to live on lush land where we were owned by others.

Chapter 13

Shivali's Elephants and Evenings

Uma worked at the quarry not too far away from home. It was hard, backbreaking work and sometimes involved long hours. My poor girl was so tired when she came home, but I saw the happiness generally on her face. She liked working and being independent. She often wanted to pay for things, and we could use the money, so Uma and I decided that she would work. Hari worked as well. There was a small store that sold everyday supplies, and Hari helped out the owner, an older man, with deliveries to the homes, especially for the heavier loads like flour and rice. The dairy close by also served the community around us, and Hari delivered the milk in the mornings. He wasn't the only one, though; many other young boys, and some young men Uma's age, also delivered milk and curd. Hari was busy in the early afternoons with the store deliveries, so he was usually home before the sun set.

Uma came home late sometimes. I worried about her being out so late or working so hard. I never took Uma to be the girl that worried about how she looked to everyone, but I saw that she bathed before she came home.

"Uma, why do you wash before you come home?" I asked.

"The dust is too much. The lady's washroom has a tap, and no one uses the washing area before they go home, just the toilets, so the washing area stays somewhat clean," she said.

Sometimes she smelled nice too. Uma looked like my mother. Long, dark hair that reached below her shoulder blades. She parted her hair in the middle and tied her hair into either a long plait or a loose bun at the base of her neck. It wasn't often that Uma left her hair down. It was too hot and sticky to have long hair.

Uma's face deserved its own spot in the sun. She had the sweetest, round face. Her features were finer than mine. Gentler. Her eyes were slightly almond shaped like my mother's. She had a small nose that had a slight uptilt at the end and prominent cheek bones. Hari would say that Uma had sharp cheekbones but no sharp words! Her face was darker than wheat, darkened even further by the quarry sun, with the tiniest of black dots sitting just in between her thick bushy eyebrows. While her hair was long, Uma was average height for an Indian girl and thin. Her hair weighed more than her body.

Uma heard so many stories at the quarry, and we waited to hear them, but she wasn't one to easily share stories. They seemed too frivolous. She was the first person who told us about the elephants that roamed nearby, though. The day was warm, not sticky, and the evening offered a cool, salty ocean breeze. Some of the trees had started losing their leaves, but few trees changed with the seasons here. Uma had arrived home from work later than normal. She smelled of the sea, and I wondered why.

"Uma, was it windy today at the quarry?"

"Not really, why do you ask?" Uma looked away as she washed her hands carefully before eating. The dust from the quarry never seemed to leave her.

"You smell of the ocean, so I wondered."

"Maybe, the afternoon got breezier just before I left. But let me tell you a story my friends at the quarry were talking about today at lunch." Uma looked at me excitedly, telling me the story as she sat to eat. I totally forgot about the sea smell as I got lost in Uma's story. After all, it wasn't often that she shared stories, and I loved seeing my girl child smile.

"I also want to hear, wait for me!" Hari rushed to wash his hands and sit with us. "Let's start, I'm here."

Both Uma and I laughed at how excited he was. Any news was good to break the sameness of the day.

"So, the quarry overseer, Nigel Sir, was telling us about the elephants that roam the high ridges of Durban. The hills are the ones that we can see from here."

"Didi, that's so close to us!" Hari looked more excited than nervous at the thought of the elephants being close by.

"So, the English men are thinking about creating some sort of road where a herd of elephants walk to the Greyville marshes. They walk this path to drink every evening and now they have made a path from the top of the Berea ridge, right down to the marshes."

Hearing about elephants reminded me of home, even if that memory was fuzzy. I think that's why this story stuck with me.

"An old house, built on the path to the Greyville marshes, stands in the way of the elephants. The elephants damage the house all the time. Maybe they think this is their pathway, and the house is in the way. Nigel Sir called it Elephant House."

Hari's eyes widened. "Do you think they will come close to us, Didi? I would like to see the elephants too. Sometimes it would be nice to have something more than everyday Hillary to see."

Hari's voice sounded wistful, and the ache in his words hurt my heart.

"I don't think so, Hari baby. But who knows?"

They looked at each other and giggled, and I was reminded again that they have their own world without me.

"The overseer said that they're building a tollgate between Durban and the inland places like Pietermaritzburg," Uma went on.

"The wagons have to pay to enter the town. They may even charge the people who are walking."

"What is a tollgate, and where would they build that, Didi?"

"It is a gate where they make you pay before you use the road. That's why we spoke about the elephants because the tollgate is going to be built close to the Berea Ridge where the elephants walk."

"I wonder if the elephants will also have to pay the toll?" Hari said cheekily, and we all laughed.

How I wished this moment would never end. But like everything, time and people interfering in our lives made these moments pass rather rapidly. Over the last months, the older ladies had started to nag me at every opportunity.

"Have you found a match for Uma? You should start thinking about her wedding." That was all they thought about, so they wanted to make it my worry too.

"If she gets too old, no one will want to marry her. Her age to have children will pass by, and then she will be your burden!" Some of these "old" ladies were still having babies when their daughters-in-law were pregnant, so I didn't think being unmarried at nineteen or twenty was a problem.

"If Uma is unmarried, she will bring bad luck into your house." I had to laugh at this unneeded comment. What did they think my life had been all these years? Uma had been my luck. They didn't even want to think about that question.

"What if Hari's wife doesn't want Uma. Where will she go?" Well, she would be with me. She was a strong woman, capable of taking care of herself. She didn't really need Hari or me for that matter.

The nagging and comments were not just affecting me. Over the last weeks, I had noticed that Uma had become more withdrawn, her temper was shorter, and she was dismissive of Hari. Her cheekbones were definitely even sharper, like her words. I thought she had lost more weight, but I didn't know how she could look thinner. Uma's beauty came not just from how pretty she was but how her eyes glowed when she spoke to you. She had a way of making you feel like the most important person in the world when you were with her. Now, her eyes were duller. She still smiled, but her eyes looked sad. I felt like this child was disappearing in front of me.

I needed to talk to her. I needed to find a moment alone with her, but these were so rare with us both working and then Hari. My stomach had been in knots for these weeks. I could see my child slowly slipping away, and I felt the hot red sword of fear slowly snaking its way from my gut to my heart. These people could make life so miserable. She didn't have to worry about them. She could choose when and if she was ready to marry. When she was younger, Uma said that she would never marry anyone. After all that she had been through, I couldn't blame her. I didn't know if she still felt that way. It had been years since we'd had that conversation.

I needed to tell her that who she loved and married was none of anyone's business. Just look at me. I was from a Brahmin family, and I married a Brahmin man. There was no joy in that marriage, no love. Because of that, I refused to bind myself to another place or man. I wore my dhoti with pride, and when I stared at my face, it was a steady, hard gaze that acknowledged my freedom. Someone you love needs first to see you as a human being before anything else and not as a possession to be marked, paraded, or owned. I saw myself as that human being and didn't need a husband for that. The person Uma married must see her as a human, an equal, and a partner in their life together. I needed to tell her that if she chose not to marry at all, that she would still be a whole person. She didn't have to have children or a husband to be a whole person. She was born whole and perfect. And, if she chose to marry, I would be the first to rub *hurdee* (turmeric) on her.

Every day, I thought of talking to Uma about these topics. But the toil of the day pushed the thoughts to the back of my mind. My body burned with fear for Uma the evening Madan came to visit, and the tucked away thoughts came to the front and sat like a burden on my neck. I was so used to seeing Madan and Mohan together, so it was odd to see Madan only.

"Madan, beta. It's been so long." I hugged him tightly. I missed Madan and Mohan. "You forgot your mother!" These two were like my other sons. Their house wasn't too far from us. I didn't think anything would separate those two.

As I kissed his forehead, he said, "I was missing your face, Mama."

"My face is not worth missing. My food, on the other hand, is worth more visits."

Madan laughed and said, "Then dish out for me, Mama. I'm hungry."

I loved it when my children wanted to eat as soon as they walked through the door. There was little that I could do for them as they got older. Food was one comfort I could give. Today, I made boiled egg chutney and roti. The days of being a vegetarian were long gone.

"I love boiled egg chutney," Madan said as he lifted the lid and investigated the pot.

He washed his hands and got ready to eat. He was sticky and sweaty from working at the new printing press that just opened. They wanted to print newspapers for the Indians in Durban. I wanted to read the newspaper, but it was in English. I needed to learn to read and write English.

Hari returned with the water pot after visiting the tap, which was about fifteen minutes away.

"Hari! I missed you!" Madan hugged Hari and slapped him hard on his back.

"Uncle Madan! So good to see you. We haven't seen you and Uncle Mohan for so long." Hari sat next to Madan after washing up.

"You must stop calling me uncle. You are almost a man now."

"I don't think so Madan, because you are Hari's elder." I saw them look at each other and smile. Madan winked at Hari, and Hari rolled his eyes. They might have thought I was old fashioned, but my children would show respect.

"How is the job? Have you learned to read English yet?" I asked.

"Not yet. I'm still trying to learn how to operate some of the machines. But Mohan and I are learning. We want to open our own printing press one day. It will print a weekly newspaper, and we decided we will call it *The Port Natal Weekly*. It will be in English, so we better learn quickly, eh Mama?" Madan said with a laugh.

Mohan was the more serious of the two. But these young men were determined. Even on the farm, they were certain they would make a success of their lives.

"You boys always wanted to live life your own way. You even left your village to come to South Africa alone. The both of you can do anything!"

"Not just us, even Zweli will join us." Zweli was Hari's old friend from the plantation. Why Zweli and Madan became friends was easy to see! Both saw joy in everything. I had never seen them without smiles.

After we left the estate, Madan had reconnected with Zweli in Tongaat town. When they moved Zweli from our plantation, he went to work on a farm closer to Durban. But Zweli had no need to work for these White men, and he left that job quickly and took a job at a printing press.

"Zweli told me about the printing press. He already works there. His job is to clean the press properly before every printing," Madan said.

He told us Zweli knew the owners were looking for men who could work hard, long hours and way into the night, especially just before the newspapers had to go out. The newspaper was a daily, so they worked late every night, Sunday to Thursday. Sugarcane workers were good at working hard, and single young men were ready to work. The boys were perfect for this job.

"The owners don't know how ambitious we are, though! Soon we'll have our own paper! But first we must learn how to read and write English," he said.

Madan's determination was impressive for someone who was illiterate, and his mention of Zweli reminded me of a day Mohan, Madan, and Zweli came to visit us some time ago.

"Uncle Zweli! I can't believe it is you! I missed you so much." Hari's eyes flooded with tears as he gasped between sobs. "My first friend here!"

Hari had become a small boy in an instant. He loved Zweli then, and that love never left him. Zweli became our family friend. I loved watching our small family grow. First it was just the three of us. Now our family included Madan, Mohan, and Zweli. I shook myself back into the moment. That memory was sweet, but what these boys were doing was very exciting.

"You will have to learn quickly, yes! I think we must teach every-one English so that they can read the paper. How else will you make money? People must be able to read the newspaper," I said.

"Next, you will ask us to build a school, Mama. You already made us build the temple." Madan smiled.

Mohan and Madan joked with me that I made them work so hard and with no wages to build temples, dig wells in the community, and put in taps, but we had to do this for ourselves since no one else cared about us or our people.

"Where's Uma?" Madan asked between mouthfuls. He used the back of his hand to wipe the chutney off his lips as he spoke. The sunburn from the long days in the fields under the Port Natal sun never left us. Many of us came much lighter to Port Natal, and now we look much darker.

"She's in her room. Her head was sore when she came home. I think it's the heat and her being in the quarry the whole day," I said.

Madan looked toward the rooms and kept eating. I felt a tinge of worry at the way he looked toward Uma's room. Madan and Mohan had taken the children under their wing. They would watch over Uma and Hari on Sundays and play with them even though they were more than ten years older. Uma and Hari were most likely to tell Madan and Mohan if they were worried or sad.

"Eat more, Madan. Take one more roti," I said.

"I'm so full. Thank you. The egg chutney was tasty," he said. The way Madan sucked his fingers made me believe him.

"I'll have another roti, Mama!" Hari certainly could eat. I frowned playfully and gave him the roti. There was one more left. Maybe Uma would eat later. She didn't eat when she first came home.

"Can I go say hello to Uma?" Madan asked after he washed his hands and wiped his mouth.

I nodded yes. "Please see how her headache is and if she wants to eat. I gave Madan a glass of water to take with him. "Give her this. Tell her I put some sugar in it. Sugar water will help with the headache."

As Madan walked toward the room the children shared, I thought about when we first met and how I was scared of him. I could hardly believe I was ever frightened of those two fools. They were my fools, though. I loved them so much.

I could hear Madan and Uma talking. *Maybe she's feeling better?* I would make the roti and chutney hot for her. Madan and Uma spoke for forty-five minutes. That strange fear crept back up as Madan came out of Uma's room.

"She still doesn't want to eat. Her head is still paining. Let her sleep. Let's check on her in the morning."

"What's wrong, Madan? You look so worried," I said. Madan usually smiled. His serious look now made me shift uncomfortably in my seat.

"I'm fine, Mama." Madan smiled at me, but it wasn't his normal smile. "I think it's the heat that is troubling Uma and maybe me too. I'm going home. I'll see you next Sunday. I haven't heard you read the Ramayana in a few weeks."

"See you next week, Madan. Tell Mohan to come too. I haven't seen him in a long time. You boys are working too hard. You need to take a break with us. Bring Zweli too. Tell him we haven't seen him in weeks."

Madan nodded. Zweli had come on a few Sundays to hear the Ramayana. He just liked being with all the boys. Our community had people of all colors. Some Black men worked in the towns and their families lived with them, and two White families lived nearby. When Zweli came to be with us, some of the Indians acted like Zweli shouldn't join us. These were usually the ones that didn't even like me reading the Ramayana, so we ignored them.

The unsettling feeling had appeared at Sunday readings, too, lately. The background noise had grown over the last two Sundays, especially from those who were here grudgingly and stood on the fringes. Last week, one of the men even spat on the floor as he walked past me. I had seen the judgment in their eyes and heard it in their words, but this was the first time it was physical. Hari saw what the man did and was ready to say something, but I just shook my head. Why bother? These bigoted men would never change.

But it wasn't only the men. The women whispered under their saris even while I read the story. I tried to finish the story I was reading. It was an important one. The lecherous King of Lanka (Ravana) captured Sita (King Ram's queen), and she was defiant and would only leave her prison with her husband. No one else. Her adoration for the noble man she loved extended to holding his honor as a king. No matter how much I tried to hold my focus, the voices distracted me. I finished quickly, hoping they would tell me what was happening when we drank chai afterward.

Uma was usually the one that served the tea, and I watched as she brought it out. Uma didn't like to dress up most of the time, but she did wear her favorite flowers in her hair every Sunday. Last week there were no orange flowers in Uma's hair, and while she usually smiled, hugged, and kissed everyone, she was silent the past week.

I heard Uma's name mumbled under many a breath. Uma had heard it too. I wondered if they all were seeing the same thing I was seeing. Did they also feel like this wasn't our Uma? Uma asked Hari to serve the tea to the men at the back. They looked scornful and defiant. But Megha was the one who took the tea from Uma. She told her to rest and said Uma looked tired. Megha served tea to these people that smirked and looked at Uma, Hari, and me. Uma sat far away from the syringa tree, near the edge of the flat ground. The storms in her eyes were turbulent and frightening. I asked Megha what the whispering was about. She just said that people were bored and had nothing nice to talk about. They were speculating why Uma wasn't married and was looking so thin.

I was so angry last week. I left, but not before telling them that I would not read the Ramayana anymore that day. I needed to have some space from these people. I knew I was fierce, but they were disrespectful. No one wanted to tell me what was happening. People feared me, some hated me. But everyone was silent to my face.

Tonight as Madan started to walk out after dinner, Hari said, "I'll come with you."

"Mama, I'm going to walk with Uncle Madan to the bottom of the road. It's too hot in the house, and I need some air. Anyway, I ate too much. I need to walk it off!"

Hari craved the company of men at times. I saw how he was thinking about his life, and he looked for ambitious men like Madan and Mohan to look up to. He talked a lot to Unni even though I didn't like him too much. His drinking scared me, and I didn't think he liked me after Megha came to live with me that time.

I put Uma's supper away. She might feel like eating later. When she woke up, we must talk. She must not let these people get to her. It was too much for her to worry about.

Hari was gone for so long, more than an hour. I thought they must have met Mohan or someone else. When those boys got together, they forgot the time! I went into my room to rest a bit. I still had to finish sewing some of Hari's shirts. His shirts would get torn at the elbows, especially the ones that came from the general store. After another half hour, Hari opened the door. I finished sewing the last button before I walked into the sitting room.

"You were gone so long, Hari! What were you talking about?" I still had my sewing in my hands, ready to playfully scold him. He was sitting on the chair in the corner staring into the passage opening. He looked directly at me, but he didn't see me. His eyes were red and watery. His face was flushed, and his cheeks had a reddish tinge that was still evident through his sunburnt face.

"Hari? What's wrong, beta? Why are you crying?"

Hari didn't answer me. He just looked straight ahead like I hadn't spoken.

"Hari?" My sewing fell to the floor. What could have happened to my child? I grabbed him by the shoulders. As I leaned into him, his body felt even more bony than normal. I shook him violently, hoping to wake him from this trance he had fallen into.

"Hari, you are frightening me. What's wrong? Did someone die?" That was the only thing I could think of that would make Hari so scared. "Did something happen to Madan or Mohan? Hari, did something happen to my sons? Tell me."

"Mama, Uncle Zweli." Hari's voice broke as he looked at me and uttered Zweli's name softly, like a prayer only with pain laced through it.

Oh my God! Did something happen to Zweli?

"Hari, what happened to Zweli?" I said.

"Uncle Zweli was at the general store."

"Did something happen at the store?"

Hari got up, looked at me, and took my hands. "Mama, Uncle Zweli was at the store. He told me something that I need to tell you."

Hari took a deep, long breath before he spoke. The air around him knew his news was sad before I did.

"He said that everyone is talking about Uma Didi and Mr. Thompson's son, Richard. They are saying that Uma is his girlfriend. I told Uncle Zweli that I don't believe them. They are lying. At first, I thought Uncle Zweli was making this all up, but why would he lie?"

What was Hari talking about? This sounded so stupid. How can Uma be with the owner's son?

"Hari, what are you saying? No, this is wrong and not true. I'm sure Zweli misheard this."

"Mama, Uncle Zweli told me that the sardar saw Uma Didi and the White man together at the terminals. He saw them kissing, and they saw him. He told them that he was going to tell everyone. The sardar told everyone that Uma. . ." Hari stopped. His hands fell. He looked away, and I knew that there was more to be told than what Hari had said.

"What did the sardar say, Hari?" My eyes told their own story of my anger. I was so tired of people talking about us. *This never stops!* All they did was gossip and yet we did nothing to them. Uma took care of everyone. "Hari! Tell me."

"I'm so sorry, Mama. I don't know how to tell you."

Hari focused his eyes on my hands and not my face. I had no time for that. I grabbed his chin and made him look at me. We were eye level. I wasn't a small woman. I squeezed his chin, hoping the words would squeeze themselves out of him. I hurt Hari. I knew that. But I had to know. I kept squeezing until he had to speak.

"This man told everyone that Uma is like you. That you got

money for sleeping with all the workers, and that is what Uma learned to do. Now she is with White men. He told everyone that he thinks Uma has many boyfriends and not just Richard. I know that's not true, Mama. They are just making up stories. The sardar said that the White man pays for Uma and that he gives her money, and that's why Uma is with him."

Oh, my Uma! My child! What was this? Why were these people doing this? Why couldn't they leave us alone?

Hari looked at me, and the tears in his eyes softened his face. "Mama, I know what happened when we came here. The other people from the plantation told Uma and me a long time ago. We knew, but we also knew our mama and how strong you were for us. We don't blame you. But now even this taints Uma. Can we not escape this?"

I didn't know how to look at my son. He knew that I had prostituted myself when we got here, and he was telling me that it was acceptable. His mouth was saying the words, but I was sure his heart and his head thought of me as the dirt that lined the streets. They could think what they wanted of me, but how could they talk about my child? Why would they say that about Uma?

"The people in Hillary all know what the sardar said. Uncle Madan told me that's what they're talking about. Some of them went to his house and told him and Uncle Mohan that they must tell us to leave this place. They think we're dirty people, and we must not taint their communities or homes. That's why he and Uncle Mohan didn't come last Sunday. They had gone to the sardar's house in the morning to talk to him before work.

"Uncle Mohan and the sardar got into a fight and the sardar hit him. Uncle Mohan had asked the sardar to stop spreading lies. The sardar said that he saw Uma with the White man with his own two eyes, and that nothing the uncles said would make him take back his words. Uncle Mohan almost broke the sardar's jaw, and Uncle

Mohan's nose was broken. His face is swollen, and he didn't want you to see that, so he didn't come with Uncle Madan today."

Hari's eyes carried the weight of more than his years. The burden of what Zweli and Madan had shared with him sat heavy on him.

"Uncle Mohan met me at the store tonight too. I remember the owner's son, Mama. He's a nice man. But I don't know why they're saying all this about Uma. Last Sunday, the men were talking about Uma while sipping their cups of tea. I heard Uma's name, but they stopped when I came close. I didn't hear any of the gossip of Uma and the owner's son, but I heard Uma's name. Uncle Zweli said that the sardar has been saying that Didi could also be pregnant. They keep on saying horrible things about her!"

I had overheard chatter that now made sense: "What could you expect from the girl whose mother doesn't know her place? Why keep daughters unmarried if you don't know how to be respectful?" I thought they were gossiping about getting her married. My knees couldn't hold me up anymore, and I fell. Hari caught me before I hit the floor and made me sit on the sofa.

"Hari, go call Madan, Mohan, and Zweli if you can find him. Tell them to come here now. I want to talk to them."

"Are you sure?" Hari raised his head.

I saw he looked frightened. But I wanted to hear everything from the others. I wasn't going to ask Uma anything before I spoke to them.

"Call them. Then we will speak with Uma."

"Let's wait until morning, Mama. They just left, and it will take me more than half an hour to fetch them and bring them here. It's already nine o'clock, and they start work in two hours. They finish at eight in the morning. I'll call them tomorrow."

"You're right, beta. But tomorrow, please call them. Let's talk to Uma now so that we know what's happening. Uma knows what they're saying. I thought she was worried about all the marriage talk, but I think she knows the lies they're spreading about her."

My anxiety for Uma now had a name, a voice. I knew something was wrong. I had known it for days, even weeks.

"Do you think we should talk to her, Mama? Uncle Madan said he tried to talk to her when he was here, but she was so quiet."

"Did Madan ask her about what the people were saying?"

"Yes, just before he left. Uma was just lying there. He said she looked haunted, and her eyes were empty. I'm worried about her."

I didn't know why, but Hari's words about Uma being empty made me stop cold. A scared murmur entered my head, growing louder with every passing moment, and I knew in my deepest place, where my love for Uma lived, that I had to get to my baby girl.

Chapter 14

Shivali's Locked Doors, Open Windows

As I ran to the bedroom, I realized that my heart never left Uma. It was sitting there, at the door, waiting to enter the room. My body had existed just for me to function for the day. But my heart knew that Uma needed me to be with her. My heart was sitting vigil with her. But sitting vigil for what?

"Uma, open the door, beti." There was silence at the other end of the door. The air around me felt heavy. "Uma! Uma, open the door!" I banged harder. Maybe she was sleeping because the headache was too much? I just needed to be louder or make more noise to wake her.

"Didi! Open the door," Hari said. His voice trembled. "Didi, please open the door. Mama and I know what they're saying about you, and we don't care. Didi, open the door, we love you."

As Hari spoke, I realized I didn't really care what anybody said about Uma. If it wasn't true, then I would deal with those horrible people who just take from me, from us, and throw us to the side. But if Uma loved this White man, Richard, then she should be with him if she wished. Why did my Uma not tell me about this?

"Uma, I don't care if you love Richard. I'm happy for you. Just open the door, beti!" The room was spinning, and I was back on the dusty floor, bangles making half-moons in the dust and blood everywhere. I was back where a sacrifice was made, holding my two small children, praying that for once we could be spared from all this. I prayed to my baba. "Baba, please help us. Let Uma be safe. Please get her to open the door."

"I'm going to break down the door." I heard Hari through the prayer and the spinning room. He rammed his shoulder against the door. We're so poor that everything falls apart at the gentlest nudge. But even the door decided to be strong for this day. Hari kicked the door this time, and it budged a bit more. The third time he kicked, the door gave way, swinging as it hit the wall behind it.

I wished it hadn't opened.

All the while the door was shut, my Uma was sad and worried and didn't want to talk to us. A closed door was a worried Uma. An open door brought absolute, total devastation. My Uma wasn't here. I looked everywhere. I searched by the rivers of my mind, near the rocks that held a memory of *my* Uma, not the Uma that was lying on the bed. Not the Uma whose wrists were draped in blood. Who was this person still holding the knife of my past sacrifices in her hand? This was *not* my Uma.

I didn't hear or see anything around me. I was with my Uma, journeying through all that she loved with her.

"Didi!" Hari's face twisted with a grief that burrowed down into his soul. He grabbed Uma and tried to wake her. "Wake up, Didi!" Hari slapped Uma across her face to rouse her. But all that did was show us what a rag doll Uma had become. "Didi, no! Wake up! What did you do! What did you do?!"

I watched Hari from the door. Hatred and pain etched the planes of his face. Hatred for those who drove Uma to this, and infinite pain for his dear Uma. Blood-bound Hari and Uma, as her blood covered him. There was so much of this blood, everywhere. But where was my Uma? This person lying with the legacy of our family in her hand wasn't my Uma. Yet there she was.

As I looked at Uma, serenity and peace etched the ghostly planes of her face. I was looking for my live Uma, but there was some other Uma lying in front of me. A lilac bedspread held my baby girl in its soft folds. She was slumped over a darker purple pillow. This was the room that Hari and Uma shared, yet it felt like Uma's only. Her colors, her scent, her life. The folds of the bedspread filled like pools with her blood, slowly drying into damp red patches that held the lifeblood of my daughter.

The patches called to me. "See what happened. See what you started, Shivali. See what Uma finished, what she did." I started this in Ishapur. The voices were right. I had killed him, and now Uma was gone.

"Uma! Uma! No! Not my Uma!" I couldn't control the screams that left me. My baby girl was gone. She took her life. She killed herself because they thought she was like me. She was nothing like me. She was innocent! She was beautiful! She was divine! She wasn't like me. She wasn't a murderer, not a prostitute. She wasn't anything like me. And she was still *gone*.

Uma's body felt like a rock when I tried to pull her into my arms. This tiny girl was the heaviest thing I had carried, ever. Her voice was forever silent. Her future stolen by the whispers and sniggers of the people around us. Taken by our own people. The people who came across the Kaala Paani with us. The friends we built temples for and the lovers we sang songs for. All of them responsible for my darling Uma's silence. But more than that, I was responsible for my beti's death.

"Oh, my baby! How can you ever forgive me? How could I let this happen to you?!" I rocked Uma's lifeless body back and forth on the lilac bedspread, spreading the pools of blood that hadn't congealed all around us.

"How could I not see how people spoke about me would affect you! I'm so sorry, my baby." I looked at her face. Soft now, like when she told stories of the elephants in Berea, not how she looked this past Sunday. I wanted to remember every line, every edge of her face. I couldn't bring myself to look at her wrists, though. I didn't want to remember this part. I looked at her fingers and her hands, and I remembered the six-year-old girl who handed me the knife that she had now taken her life with. I remembered when she held Hari's hand on their walks. I remembered her taking my hand to show me Megha's dead baby. I thought about those hands working the quarry. I thought about how those hands had taken my baby's life. I loved those hands and hated them at the same time. But those hands wouldn't hold mine anymore, or Hari's for that matter. Those hands would give no one support any more. I rocked Uma while Hari sat at the edge of the bed, tears in free fall.

The window was open, but the night was still hot and sticky. I felt like Uma's soul had just flown out of the window. The curtains were waving a sad goodbye as the breeze whispered. I couldn't sit there with Uma's body. I couldn't. I got up, walked to the kitchen, found a small clay lamp, and lit it. For my baby girl. I placed the lamp on the veranda and that was where I sat, in a corner that was small enough to hold what was left of this Shivali, Uma's mother. When Hari found me, we held each other for a long time.

"Mama, what will we do? How will we live without Didi?"

Hari's voice dripped with so much pain, and I couldn't handle seeing the death of both children at the same time. One dead by her own hands and one dead from watching the aftermath. Hari looked like the small boy who played with Shanti and Ram, the boy who looked for his Didi all the time.

"I don't want to live without Didi."

"Me either, Hari, me either. I want my Uma back. Give her back to me." I held out my hands, palms turned up, cupped, begging for my child's life again. "Bring her back, Hari Beta. Don't let them take her."

Hari and I collapsed into each other. Two souls begging each other for the most important of them. What would this boy do? His true mother was gone. Where there were three, there were now two.

"Go and get Madan, Mohan, and Zweli," I said. While Hari was gone, I thought about all the people who loved Uma so much: Dada, Tara, Shanti, Mohan, Madan, Megha. So many people. How did I tell the ones alive that Uma wasn't here anymore? How would I face the ones who left Uma in my charge? I sat with Uma's lamp on the veranda, Uma's body in the bedroom, and Uma's soul roaming the land of Port Natal. I sat in the pain that I would have to face this world without my Uma.

Chapter 15

Hari's Summer Tears

That night, Mama never moved from her spot on the veranda floor. She lit Uma Didi's lamp when I went to fetch the uncles. It was too hot to go inside, or maybe she just couldn't move, but she protected the flame with her body. My mama was the wall that held the breeze away from Didi's lamp. The lamp rested against the outer wall of the house. The flame danced playfully on the wall. Sometimes it hid the peeling blue paint and sometimes revealed all. We never knew when the flame would be bright, or dull, or when the flame would never light again like my didi.

Mama looked like a discarded stone kicked too many times. Why did she look so small? My mother was a tall woman, but in the veranda corner sitting against the metal railing, she looked as tiny as Didi. Her life was one thrown away stone, heavy, hard, and exhausting.

Why did we have so much to deal with? The rage in me curled like the smoke from the lit incense sticks next to Didi's lamp. My anger and misery needed a place to go. I couldn't bear to watch Mama like this. What was wrong with this God? Was he angry with us? Whenever we had some happiness, he took it away. Today, he was making us cry for Didi. The only person who knew me. The only person my mama could depend on. Why was that? Mama said that Ram loved us, but could I believe what she told us? If he loved us, then why did he do this? Why couldn't he stop Uma from doing this? Why couldn't he stop everyone from saying terrible things about us, about my didi? Why couldn't he make us get to her quicker? Why did he want us to suffer? What did we do to him that he was angry? What did my didi do? I didn't think this God deserved my prayer anymore!

Mama read God's book every week. But what was the use of telling us His story when that Ramayana didn't turn the people listening into better people? Did the God of the Ramayana enjoy watching the devastation of two people who had just lost their everything? Did this God know that Uma's leaving us had created a shell of a life for us? This desolate shell held even the light at a distance, making the air afraid to fill it. That sorrow silently churned in the darkness, twisting the open door, tempting me to step in and find solace and silence in its darkness. I couldn't breathe. No air wanted to enter or leave my body. All I could think about was the light and breath that abandoned Uma Didi's body. How would I breathe without her guiding me to exhale? Where would my light come from? My life force had left me, taking all my joy and happiness with her.

I lost my belief in Him. How could a God watch my mama break with all that she did for us? I was used to seeing determination, love, and anger on her face all the time. That was what made my mother what Uma and I knew of her. Today, her face held no expression, no determination, no anger, no love. Today, she looked like she was waiting for something, staring into the distance, her eyes searching for something she knew wouldn't arrive. Her body showed me what her face couldn't. My mother had lost her will to be. How could I keep my faith in him when I saw my mama like this? Fractured and broken. No longer the unmovable Shivali. When she held Uma on the bedspread, I saw the pieces of the Shivali who killed her husband. The pieces of the Shivali who left her land. The pieces of the Shivali who made a new life in this place. The pieces of the Shivali who held her head high, and now the pieces of the Shivali who held her dead daughter in her arms. All the pieces of the Shivali who was my mother.

No, for now, I had no belief in Him. He must fill all this emptiness if He wanted me to believe in Him. He must make my mama whole again. She was cracked and broken in too many pieces, and He made that happen. My didi must come back. We left Sakshi and Ram behind in Ishapur, and no one filled that emptiness. I couldn't even remember their faces. This God took away the only Dada we knew, Aunty Tara, anyone that loved us, anyone that loved me. He took them away.

The weight of sadness and grief set in as I watched my mother sitting next to the lamp. I couldn't breathe not just because Didi died, but because I realized watching Mama that she was all I had left. She was all I had left! *Oh my God . . . that was all that I had left.* I loved my mother, but a world where she was the only person left for me? The joy of Uma Didi was gone. I was alone now because all I had was my broken, sad Mama. I hated myself for feeling like this. The days and years alone ahead of me seemed like the heaviest burden.

What was wrong with me? Why was I thinking about that now? Mama needed me and I was selfishly thinking about how hard it was going to be to live with her without Didi. My mama made this life for us. I loved her. I needed to be strong for her, and I needed to stop being selfish. But the voice in my head continued, "Is this what life is going to be? Is this who I'll spend the rest of my years with?" I couldn't stop the feeling of drowning in a future with Mama alone.

"Mama, Uncle Madan and Uncle Mohan are here," I whispered close to her cheek. She didn't look or turn to me. Shivali wasn't there, only her body sat protecting the lamp. "Mama, look who is here," I said.

171

Uncle Mohan stepped in front of Mama. My mother's other son. He held her shoulders. His face was a red and blue color from the fight with the sardar. His nose was swollen, his eyes darkened by the sardar and his tears. He leaned into Mama to hold her as she woke from her memory. This man whom my mama had made her son when she drew his blood held her as she stood up.

"Mama, our Uma," Uncle Mohan whispered. He held Mama's face in his hands. "Our Uma is gone."

"She left us, Mohan. She left all these people. She left me and Hari alone."

My mama didn't raise her voice. She didn't bang or beat her fists against Mohan's chest. She merely leaned her face into Uncle Mohan's left palm, her tears wetting his already sweaty hand. "She's gone now. My baby girl will have some peace. But where will our peace come from now, Mohan? How will Hari and I live?"

I hated myself for thinking about living with Mama when all she was doing was thinking about me. I wasn't a good son. Mama was sinking without Didi just like I was. I could hear it and see it. Uncle Mohan held Mama's face and cried hard but without any sound. His shoulders jerked as the silent sobs found a place in every fiber of his being. His damp palms never moved from the mother's face he had known for more than ten years. His head was bowed in the heaviness of sorrow. Uncle Mohan's sorrow was as silent as my didi's pain. No voice, just pain. Too much pain that just rolled on day after day.

Mama and Uncle Mohan never hugged. She just couldn't close the space between them. That changed tonight. Uncle Madan moved Mohan's hands off Mama's face and kissed the forehead of his brother-cousin. Mama had no energy left to give, and Uncle Madan caught her just as she was about to fall. Taking Uncle Mohan's hands away from her had removed the anchor that was keeping her upright. Uncle Madan held Mama tight in his arms, squeezing life and energy back into her. The smell of egg chutney still lingered on

Uncle Madan's clothes, a reminder of a time earlier this evening that now felt like forever ago.

"It's my fault. I should never have spoken to Uma earlier. I shouldn't have come." Uncle Madan's expression of grief was opposite to Uncle Mohan's. Silent grief and outwardly intense grief are two sides of the same coin. Just like my uncles. Uncle Madan poured his pain into a steady flow of tears and heavy, loud, heart-wrenching sobs. "I shouldn't have said anything. What's wrong with me?"

"No, Madan. You didn't do anything. Uma knew what these people were saying long before you said anything. I could see how upset she was." Mama held onto Madan because she couldn't stand on her own.

"I told her about the sardar and Mohan, Zweli, and me. I told her not to worry, and that we would sort it all out. That all these gossipers had nothing to do but make trouble. Maybe when I said that it made it worse for her?"

The news had spread, and all our neighbors had started to arrive. Aunties brought pots of tea. Some arrived with containers of rotis. I saw many eyes look away as Uncle Madan spoke about the gossiping. Many of those bringing food were sitting there on Sundays talking about Uma and Mama. These same people that came to comfort us today had brought on the grief in the first place.

"They made it worse with their nastiness not you, Madan." Mama's voice was still so soft. But even her soft voice could make you stop and take note because it was dipped in steel and fire.

When Mama sent me to call the uncles, I didn't know how I got to their house at all. My legs knew the way to their house, but my mind was sitting on the bed, holding my didi, sitting in the blood pool in the folds of the bedspread and staring at the window. Their house was made of mud with just one room and a tin roof. I went there often It was the place I could be with men. They spoke about the girls they liked, the printing press they wanted to open, and the people they wanted to be. I wanted to be like them, and I wanted to be like my didi too. Tonight, my legs carried me to their house while my heart rode the wind searching for my sister.

"Uncle Madan! Uncle Madan!" I banged hard on the door with both fists. They couldn't be sleeping because I had just left them at the general store. "Uncle Mohan, open up."

"I said don't call me 'uncle' when Mama is not around!" Uncle Madan flung open the door, shirtless and laughing. His laughter dried midair. "What's wrong, Hari? What happened?" Uncle Madan grabbed me quickly as I sank when he opened the door. Then Uncle Mohan came running out. They knew something had happened.

"My didi is gone. She is gone."

"What do you mean, Hari? Uma is gone? Gone where? Did she leave you and Mama to go somewhere? In the night? She ran away?" Uncle Mohan couldn't even think about a world where Didi was not around.

"Didi left us. She left us all. Forever."

They both still looked at me bewildered, not understanding.

"Didi is dead," I said.

That still didn't get a response. I was becoming hysterical. I needed someone to understand me and to hold me.

"She killed herself! She cut her wrists! She killed herself," I screamed into their faces. "She is gone! My didi is gone! Oh my God, my didi is gone."

Uncle Mohan grabbed me. They both held me tightly. My brothers. I relived those moments every second. My mind kept taking me back to when I told them. It was Uncle Madan's voice that brought me back to the present, to this place on the veranda with Mama.

"Hari, we need to arrange the funeral," Uncle Mohan said as he held my hand and led me toward the sitting room. "Let's talk inside, where it is quiet. Away from Mama."

The uncles knew there was a lot to be done. Dr. Govinder had come earlier and taken Didi with him to his surgery. He knew Mama from reading the Ramayana, and he knew Didi from serving tea. We didn't go to the doctor at all. Mama took care of us when we were sick, but today Didi had to go with him. This time Mama couldn't make her better. The uncles discussed the funeral while I sat listening. But focusing on the practical things to get done helped to pull me out of my own head. At least I wouldn't think about being alone with Mama.

Uncle Madan said he would go to bring Uma Didi home before the funeral. This wasn't Ishapur, and cremation wasn't a given. We had to fight to cremate Dada because they wouldn't let us cremate him on the farm. We had to go all the way to Verulam. Many of our people worried about how they would be reborn if their bodies were not burned. But in this land, new rituals had to be created, and the gods would just have to accommodate us.

"There's the coolie cemetery not far, I'll check," Uncle Madan said.

"I think the new crematorium is now open," Uncle Gopal said. He and Aunty Savitri had just arrived. "Hari Beta, I am so sorry. We loved our Uma."

Uncle Gopal folded me into his soft body, and I heard Aunty Savitri talking to Mama outside. They still didn't have children. We had been their children. Seeing Uncle Gopal reminded me of our journey to get here. While Mama, Uma, and I were blood, uncles Madan and Mohan were our brothers and family too. The five of us were a family. Dada, Uncle Gopal, Aunty Savitri, Megha Aunty, Unni, and Uncle Zweli were our extended family. We had people who loved and cared for us. This was the most tragic thing to happen to us. When Dada died, we knew he was old, but Didi was young.

"They opened it in Clare Estate. They can do Sanatan Dharma (Hindu way of life) rites there. We need to check if we can use it," Uncle Gopal offered gently.

No one wanted to say that some places refuse to hold funerals for

175

suicides, but it was common. People thought it was bad luck. Wasn't it bad luck enough that we lost Didi?

Between the uncles, they made the plans to bring Uma Didi home later in the day, it was already after three o'clock in the morning.

The word of Didi's death had spread quickly, and Megha Aunty and Unni had arrived. I heard her scream as she came through the gate, and she kept screaming as she walked to Mama. We all went outside when we heard her.

"Shivali! Uma! What did Uma do? Shivali! What did our baby do?" Megha screamed. Unni was holding her, but she was looking franticly for Mama and crying. Unni and Megha had bought their freedom with help from the owner's wife and came to live close to us.

"Our baby is gone," Mama said.

Megha Aunty screamed and cried as she held Mama. "What did my baby do, Shivali?"

They cried together. "What did I do to my baby, Shivali?" Megha Aunty kept asking about what she had done to Uma Didi. Mama and Unni just held her. Unni touched Mama's feet, and Mama held him too. There was no lack of tears in this early morning. Megha Aunty was screaming uncontrollably. It was distressing for us all to watch.

"Unni, please take her inside and let her lie down. Maybe give her some sugar water. It will make her feel better," Mama said.

Gopal, Madan, Mohan, and Aunty Savitri returned from making funeral arrangements. It would be tomorrow. They couldn't get Uma Didi home early enough today to have the funeral and cremation on the same day. Didi would come home today, and tomorrow we would cremate her and release her from this place.

When Didi came home, Mama didn't come to see her on the cart immediately. The uncles and I brought her wrapped body toward the veranda. Aunty Savitri had washed her and dressed her in white cloth. Mama stopped them from entering the veranda and met us at the stairs. She kissed Uma Didi on her forehead and cheeks. Then she held Didi as we placed her in front of the lamp. Aunty Savitri had laid out a *chatai* (knotted grass mat) on the floor, and we placed Uma Didi on it. Mama didn't want Didi to be on the floor. The neighbors had brought purple and orange flowers to keep around her. Didi loved those colors. She had planted bird-of-paradise flowers in the garden and tended to them carefully. I wanted her to be surrounded by the things she loved, so I placed the orange bird-of-paradise flowers at her feet. Better they sat at her feet than on the stem. They served themselves better to be in the presence of my divine sister. I hoped she kept them close to her through her journey. She deserved beauty and love.

My big sister. My bossy, caring, darling Didi. She told me about the river and Shanti. I remembered a bit, not too much. I did remember her being mad when I brought Ram and Sakshi to the river because she loved playing on the flat stones with Shanti. When I used to ask Didi to tell me stories or play the house-house game when we were smaller, she would describe her house with a river, a large tree, and rocks. She wanted to be a warrior princess.

Uma Didi was the keeper of all our secrets. She kept them buried deep. My sister held my hand while she gave Mama the knife to kill that man who hurt us. She was the one who squeezed my hand tight on the boat to let me know I wasn't alone. She was the one who knew how to keep me out of trouble on the farm and who never had a chance to let the pain and guilt buried deeply within her escape. All this time, my sister had grown into a woman in front of us. I thought of my didi as still lying on rocks watching clouds, but my warrior princess had fallen in love quietly without anyone knowing. She deserved love and not shame. She deserved happiness and not grief.

I hoped all the people who gossiped about my beautiful sister would be there when we cremated her. I saw them standing in the shadows, shaking their heads, clicking their tongues, and saying, "Shame, what a young life. So sad." When her body burned, I wanted to watch them hide their shame, especially those who hid behind their cups of tea and gossiped about her. Surely, they must find peace in her death if this was what they wanted when they spoke about her in such an unkind way.

Didi was my peace, whether she was here or not. I wondered if all her pain left when she cut her wrists, or if she was in more pain when it happened. Did the pain of the cut release the light and breath from her body? I couldn't control myself thinking about how much pain she must have been in to make herself feel even more by using that same wretched knife on her wrists. Did the pain of the cut ease the agony that these people created for her? I didn't know. I knew that my heart was cut deeply. It was wounded and permanently damaged, and no amount of tea and food from these people could make it better.

Didi was in the wind, saying goodbye to Shanti in the place where they lay on rocks and looked at the clouds. Becoming a warrior princes on the small patch of grass. Closing her eyes while looking at the sky, and finally getting some peace.

"Hari, my son." I heard the words, but I was still thinking about Didi in Ishapur. Let me be with her. It's the place she was happiest. I wanted to be there with her.

"Hari." I heard again and looked up. Uncle Zweli had tears in his eyes. He hugged me and sat with me as I broke down. All the tears that were held back after telling the uncles came flowing all over again. Uncle Zweli said nothing. He stroked my hand and let me cry. I buried my face in the ebony wall of Uncle Zweli. His steady, calm presence gave me permission to be Uma Didi's baby brother again.

"Hari baby," he said the same way Uma Didi said it. I wanted to be that small boy again for a few minutes, and Uncle Zweli let me.

"Hari, we need to tell Richard, the owner's son. I think Uma would want him to know."

"No. We don't even know if it's true or not. I don't want to have him here. She's dead because of him."

"Uma is dead because of gossiping, and not because of Richard. And if Uma did love him, he deserves to know what happened."

"No, Uncle Zweli. I will not let him come. That would be too much for Mama, and she has gone through enough." I had so many bad thoughts about Mama already, and I didn't want to make it worse. I had to protect her.

"Don't you think Uma would want him here?" he asked.

"No." I jumped up and everyone looked at me.

"Ok," he said. "We'll do what you want. Just please be calm."

What was Uncle Zweli asking? How could I stay calm? Didi was gone. I didn't care about this Richard, but I cared about my mama. All the gossip and Didi's death was making Mama a shell. I didn't want the reason for that to be here, in this place. Uma's death broke Mama. What would Richard bring if not more pain?

Mama and I sat through the night, keeping vigil for Didi and making sure her lamp didn't go out. People came and went all the time. They drank tea on the veranda with soft murmurs of conversation now and then.

"Such a beautiful girl," someone said.

"What a loss, so sad," another said.

"What will they do now? She worked at the quarry."

Many of the people Uma worked with came to say how sorry they were. They shared stories of how generous she was, and of how she took care of the people around her. Mama nodded when they spoke. She had nothing else to give them. These people said they were sorry and expected Mama to say thank you. Neither of us had anything left in us.

It was Megha Aunty's story that cut through to Mama.

"Uma found my dead baby. She was just a baby herself," Megha said. She sang about her pain in the most lamenting way as she rocked back and forth in a sad dance. "Uma found the baby I killed in the river. Uma, you were too small to see what I did. You should have never had to deal with that. I'm so sorry, Uma.

"Shivali, I'm so sorry! I left my dead baby, and your baby girl found my baby. I killed my baby, Shivali! Oh, Uma, I made you do something no child should do. I killed my baby, and Uma had to bury him, Shivali."

The neighbors played their role of indifference well. They were interested in this new gossip but acted aloof. No one knew that Megha Aunty had killed her baby. No one knew that Uma had found the baby or that she buried it.

Megha Aunty's collapse was happening in front of us now, but it had started a long time ago on the boat, continued through the death of her baby, and even through her marriage that was built upon all that sorrow. Didi's death made it happen now, in front of us all, while Mama and I were still dealing with the real pain of having to cremate our Uma tomorrow. How could we deal with two deaths?

Unni took Megha Aunty to the kitchen again, but we could hear voices and crying. We all knew the crying was not for Didi.

Mama held my hand. She didn't pick her head up from the railing of the veranda. "Hari, please tell Unni to take Megha home. Tell him to come back tomorrow for the funeral and cremation. She needs to be alone with Unni and not with these people watching her."

When I said such to Unni and Megha Aunty, she screamed at me. "I am not going home. I want to be with Shivali and Uma. I am not going home!" She ran outside and placed her head in Mama's lap, her eyes buried in my mother's dhoti. "Shivali, please don't make me go home. I want to be here, with you. Please, Shivali! Please!"

"Megha, all these people are watching you. Won't you feel safer at home? You will come back in the morning. Go be with your children." Mama tried to lift Megha Aunty's head to look at her.

"I want to stay here. I don't want to go home. My children are all right. Don't send me away, Shivali. Please don't send me away. I won't be able to cope. I need to be here with you and Uma. I must be with our baby girl."

Mama held her for a while before she sighed and said, "Megha, please don't scream any more. Stay, but please be quiet."

Mama looked at me, and we both knew that Megha Aunty would be quiet for now. We had delayed her breakdown by a bit. And so the night passed, in vigil for Uma, on high alert for Megha Aunty's breakdown, and in murmurs from the neighbors. I must have fallen asleep at some point. Uncle Zweli woke me up. The heavy air surrounded us even though it was morning. I didn't know if it was the heat or today, another day I faced without Didi. The summer day was shedding tears, trying to wash away the loss of innocence. As I wiped my face, I realized the dampness was more than the heat, I had woken up crying.

Zweli shook me. "Hari, time to get ready. We have to leave by nine o'clock, and we still have to do the prayer."

The older aunties told us not to bathe. We must only bathe after the cremation. They told us to just wipe ourselves and change. I smelled so bad. How could I not bathe? Didi would wash all the time. Even when she came back from work from the quarry, she was immaculate, clean, and smelled nice. She had a sweet smell on her, like the flowers she loved. Didi never liked to be dirty, so how could I be dirty when I saw her? I said so to them, and Mama just shook her head at me and beckoned me to follow her. They clicked their tongues and wagged their fingers at me.

"Don't argue with them, Hari. They will tell you that it's tradition. That's not tradition. It's just nonsense. Let's just get ready. Zweli, please bring a bucket of water for Hari and me. Bring it to the back. No one will ask too many questions then."

Putting on my clothes felt extra hard today. My white shirt felt like paper scraping my chest and leaving red marks against my skin, Except the marks weren't really on my skin. My heart and soul were slowly scraped by the clothes I put on my body to say goodbye to my sister, my real mother. I was so tired, so drained, and no light was left in me. I sat down on the edge of my bed. A bed that I had shared with Didi. The same bed. The purple bedspread had been changed. It was green now. Not Didi's color at all. She liked green in sugarcane, not on her bed.

"Hari, are you ready?" Mama asked from the doorway. The lady standing at the door didn't look like my mama. She was small, old, and had an ugliness that she brought to all of us. What was wrong with me? This was my mama! I loved her.

A persistent voice whispered, "She is the reason that Didi is dead. People talk about Didi because of what she did. You know she is what they say she is."

How could I blame Mama for what happened?

The voice continued, "Now you are the only one left with her. You have to be with her for the rest of your life, and there is no more Uma Didi to turn to."

I tried to push the voice out of my head and turned to Mama. "I'm dressed, but I'm not ready."

I had never known a world without Uma Didi. A world without white guavas, and tightly held hands. Hands that left imprints on each other's bodies and each other's hearts. A world without my big sister. A world alone.

"I'm not ready either," Mama whispered. Tears filled her dark eyes, which stood out on her turban-less head. "I don't want to go to the crematorium. Ladies don't go to the crematoriums, do they? I'll stay at home. I'll stay here until Uma comes back home."

I held out my hand to Mama to come and sit with me. My bowed head was just so heavy to lift and look at her. Seconds passed before I could look at her.

"Mama, come sit with me." She was leaning against the door frame. She couldn't cross the floor to come to me. My mother just looked at me. The vacancy in her eyes expanded as she scanned the room from the open window, whose curtains danced in the breeze, to the bedspread, whose cover had held Didi last night. I crossed the room to her and led her to the bed. I held Mama's palm, and she wrapped her dry fingers tightly around my damp, hot hands. Mama and I, we are the same yet so different. We were creating a new pair of hands to hold and leave imprints on each other. Uma wasn't here anymore. The edge of the bed held us so as not to let two drowning souls sink into oblivion.

Mama brought our hands to her eyes, and her tears dampened our fingers. Her body shook with a pain buried so deep that it had to find its way through the layers of stories Mama told herself throughout her life. Uma Didi's death gave her pain the power to break through those layers. I had never heard my mother cry like this. This pain was the exorcism of all her ghosts and the spirits that had walked her entire life with her. It pierced all the veils covering the wounds that made up Shivali.

I hoped Mama's God was listening and felt comfort in her pain, because I couldn't see why a God would want this wounded sound. Uncle Zweli came to the door, but when he saw me, he closed it. This wasn't for anyone to see. This was a pain so private that even I felt I shouldn't be here. But who else did my mother have? My sister wasn't here anymore.

Mama told the world with her screams that she was tired of carrying these burdens, these secrets. She shook violently and relieved herself of all the tension that had built up over the years. The rising power of her pain burst the bubble of the mask she had worn all her life. It needed to come out. Like poison, it had buried itself within Mama, taking hold and making a home in her body, her mind. Her screams allowed this vileness to escape and left space for grief.

"Hari, I'm so sorry, my baby boy. I'm sorry that my life has been so hard for you and Uma. People talk about us because of me. My girl is dead today because of me." Mama's cries were replaced with a deeply sorrowful lament. It sounded like she sang out her anger at herself. It was what made her cry even more painful to hear.

"No, Mama . . ."

She placed her fingers on my lips, unwinding our hands first and then holding my face in her hands.

"Hari, it is true. You know it. Uma knew it."

She looked at me, and all the anger that I had for her rose into my throat. It stuck there, unsure of where to go next.

"I killed your father. I was the sardar's mistress. I did things that you shouldn't have to deal with. No one deserves a mother like me. You deserve a mother who is pure. I'm not. My past has made all this happen. We're going to Uma's funeral because of me," she said.

I remembered how Baba would hit me, and I would hide behind my mother's sari. Mama saved me from him. How could my mother think that we were going to a funeral because of her? We were alive because of her. We had a place to live because of her. Mama had sacrificed so much of herself for us, and here I was thinking that I was stuck with her! I should be grateful to be left with my mama. The anger held in my throat finally had a place to go. It was directed at my ungratefulness in thinking she was a burden, and to the world that told her she was dirty and impure. This is my mama.

"I stabbed Mohan. Uma and I buried Megha's baby. Who does all that, Hari? What kind of a person does that?"

Her lament continued as my own was building. I heard a mother berate herself for all the things she did to keep everyone safe. And no one was saying thank you. Especially not the son she had done all these things for. That son, me, was thinking about being alone with her, and so angry at that thought. Angry at Didi that she left me with my Goddess.

"And now my daughter, my sweet girl is paying the price of my karma," Mama went on. "Hari, why? I'm so sorry, baby. I wish I had been a better mother. Uma would be alive today, and you wouldn't be so embarrassed by me." She left the bed and touched my feet. "Forgive me, Hari. Please forgive me. Uma, forgive me, my baby girl."

It was wrong for her to touch my feet. "Mama, please stop. There's nothing to forgive. We're alive because of you. You made our lives possible. I love you. I know I'm here because of you. Uma Didi loved you."

I held Mama in my arms and picked her up. She felt as light as a feather. The exodus of pain and poison had made her lighter. As I stroked her short hair, I wondered why she wasn't wearing her turban. Had she tried to rid herself of all that made my mother Shivali?

"Uma Didi knew how much you loved her," I said.

Mama's cries had slowed. They weren't as violent or as turbulent as earlier, but now the tears just felt like pools to drown in.

"Mama, you can't leave me now too." A sudden fear gripped me deeply. Why did I feel like Mama was now waiting to die? Did I make her think this by being upset to be left alone with her? "You have to see my children. We must live for Uma Didi."

"I can't anymore, Hari. I don't know what to do. How do I make what I did right again? How do I bring back Uma? I have to bring her back. I can't go to her funeral. I can't! She has to come back. I'll wait for her!"

"Didi isn't coming back, and it's not your fault. If it's anyone's fault, it's all those people that gossiped about her and told lies. We have to say goodbye to her, Mama. Uma needs us to say goodbye."

I knew that we had to be present for our Uma Didi, to hold her hand, to say goodbye with love, and to send her orange and purple flowers. Her heart was now free. Our lives would never be full again. They would have a hole. Hopefully, light and air would fill that hole in time.

"Mama, wear your turban," I said. "This is you. This is the you that Didi knows. This is the mother that she loves."

We sat together for some time until Uncle Zweli knocked on the door again. I promised myself that my mother would never want for love again and that no one would say a word against this woman who made us all. I promised myself that I would give her all that she gave up. She would hold her head up high. That voice that told so many lies would have another place to live, not in my heart or my mind. Together, we left the room in silence, two broken souls from Port Natal with grief as their chaperone going to bid farewell to their love, the one who had been their strength.

The uncles had readied everything for us to go to the crematorium. The trip there was silent. It took around an hour for us to reach our destination. The priest did the last rites for Didi. Mama was with us. This was important for us, for Mama, that she was there. There were those who didn't think Mama should be at the cremation, and I could just hear them whispering under their breath. This time, I had no time or energy for them, or this.

"Mama is staying with us. Anyone who feels that this is wrong, can leave." No one left. All they did was talk; they couldn't do anything else.

As Uma Didi's cremation continued, I thought the silence was unusual. These people were never this quiet. As we watched the last semblance of Didi's life, white smoke raced eagerly toward the sky, hastily trying to touch the clouds. The heaviness of the day sat on us, but it did nothing to hold back the smoke of Uma's burning body. *I love you, Didi.*

Chapter 16

Hari's White Guavas

Finding Didi on the bed was hard. Bringing her body home was hard. Burning her was hard. Everything was hard. Waiting for Uma Didi's ashes wasn't hard; it was impossible. I rested my back against the tin wall of the hall. Earlier, when the pundit did the prayer for her soul, I wondered why he was wasting his time. Didi was in Ishapur, lying on the rocks and looking at the clouds, not here in this place. When he asked me to light the cremation fire on her chest, I couldn't even look at her.

In this room, only uncles Madan, Mohan, Gopal, and I remained. Only men were allowed in the cremation room. But I wasn't a man. I was Didi's *Hari baby*. Whenever I couldn't do something, Didi would hold my hand and say, "Hari baby, give me your hand and let's do this together. You are a big boy." Just like how she held my hand while we waited for the boat and on the farm. No one held my hand now. They waited for me to light the fire. They waited for me to be the adult who lit the funeral pyre, but all I wanted to do was hold her hand. So, I held her hand first and spoke my heart to her. I told her what her Hari baby was so scared of.

"Didi, when I light this fire and it burns, your body will be gone. I know you are in Ishapur and not here. But I'm here alone. You left me here. How am I going to live out my life without you?"

My tears were not the only ones. Uncle Madan tried to hold his tears in, but they broke through when I held my sister's hand.

"Uma, how will we manage without you? What will our lives be without you as our rock?" Uncle Mohan whispered through his tears.

Uncle Madan's grief didn't give him permission to speak. Three men and one boy stood watching this body, each trying to hold back the shadows that engulfed us.

"Hari, please light the camphor and let it burn, boy." Uncle Gopal placed his hand on my shoulder.

I knew I must start the cremation, but I had things to say first. "I love you, Didi. I'll never forget you. Wait for me." I kissed her hand. It felt cold, not like how I remembered. This was my sister's body but not my sister's warmth. That warmth had left through the window with the breeze in the room where she decided this life was too hard to live with us. The flame that glowed on her chest was small at first, but like Uma, it was also strong.

We waited several hours for the ashes. I had sent Mama home earlier with Unni and Megha Aunty. It was hot and sticky, and the wait would have been too much for Mama. When I suggested to her and Unni that they go home, she didn't even fight me. Her shriveled and stooped body reflected how hard the day was for her. Besides, Megha Aunty's crying and wailing weighed us down. Unni looked hopeless, like he didn't know what to do with her, the situation, or himself. What was a man to think when everyone was talking about his wife's baby, a baby that wasn't his? Even though he knew she was pregnant when he met her, confronting this demon from the past hurt every time he opened the door, especially when new people were peering through and examining the situation.

Unni was relieved not to have others watching his wife's total collapse or his continuing humiliation at something he had no control over. Everyone now knew that Megha Aunty had killed her newborn baby. They all also knew that Uma was the one who found it. Unni knew everyone talking about Uma Didi's death and the death of Megha Aunty's baby.

The quiet when they left was such a relief. For a moment, I felt happy. Then I remembered that I was relieved because I could wait for the ashes in peace. This wasn't a relief; it was a torture reserved for baby brothers waiting for what was left of their big sisters. The anguish was so conflicting—waiting and hoping the time went quickly, but praying that it took longer so you never saw your sister reduced to ash. Maybe if it took longer, I could still have a memory of her as a person. I knew once I saw her ashes, I could never erase that from my mind.

"Hari, come to the cremation room, son. The ashes are ready," the priest called to me.

He didn't look like a man of God. But then this was the God that allowed Didi to die and Mama to break, so what could I expect from his people. He didn't look like a man of God with his round face and wobbly chins. His bald head glistened with the sweat of the day and the heat of the burning pyres. He had a large mustache and a long, unkempt beard. An orange shawl was draped around his bare shoulders, and a white thread hung from his left shoulder, settling under his right arm across his body. This thread symbolized his initiation into the priesthood.

He handed me a clay pot filled with Didi's ashes. He had an orange cloth in his hand, and as he handed me the pot, he said a prayer over it. I heard none of the words. I was focused on the pot. My hands cupped the container. *Why was this pot so small?* My sister filled my whole life. She had too much courage and strength to fit into this small vessel, but this is where they put her. The pot was filled with a white powder flecked with some brown and black bits. Holding the ashes brought no solace or pain. My Uma Didi was made to look at the clouds, lie on flat stones near blue waters, and play on grassy patches under a big tree. This was merely dust. But somehow holding this pot of ashes felt like I was holding her hand.

After his prayer, the priest covered the pot with a flat lid and tied the orange cloth over it. Uma Didi looked like she was wearing a wedding veil. The uncles were with me all the time, but the person I looked for was my uncle from Natal. Uncle Zweli stayed with us throughout the cremation. He didn't come into the cremation room, though. That would have been too much to ask. Uncle Zweli was a Zulu man. In his tradition, burning a body after death was the worst thing one could do for the dead. The ancestors had no way of returning if they were burned. Yet Uncle Zweli knew what I needed, what Mama needed, and he was with us. He held me as I held Uma Didi. He was with us exactly like when we were so little and landed on this foreign land. The Black giant held these two Indian children in his arms, and he cried. Thunderstorms raged from his eyes. His fat, hot, heavy tears landed on my shoulders and arms. They were incessant, and my tears mingled with his. We cried together for the life we remembered and for the life that we would never have again because one important part no longer existed. We would be Uncle Zweli's children no matter how old we were. It didn't matter if we were dead or alive, Black or Brown.

I would now have a memory of Didi in a pot. Someone who was reaching for the skies was now stuck, covered by an orange cloth.

"You must take her ashes to the sea and let them become one with the ocean. Take her ashes today," the priest said as he placed his hand on my head. "Bless you, boy. You are a good son, Hari."

He didn't say I was a good brother because he knew I couldn't save my didi. I nodded. I wanted to go home. The priest needed to be paid, and Uncle Gopal took care of that. Uncle Madan took us all home in the cart. When we arrived home in the early afternoon, we still had to visit the beach. The day would not end. I counted the stones under my feet as I walked the short distance from the gate to the veranda. Mama was sitting there with her head against the railing, waiting in the same spot she'd been in for days.

I used to ask my sister to play the house-house game all the time. We would imagine Ram, Sakshi, and me. I never played the game of Didi's funeral. Mama and I had never even considered that this was something we would have to experience. My eyes never left the orange cloth draped over the clay container. Mama got up when she saw me. As usual, she didn't wear a sari, but she held a white shawl in her outstretched hands ready to receive her baby girl. I couldn't look at Mama as I placed Didi in her hands. We stood, holding our love tightly, neither of us wanting to let go.

Aunty Savitri took the clay pot from us and placed it where the lamp had been. Then she placed the lamp in front of it. Few people stayed with us, just our family. Our uncles and our aunties felt the acute, massive loss of Didi, and we all knew this was a loss that would stay with us forever. Whether you were Uma's brother, mother, uncle, or aunt, it didn't matter. She was a light that kept us all bright, and she was home. Not for too long, but at least her ashes were home.

Mama wanted Uma's ashes to come home before we went to the beach. Others thought we should have gone straight to the beach, but my mother insisted we stop at home first. The murmurs of dissent never stopped around her. She wanted her daughter home. She wanted the last place she rested to be in her own home and not a crematorium. Her ashes would mingle with the rough, foaming waters of the Natal Sea soon enough.

Uncle Madan brought bird-of-paradise flowers, and Aunty Savitri placed Christmas flowers around the pot before adding more oil to the lamp. The flame flickered in gratitude—for the flowers or the oil, I wasn't sure. The heat even stood back with humility. The afternoon wind cooled everything but didn't dare touch Didi's lamp. I had no more words for her. I said all I had to say at the crematorium. I held her hand when she left. I would keep that with me. But Mama had much more to say. She had not had a chance to say goodbye to Uma Didi in her way without tons of eyes judging and ears ready to grasp every word whispered with love and pain.

Mama sat next to the orange covered cloth, her hands clasped in a prayer stance. She closed her eyes and spoke to her heart. By joining her hands, she bridged the gaping wound between her heart and her mind, two things she kept separate from the time I had known her.

"My beautiful girl. My darling Uma. I love you so much. I know that you found it hard to like me or even love me. But I love you, and I will love you forever. There's no one like you, my baby."

She didn't cry when she said those words. This was just a fact for Mama. This was her truth.

"No one besides you, me, and Hari know what we left in Ishapur. You were so small, just a baby yourself, but you had more strength than me. You knew what was happening was wrong. People think that I'm strong. They don't know that you're the reason I'm able to do what I do. You became Hari's mother, more than me. On the plantation, it was you that made sure we had a home, not me."

I wasn't sure if Mama was talking to herself or to Uma Didi. Her closed eyes and words told us that she needed to speak.

"You fell in love. You loved. You had more strength than me. Despite what life threw at us, you still had the courage to see joy and love. My baby girl, I wish I had spoken to you that night. I would have told you what was in my heart. I wanted to tell you that no one could force you to marry. I wanted so much to tell you that when you decide to marry, I would be the first person to rub *hurdee* on you. I don't care about these people. I wanted you to be the happiest always."

Tears now fell steadily. Mama couldn't control her grief when speaking of the future Didi would never have.

"You're not here, Uma, but that doesn't mean that you're gone from our lives. I have a daughter. You're my daughter. No gossip or death can take that away from me. And Hari is my son. We are still three. I love you until I die, Uma."

My mother's other sons wept with her. Both shared their love for Uma and for Mama. Both looked like lost boys who needed their mother. I watched them and thought how Didi would have laughed at them. She would have said that these uncles cry for every small thing and that they were just little boys missing their mother. She was right. Except now she would have been wrong. They were not crying for a small thing. They were missing their sister.

Uncle Gopal reached over to add more oil to the lamp. "We have to leave for the beach now. We should put her ashes into the ocean before it gets too dark. We still have the prayer to do when we come home. Should I call the priest, Shivali?"

"No, Gopal-ji. I don't want the priest. I know what to do for my child," Mama said.

"But the priest would be best to do the prayer, don't you think? He knows what last rites to complete."

Mama looked at Gopal. "I know what to do. I know more than they do. I know what is important for Uma's soul. Don't worry, Gopal-ji. My baby will get *moksha* and peace. She's already at peace. Let us just do what we have to for her." She looked at Aunty Savitri. "Savitri Bhen, please let everyone know that just us here will be doing Uma's prayers for the next ten days. We are happy to have people come home. Everyone loved Uma. But we will decide what we do."

"Don't worry, Mama. I'll also tell everyone. They're a bit scared of me too. They will listen," Uncle Zweli said, bringing a tiny smile to her face. They were frightened of things that were different from them, especially the Black Zulu men of Natal. "Let's go. Madan, get ready to leave."

"Can we wait a little longer?" I asked. I wanted to stay longer with just us and Didi. I didn't want her to leave just yet. I was tired of being strong. Hearing Mama talk to my sister stopped my breath, and my heart slowed down. My mother's words stopped my world, and I didn't want to do anything more. I just wanted to sit here on the veranda and think about Didi.

"We can wait a bit more, Hari. But not too long." Uncle Zweli stood next to me, his large hand on my shoulder. He leaned in to pull me against him, and I let him.

"I grew up in a place far away from here. Far north from here, where the elephants and rhino are plentiful. They roam the land freely, because it is theirs and they were here before any of us. The two rivers that give my home its name are the White and Black Umfolozi Rivers. One is dark and deep, and the other has so many rocks that it feels like the water is boiling all the time," Uncle Zweli said. His voice took on a wistful quality, like it was searching and remembering his ancestral home.

I loved hearing those stories, but not today. I was too tired. "Not today, please. I'm not in the mood for a story."

"This is not a story, Hari, but a truth of this land. The Zulu people know that this land is the land of the elephant, the rhino, the lion, and so many other animals that came before us. But we learn the most about being a family and the pain of losing a loved one from the elephants."

He spoke with an intensity that made everyone listen.

"Elephants are the storytellers of the animal world," he continued. "They hold the memory of who we are. When an elephant dies in a herd, the herd will circle the dead and touch their loved one with their trunks. Once all the elephants have said goodbye, the mother and siblings will do the same. They cry and they hurt. They feel the pain of their loss. When they have mourned, they walk away. They leave the dead elephant behind. Not because they don't care, but because they know to survive, they must take care of themselves and keep walking. It is the way of the elephant, the way of the world. They are the storytellers because they hold the stories, but they don't let it engulf them. They remember their loved ones but focus on walking forward. They tell the stories of their loved ones, keeping them alive in their memories."

Uncle Zweli touched a place in me with his story of the elephants. He nudged the memory of Didi telling us about the elephants of the Greyville marshes. How happy she was. How happy we were.

"Let's keep Uma's memory alive, Hari. But we must keep on walking."

Usually, a trip to the beach was such a joyous occasion for us. Everyone from our community would be there. Food and fun were the order of the day. The sun burned us all browner, but we didn't care. Didi especially loved the ocean. She said that it reminded her of us crossing the Kaala Paani. She said that was where our family with all the uncles and aunties were made. She loved to sit at the water's edge and wait for the waves to break on her. Oh, her screams! Once we thought that she was hurt! But she was laughing. Laughing so loud and so hard, it made us all want to sit at the water's edge and enjoy the waves breaking on us. Today, it was Mama and I who trudged to the ocean's edge with Uma Didi in her orange veil.

My feet sank into their porous and wet depths. Each step was a hug that grabbed my feet, trying to hold me back from releasing Didi. It took time for an awareness that someone was next to me to filter in. Heavy sobs fell into a rhythm with our footsteps. I lifted my eyes off the pot of ashes to find a white face, awash with red as tears rolled down his cheeks in a steady stream. Every bone in my body tensed, ready to attack the coward daring to share my space with Didi. How dare he walk here with us? And who brought him here?

"Hari, I asked Zweli to bring Richard here," Mama said. "Uma deserves to be surrounded by all the love that she had for everyone. Richard, come with us to send Uma off."

"Why, Mama? Why did you call him here? Didi is dead. We don't know him, and we don't need him."

"Uma needs him, Hari. Even if you don't think so, I know we need him. He loved our Uma. I want to know that side of my child that loved this man. Did you ever wonder why Uma didn't tell us that she loved someone?"

"We don't even know if that is true," I said.

Could there ever be any peace in this place? Could we just have a few minutes without feeling torn and broken over and over again? I was ready to sink my fist into the blue eyes that I knew I would meet. I needed a place to leave my anger at my sister's death, and that place had a name—Richard. Not often did the plantation owners want to mix with the Indian coolies, even if we hadn't worked for them in years. But here he was, standing alongside the brown Indian boy who carried his darling sister's ashes, ready to surrender her to the wind and the water. As Richard continued weeping, I wavered. A bit. For my didi.

"It's true," Richard said.

My eyes found a strange uneasy companionship in the window of a sorrow that mirrored mine. But his eyes were not on me. They rapidly and incessantly scanned the orange covered clay pot.

"I loved her. She loved me. I wanted to marry her, but she was too scared. We could have left this place and made a life together. But Uma never believed that it was possible for us. Even when she told me she loved me. I knew that she loved me, but she believed that we would never be together."

How dare he talk about my sister like he knew her so well! There was so much I wanted to do to him! But my heart held sway hearing the man that loved my Uma Didi. A man that my Uma Didi loved. He told us that she had told him people were talking about an unmarried Indian girl being with a White man. He said the old sardar saw them together and told others. That we knew. The uncles nodded. The sardar that Mama hated was responsible for all this.

"Hari, I think we should do Uma's prayer and let her ashes go into the sea, and then we can talk. But first let us send my daughter in peace. Richard, join us please," Mama said.

I wanted to do what was right for Didi now, so I listened to Mama. We reached the water's edge, and my mother removed the orange cloth. She held the pot in her hands, offering it and its contents to the elements. My mother knew the prayer to say. You could see the remnants of Shivali returning. Mama wasn't lying when she said that she knew the right prayer to say. The only reason we needed a priest in the crematorium was because my mother was in no state to do anything. As she uttered the prayer, we felt Didi's presence all around us. Uncle Mohan gasped and held my hand.

"Uma is here," he said with sadness.

"Richard, please say goodbye," Mama said, holding out the pot of ashes to this White man. As she placed the container in Richard's hand, his tears fell on the orange cloth.

"Goodbye, my dear darling girl, in this lifetime. Your love is the greatest gift I have ever received, and I will treasure it for all my years. However long I am on this earth, I will honor our love, my darling Uma. Wait for me so that when my time is over, we can be together. In the meantime, I shall meet your laughter every night in my dreams."

We stood with her. We realized that we only knew parts of her. Uma wasn't just the keeper of our family secrets but her own too. Richard's tears never dried as he kissed the container and handed Uma's ashes back. "I love you, my Uma. My sweet angel," he said.

Everyone kissed the pot, and Mama tilted it and held it to the wind as an offering to the earth, the sea, and the sand. Didi swirled all around us as she said goodbye. Strange how the ocean brought us to this land, and the ocean was where we went when we were no longer a part of this new world.

"Leave the container and the cloth, Shivali," Uncle Gopal said.

He spoke to Mama, but it was Richard who asked, "Can I please keep the cloth? It was the last thing that touched Uma, and I would like to keep it. Please?"

There was an earnest plea and hope in his voice. A body that lost hope found a small token of light to hold.

"We don't keep anything from the funeral with us, Richard." Uncle Gopal spoke kindly to Richard, but his eyes sought out Mama.

"Keep it, Richard. Keep something of Uma with you," Mama said.

My mother had no time for tradition and custom. None of that had served her well in her life. She wasn't going to start now. Richard took the orange cloth, folded it, and held it in his hands.

"Uma's laughter is my favorite thing about her. I hear bells every time she laughs. But she doesn't laugh often. I wish she laughed more. It's the most beautiful sound. She told me that her life was happy but hard, so when she does laugh, the universe celebrates my beautiful girl," Richard said.

He seemed lost in his memories. When he spoke of Uma Didi, it was as if she was in the next room. *Was she?*

Richard continued, "When Uma laughs, the wind claps in delight, the clouds clear, and the sky beams its widest smile. They know. They know that this is a rare moment, pure, ethereal. Uma has had sadness in her life, yet when she smiles, one small smile, all the moments of sadness are worth it."

We all listened to Richard speak about this Uma that we knew, but only in parts that she allowed us to see.

"Uma's joy, her playfulness is like a spiritual experience for me. I find God in her happiness. I can live lifetimes of pain just to experience the beauty of that one moment of ecstasy," he said. Richard's breath dragged, scraping away at his soul as he shared the joy of

Uma. The air stilled for just a second so that we could all experience Didi with him.

As we prepared to leave, Mama asked Richard to come home with us. She said she wanted to hear more about them and the love they shared.

Uncle Zweli, ever protective, said, "Mama, there might be people there. Are you sure you want to bring Richard with all those people around?"

"I never worried about them before, and I won't start now. I want to hear about my daughter and the love she had. Come, Richard." She held his arm, and he placed his hand on hers.

After a funeral, the first thing we would all do was sprinkle water on ourselves. Aunty Savitri was waiting for us at the gate, and we all cleansed ourselves as we entered our home. Mama and I went to bathe.

"Richard, please don't go anywhere. Please wait for us," she said.

"I'm not going anywhere, Mama." Richard was built like my mother; he was scared of no one.

Bathing was the first time that day I had time to reflect. It was painful, thinking about the woman that Richard described. Who was this Didi? Was life with us so hard that she couldn't tell us what she was thinking or feeling? It was hard enough for her to decide that this wasn't where she wanted to be anymore. She would rather die.

While Didi was busy being a mother to me, I didn't see that she was also a young girl struggling to be a woman in this horrible world of ours, trying so hard to find love and joy in a place that was built only for work. Mama knew this. This was what I felt this morning when we sat together. Didi was never a child; life in Ishapur saw to that, and even this place took what little childhood she had left. These people never even allowed her to be a woman either. She was hiding her love. Hiding that she found a way to be happy. Didi kept all our secrets and now her own too.

Could I ever be like my sister? I didn't know. All my life had been with her. How was I going to be able to be Hari without her? As I finished my bath, I thought about my didi who gave me guavas even when her heart was filled with secrets. She found the white ones, not the red ones. She knew that I didn't like those. This was the same Uma Didi whose laughter made the sky smile for Richard. She had a way of making everyone feel so special and like she was made only for them. So as much as I didn't know *all* of my sister's life, I knew my didi. And she loved me.

Richard and Mama were sitting on the veranda. Aunty Savitri and Uncle Gopal were making tea in the kitchen, and Uncle Mohan and Uncle Madan were sweeping the house. We swept the house after the funeral. We cleaned.

"Come, Hari Beta. Come sit," Mama said.

I was still wary of Richard, even though Mama was comfortable with him here. My heart now believed that Didi loved this man. I knew that he loved her. That was clear. But he was still new to me in this form as my didi's love. I knew him as the owner's son who lived in the main house. The young man that gave me mangos to eat.

I told him so. "The last time I saw you, I was small, and you gave us mangos to eat from the big tree in your garden." I sat against the opposite wall, making sure that there was a small distance between us. "When did Didi start to like you?"

"Uma and I used to meet at the spring on the farm. It's been some time now, years in fact. Once you all moved from the sugarcane plantation, Uma and I used to meet after her work at the quarry. She loved to go to the harbor," Richard explained.

I saw Mama look at him with a sense of recognition.

"That's where the old sardar saw us. I wanted to tell my father, and I also wanted Uma to tell you, Mama. I wanted us to get married."

His eyes looked pained as he said that. He told us that he had promised her they would build a house next to a river, far away from here, where we all could live together if we wanted. Uma Didi had wanted a house that had a garden and a river with flat stones and grassy patches. His voice echoed and seemed far away as he spoke. It had a pain that intertwined itself into the fibers of the muscles, settled in, and planned to stay forever. Ours was a shared grief, but one that each person held as unique at the same time.

Richard looked at me with a sadness that was specially made for broken boys. "Hari, how Uma loved to talk about you. She said that you are the best brother a sister could ever want and shared stories about you both growing up. Uma loved to talk about Shanti and how upset she would get when you brought your friends to play by the Neel River. But she really liked Sakshi and told me that she hoped that you would find a girl like Sakshi when you are ready to get married. Mostly, she told me about her little brother who kept her alive with his stories and with his games and laughter. She loved you so much, and she said that any child she had would be her second child because you were her first. Uma said that holding your hand was her most precious memory from the ship."

I looked at my hands. It wasn't my imagination that told me how important holding Didi's hand was. She even spoke about it to him. I remembered holding her cold hand before she burned. I thought my tears were finished when we came home with her ashes, but Richard's words brought a new set from deep within the wells of agony. Every word drilled even deeper, sending tears spilling to the surface. But Richard wasn't finished. He spoke to Mama.

"Uma was in awe of you, Mama. She said that you were the strongest person she had ever met. I couldn't believe the things you had to go through to keep them and yourself alive. When Uma told me about the farm and the sardar, I was so angry. I wanted to tell my father immediately, but she stopped me and said the sardar had a small child too."

Mama looked away and bowed her head. Even now, embarrassment filled her when we spoke about what she had to do to make sure we had a place to stay.

"Uma told me about her father in India, and she said that no one was like you. You made sure that they survived. As an adult, she couldn't believe how much courage you had to leave India alone with two small children."

Mama cried, and Richard held her. "Uma loved you, Mama. She told me that sometimes she didn't know how to tell you. You were the person she looked up to the most. She worried about only you and Hari. And now I'm all alone. I have no one. My love is gone forever. How will I live alone now?"

Richard wept with Mama like she was his mother. His family didn't know this Richard, and they would not understand the depth of love he had for a beautiful, Brown girl that made the world smile with her laughter.

I thought that it was just Uma and me, that we were the pair that had our own world. But Richard was showing us that their pair was another secret that Uma kept deep within her. We didn't experience that part of her, the part that loved Richard. She didn't tell us or believe in us enough to share the love she had for this man. Didi was my world, but Richard was the place where she felt safe. So safe that she could speak about us to him. It was with him she could be a joyful Uma, a pain-free Uma, a happy Uma. My didi of the rocks and clouds, his warrior queen. Richard brought her joy and love in a place that sucked it all from you if you weren't careful.

"The one thing that Uma believed in was that your reading of the Ramayana was what kept the three of you safe," Richard said. "She said that you got your courage and strength from the book and that she and Hari were the luckiest because you believed that they were equals. You didn't believe that girl children were less than boys."

Richard looked at Mama and held her hand. "Uma loved that you read the stories every Sunday. Sometimes I would come and stand far away to listen. She made me! She told me to love her was to know why she is the way she is, and Uma spoke about you reading to her when they were little under the tree. Once you read about Sita, Uma told me that she wanted to be like Sita. Full of love, but free. For her, God was you, Mama, being the free woman who made life happen for her children."

"I don't believe in God," I interrupted. "He didn't stop Didi, nor did he stop all the gossip. That is not my God. Why should I believe in this God?"

"Sometimes I feel the same, Hari Beta," Mama said. "I even wonder whether I'm ever going to read the Ramayana again. But I have never believed that my God could stop things from happening. My God is what we choose to do. And every choice I made, my God was with me. Now I have to think about how I'm going to be without Uma. So I don't know if I'm going to read the Ramayana again."

Richard was still holding Mama's hand. "Uma said that every choice you ever made in their lives was an act of God."

I held my memory of Didi in my mind's eye. I almost expected her to enter through the front door with something from the kitchen as she did in the afternoons. The thought about how I was going to live alone with my mother still lingered, settling in place at the bottom of my heart. Maybe it wouldn't be so bad. Richard was here, too, or perhaps it might be even worse because she only had me now. I kept telling myself to breathe. These last days had brought rising tides of panic. I never knew when they would hit me. Didi was gone and Mama was here.

Aunty Savitri brought out the tea and the rotis the neighbors brought the night before. The uncles joined us. Uncle Zweli sat next to me, opposite Richard. None of us had eaten since the day before. When I saw the rotis, my stomach growled, but I couldn't get myself to eat them. I walked into the kitchen and found the one thing Didi always brought for me. The white guavas. Didi made sure that I had them to eat. We promised each other that when we were older, we would only eat the white guavas.

I brought them out. Mama saw them and immediately came to sit by me. We ate the guavas in silence, saying goodbye to the girl we all loved.

Chapter 17

Shivali's Honor Returned

1903

The Hindu community, indentured people from the length and breadth of India, had come to love listening to the Ramayana on Sundays, and how the crowds had grown! The language it was sung in didn't matter when the story was universal. I read in my language, and now my Tamil and Telegu family read alongside me in their mother tongues. Everyone got to experience the grace of the rhythmic song and hear the words of this eternal story. It started with a few people attending and now the crowds stretched past the tree's plentiful shade. The community had set up a tin shelter to provide some cover for us from the scorching sun. The men still whispered about me over their cups of tea or cane, but the murmurs have quieted down. At least it wasn't openly now, not under the tree and not under the shelter. Our community, our people were slowly making a new world around work, family, prayer, and a new life.

I was one of the few who read the Ramayana in my community, but there were many around Natal. Mostly men read this story, but others, both men and women wanted to learn to read. Soon, others would take over the reading from me. I was getting old, and I was tired. My legs hurt and my feet never lost their swollenness from working the plantation, but mostly I was tired from taking care of everyone and feeling empty all the time. I wondered why they thought I could do anything when I couldn't fix my own life.

People looked for me whenever they needed help, even if secretly, sometimes openly, they didn't like me too much. I wondered if it wasn't my time to close my eyes and rest for a long time. So much pain and toil. It took all it could from you. Other times, when I saw people coming every Sunday, I knew that I wasn't finished here. But I was ready for someone else to take over. I thought Hari would take over when he was older. This boy, whose faith was and is severely tested, still yearned to bring everyone together, and he had learned to read the Ramayana. I had taught him well. He knew the stories, and he could read the book, but Hari wanted more than to read the Ramayana himself. He said he wanted to build a school so that everyone could learn. Even with all this boy had gone through, he still wanted to make the lives of those around him better. Hari said that Uma and he spoke about going to school, so he thought if people could learn to read and write, they would be able to have better jobs and make better lives for themselves.

I worried about him, though. The boy was gone, and a thoughtful young man had replaced him. Gone was the boy that liked to laugh at everything. He laughed now, but less, and a lot less with me. At times, Hari was more grown up than Madan and Mohan, who would always be the eighteen-year-olds that ran away from their village. They were still working at the printing press company. I heard them discussing with Hari that they wanted to buy the machine the printing press was throwing out, and they were trying to find the money. Hari was helping them talk to the store owner, Abdul Cassimjee. The general store became the place for groceries and also served as a bank of sorts. Many people borrowed money from Mr. Cassimjee, and Hari knew him well. He was an older man, his legs couldn't carry him far, but his mind was sharp. Nothing passed Mr. Cassimjee's notice. When Uma died, he brought groceries to us for a week.

My boy had become so much like me, and I didn't like that at all. I wanted them, Uma and Hari, to be free and not fearful or scared like me. I had hoped that they would live happier lives than I did. Uma tried to be happy with Richard, but even that didn't last. At least she had love and happiness for a short time. She just chose not to tell me. Sometimes, I would catch a look of fear or dread on Hari's face, especially when he thought I wasn't looking, or when he lost himself in thought. A particular sadness sat on Hari. Sometimes I thought it was less sadness and more loneliness. For Uma or for himself? I really hoped that this passed with time.

I thought the school he wanted to build, or even the newspaper, would give him purpose and bring him some happiness. Hari outwardly showed a happy face, but when he entered our home, he left that face at the door. It was a sadness reserved for me, away from prying eyes. It was a vulnerability that needed a safe place to reveal itself. Only Hari and I shared the loneliness of Uma's death. Richard felt Uma's absence, but he couldn't share our pain. Our story was one that stretched over lands, oceans, and plantations of sugarcane.

This community had grown to love my boy. Hari was becoming the person that people wanted to be around. What I saw as sadness, they saw as calmness and peacefulness. He made everyone feel cared for, and people cared for him. Me, they slightly feared with some grudging respect. Hari, they looked for because he was gentle and yet so determined. Be it Mr. Cassimjee or Father Elias or Gopal-ji, people were pulled to Hari's strong inner light. He filled any place with his presence, and he was still a boy. Hari brought everyone together.

Often on Fridays, Hari came home late. I had stopped worrying about what time he came home now, but at first, I was so worried that he was drinking like Unni and some of his friends, or that something more sinister was happening. The first time he came home late, I was so scared that my fear turned to anger as he walked through the door. Every time I couldn't see Hari, I worried whether he was hurting himself like Uma. I couldn't get rid of the gripping, excruciating fear. It filled every space in my body and left no place for trust or wonder or hope.

"Hari! I've been waiting for you. It's so late. Where have you been?" I was so relieved to see him. I wanted to hug him and hold him tight, but my anger just spilled out of me. "I hope you haven't been drinking or smoking with Unni and his friends."

Drinking was becoming a regular pastime for the men. The drunkenness got rowdy at times. I saw broken arms, painful bruises, and dark eyes on Sundays, mostly on the married women, but also on the men.

"Mama, I was with the uncles. We finished late at work and then we just talked," he said.

Hari's voice was a counter to mine. People loved his calmness, and I did, too, but in this moment, I didn't need Hari's peace. I wanted him to also be shameful, like me.

"You didn't think that I would be worried about you? That I would be thinking that something happened to you? It's dark and late!"

A look of loneliness shadowed Hari's face quickly before it disappeared again.

"Sorry, Mama. I should have come home. But the uncles and I were deciding what we wanted to do with the newspaper, and we needed to talk. Next time, I'll bring them home with me. I'm sure they would love to eat your cooking." Hari smiled at me and asked, "So, what did you cook? Dish for me. I want that mango pickle you made last week."

I grumbled and hid a smile. Did my son think I didn't know

when he was trying to deflect my anger or calm me down? I knew it, and I let him. I was glad he liked the pickle and that he still wanted to eat with me.

"I have something I want to talk to you about. I need your advice. The uncles and I spoke to Mr. Cassimjee, and we're going to take a small loan from him. He said that he would help us, and we can pay him back when we make money with the newspaper, or he can be a small part of the business," Hari said and then took a bite of the mango pickle.

I hoped he liked it.

"I'm thinking we should take the loan and pay him back. What would you do, Mama?" Hari took a sip of water.

I hoped the pickle wasn't too spicy.

"How would Abdul-ji be a part of the newspaper?" I said and sat next to Hari to eat with him. I knew Abdul Cassimjee well. To me, he was Abdul-ji, to the boys, he was Mr. Cassimjee. The old ways were passing so quickly, and the boys were learning the ways of the English. It made me sad to think about it, but this was a new land and a new life.

"He said that he would be a silent partner and only take a twenty percent share of the profits. He knows how to run a business, so he could help us learn quickly." Hari licked his fingers as he ate the mango pickle.

Rice and dhal with pickle were Hari's favorite Friday meal. Today, I also made green beans, but I noticed Hari only took a few of the vegetables. Next week, I would make some other curry.

"That's true," I said. "Abdul-ji is good at business, and his store is successful. Why are you thinking the loan only and not a part of the business?"

"I'm not sure. I was thinking we should keep this for us only."

"That would work too. Having a newspaper for our people would be a big achievement. I think it will help to bring our community even closer. Abdul-ji is a good man. I think he would help you a lot. If he has a stake in the paper, then he will want it to succeed," I said.

"That's true, Mama. Let me discuss that with the uncles. We'll tell Mr. Cassimjee on Sunday what we're doing. He said he would loan us the money either way. It was about how we pay it back. But there is something else I want to talk to you about."

"What is it?" I said.

"The uncles need to learn how to read and write. We need to learn English."

This was true. How could you start a paper when you couldn't read?

"You and I should teach everyone to read and write," Hari said. "Let's start with the uncles. I was thinking that every Friday after work, we can get the men that want to learn together. Could you get the ladies together in the day and teach them? Mr. Cassimjee said that he can make a space at the back of the store, or they can learn under the syringa tree cover."

"The ladies have been asking, Hari. But many of them are scared of their husbands. The ones whose husbands are learning themselves I'm sure will want to, though."

This was bigger than my struggles, and it was what I wanted to do—read, write, and teach. Just like my baba, and I wanted to teach girls and women.

"We must tell the ladies to bring their daughters and sons in the mornings. It's not just the older people. Or I can do a morning lesson for the children and an afternoon lesson for the ladies," I said.

Hari laughed. "I can see how excited you are! Let me talk to Mr. Cassimjee first and see what he says and when we can use his room. The uncles are excited. Uncle Mohan said he wants to know what he's printing. Now they do the work but have no idea what the paper is saying."

Hari laughed again, but it was so sad that our people did work with no idea what it meant. It was like that on the plantation. We did backbreaking work and yet we knew little about what happened to the sugar.

"Let's talk to everyone on Sunday. We can talk about Friday evenings for the men, the mornings for the children, and the afternoons for the women," I said.

"Mama, for us to learn English so we can teach the others, I'm thinking of asking Richard to help us. What do you think?" Hari looked up at me as he licked his fingers dry of the dhal and rice.

Whenever I heard Richard's name, I felt like Uma was near me. "Talk to Richard. That's a good idea, but we need to learn first and quickly. I wonder if he has a teacher that can help us. The teacher can start with a small group while we teach the others."

The excitement of a new purpose was growing, and the desire to pull myself out of my own day-to-day pain was even greater.

"We can't fail on this, Hari. We must start even if we don't know English well enough. Richard will come one of the days, and we can ask him then."

"No, I'm going to his house tomorrow. This is important, and I don't want to wait," he said.

That was Hari, wanting to do things now and not wanting to wait. Hari got up to wash his yellow-stained fingers. "Thanks, Mama! That was nice. I'm so full."

Before, the three of us would eat together, but now there were just two people. It felt so quiet with just us two. I wished the boys would come to visit more. After Uma's funeral, the boys, Zweli, Gopal-ji, and Savitri Bhen came often to see us. The boys more than the others. They came every day for the first month. Slowly, everyone had to live their lives, and Hari and I had to learn to live alone.

In the weeks that passed, Hari, Madan, and Mohan decided to make Abdul-ji a partner in their new business. In return, he helped them with the money and decided he was going to do the "sell" plan to ensure the paper was successful. The name, they had decided a long time ago: *The Port Natal Weekly*.

The boys wanted Zweli to join them, and he welcomed the idea. It was becoming harder for the Zulus and Indians to work together now. There was talk about keeping everyone separate. We had some Zulu families that lived close to our village, and we all lived side by side. What we didn't realize was that would change so much in the future and even the relationship that Zweli shared with my boys would be looked at with hatred. But for now, Zweli was Hari's uncle and best friend.

Richard's eagerness to help us made me wish for Uma. I missed her deeply, but certain moments made the longing even more painful. We felt her presence, especially when Richard was around. Madan and Mohan made sure that they were home when Hari brought Richard with him. They were excited about the newspaper, but the excitement of creating a future of our own was more compelling. We were not going to let these Englishmen tell us what to think or what to do.

As Richard sat down on the faded sofa, he said, "My mother is a trained governess."

"What is that, Richard? I have never heard that word." I had so much to learn about English.

Richard lowered his eyes and shifted in his seat. "A governess is someone that educates rich people's children. Sometimes they may also take care of them like a nanny. Governesses are always educated themselves."

As he was telling us about governesses and Mrs. Thompson, Madan innocently whispered to me behind his palm, "There are people richer than Mr. Thompson?" Our world was small.

A few weeks later, Richard brought good news. "Hari, my mother is excited to teach English again. It has been a long time since she taught, so she's nervous. Can she start with you, Mama, and the uncles? Once you all are ready, you can teach others?"

"Richard, thank you!" Hari was grateful just to start.

That was a big ask of Mrs. Thompson, of us, and of me. We decided that we would start the small class that Mrs. Thompson suggested. I also didn't want to look stupid with everyone watching. A small class was good for Mrs. Thompson and for me. My stomach was in knots at the thought of meeting this lady. I remembered very little about her from the farm.

"Does she know about Uma?" I asked.

"Uma is the love of my life and lives in my heart. My mother knows this." Richard could see how tense I was, and the hands that once held Uma's reached for mine. "She knows about you, Mama, and cannot wait to meet you."

The tension of meeting fell away when I saw Richard's mother's sad eyes. Our love for these children melted the walls between us as we hugged.

"Shivali, I hope I can call you Shivali? Please call me Eleanor."

Eleanor and I held onto each other as we spoke. No one else could feel our pain. We were mothers. I nodded through my tears.

"Our children loved each other so much. How I wish we could have been there for them," she said.

How I wished the same. Eleanor and I would never know what it would have been like to be family, but I sensed I would have liked her very much as Uma's mother-in-law.

"Do Unni and Megha live close by? I miss them terribly," she said.

Megha and Unni had settled near us a year after we left the plantation. No one knew how Unni paid off his indenture, but I suspected that Eleanor loved Unni and Megha more than just as her cook and housemaid.

"They live not too far away from us," I said. Our hands were still in each other's as we spoke. "Their children have grown so much."

"I hope I can visit them soon. Life is not the same without them."

A new friendship was developing.

Our community was mostly Hindu, but the shared pain of indenture made us family, regardless of our religions. The maulanas, pastors, and pundits cared for the entire community, not just their own flock.

The Christian missionaries from Kerala, India, brought with them their love for Christ. Their community built a rectangular-shaped, tin-roofed church on top of the hill. Every Thursday, the church provided meals for everyone. People lived on daily wages, so every meal was precious. After Sunday church service, everyone came to the syringa tree to drink chai and eat roti rolls.

On Fridays, *haleem* (meat soup) was served to everyone outside the mosque. Many shop owners were Muslim, like Abdul-ji, and they made it their duty to help the community.

"Today, Mr. Cassimjee asked us to deliver a month's worth of groceries to the Naidu family. Mr. Naidu is sick and hasn't worked for more than a week," Hari said.

He always told me when Abdul-ji sent groceries to any family, so I knew which ladies to look for after reading the Ramayana.

On Sundays under the syringa tree, many Hindu ladies would bring tea and serve rotis to everyone. Tea, roti, and potato curry became our Sunday lunch meal. A roti roll was potato curry rolled into a tube with the roti. Sometimes when there was a huge celebration, Mr. Cassimjee would bring rice, and the men would cook *biryani* (a rice dish). But mostly, it was roti and potato rolls. For years, if you asked me what my best meal was, I would say roti rolls and chai.

Everyone would share news too. It didn't matter if it was theirs to share or not.

"Did you hear about Nelson's son? He is getting married soon."

"Prema's daughter is having a baby! After so long, they were getting worried."

"Rumba and Tony had to take groceries from Abdul-ji. Lucky he was there to help them. Shame, they had no food."

No one gossiped around me, especially after Uma. Madan and Mohan also refused to engage in the gossip, but Hari was the most aggressive. No one spoke about others with Hari. The hard look in his eyes stopped everyone from gossiping around him. This boy inspired much love from his community, but he was clear on which boundaries they could not cross with him.

On such a typical Sunday, Hari shared the plan with everyone. Watching Hari made me so proud. My son wasn't his father or his grandfather. He wasn't me either. Any mother could be proud to say, "that is my son."

"We struggle to survive daily. We do the jobs that no one wants to do, and yet we still go to bed hungry some nights. Even worse, there are times that our children go hungry," Hari said to the crowd.

Some people nodded, and others just hung their heads in the everyday defeat of life in this place we called home.

"Together, we built this community. Our blood and sweat made the plantation owners rich. It is also what helped us make Durban our home. This is *our* home, and it's time for us to think about our future here, and most importantly, our children. I don't want my children to only do the work that we do today," he went on.

There was much murmuring in agreement when Hari spoke about our sweat and tears. Everyone felt this pain.

"Hari is right. I am tired of working hard and still not being able to feed my children," Thumba chimed in, rubbing his face with his weathered hand. Thumba lived not far from us and came to listen to the Ramayana religiously every weekend. The resignation in his dry, raspy voice belied the resilience that this man from the South Coast showed every day when he woke up at three thirty in the morning. to get to the Illovo sugar mills. Thumba's wife covered her mouth and eyes with her sari. No one saw her silent tears, but I knew that she felt her husband's pain.

Hari continued as more people listened closely. "Our children must be educated so that they can live a life better than ours. One that doesn't depend on whether we're too sick to work. We're not in the sugarcane fields anymore."

 The murmuring had given way to silence, and he said, "Why should we depend on the White man to build schools or hospitals or give us jobs? They don't want us to progress. They like keeping us poor and hungry. It makes us easy to control. They think help is a favor. They want us to say yes, Master, thank you, and never believe that our lives can be better than the sugarcane fields."

Hari's aura made us forget that this boy was not yet twenty years old. He spoke with so much love for this community. A young man that had seen too many things and lived too many lives already.

"Why should we wait for these Englishmen to help us? As Mama says, the stomach doesn't know when it's being kept full through someone's greed. That's for the mind to determine. That's education."

"I remember when we built the temple for Megha and Unni's wedding. No one wanted to help us, but it felt so good to have a temple of our own," Madan said. He was determined to be literate, and he wanted his community to join him.

Watching Mohan, Madan, and Hari start the newspaper made my heart swell with pride. This was now a common feeling around these boys. Maybe we did something right.

"I think building our own schools will feel just as good. If the government helps us, that would be nice. But we must do this for ourselves," Madan said and winked mischievously. "If they help us at all, we'll then say we are state-aided, but never state-owned."

"You just want us to read because you are starting a newspaper," one of the older aunties said, laughing as she chewed the corner of her sari and covering the bottom half of her face. "What's the use for me to read, boy? I'm going to die soon anyway."

There wasn't really any nastiness in her comment. Her voice echoed some of the thoughts of the older people, death always seemed close by.

"That's true, aunty. I want to sell a lot of newspapers." Madan crouched next to the grey-haired lady and turned his head toward her. "But I want to live without the White man telling me what to do. If their laws, schools, and businesses are in English, and if we and our children can't read English, the White man will own us." He wagged his finger at her playfully. "If all of us read, then we will certainly sell lots of newspapers. Mr. Cassimjee will help us sell more than the White man's papers!"

Mohan clapped hard for Madan and said, "I want to beat them. We can only beat them if we read our own newspapers."

"But you can't read English yourself!" a mocking voice piped up from the back of the crowd.

Hari spoke, adamant that this was the way for a better life. "That's true, for now. But we have already started learning. Richard and Mrs. Thompson are teaching us."

The mention of Richard's name brought some uneasiness and shuffling. They could shuffle all they wanted, but that wouldn't change what happened or what they did.

Gopal-ji voiced what the others were thinking. "Why would Richard Thompson and his mother help us? Are they not like the rest of the English?"

Hari reached out to Gopal and said, "Richard is not like the rest of the White people, Uncle Gopal. He knows what Uma wanted and he wants to do this with us and for Uma."

Gopal nodded. He wasn't totally convinced, but he trusted Hari.

Sometimes the mention of Uma's name took me back to the time just after her death, and even with all the conversation, I slipped into a memory of three years ago. Two weeks after Uma's funeral, I walked to my spot under the syringa tree. We didn't have the tin shelter back then. Hari swept the leaf covered ground and sprinkled turmeric infused water to purify the area. This was an important ritual when reading the Ramayana, and it was Uma's job.

Hari did the work without being asked. He laid out my rug, setup my Ramayana on the stand Dada had made for me so long ago, and sat opposite me, crossed-legged. "Read the Ramayana for me, Mama. Teach me how to be a better brother."

The word spread that I was reading the Ramayana again, and people came to listen, sitting in reverence. They brought their children. They brought their husbands and their wives. A few came to see how broken I was.

The stories taught us what it meant to have honor in the face of challenge. "Life can go, but your word is your honor and should never be compromised." Lord Ram taught us how to hold our honor and the dignity of others in hard times. Courage and compassion were the cornerstones of this story of Queen Sita's courage when she was abducted by the evil King Ravana and of Lord Ram's compassion in dealing with his father and his weaknesses.

This was also a story of righteousness, and about doing the right thing all the time. That wasn't the life we lead, and I didn't agree with everything I read. Often, we had less compassion for the people we loved because of the cloak of righteousness that we wore.

I said to my baba once, "Ram is a very good man, but I am not such a good person like him. I feel I will never be like him."

"Beti, it is not easy to be Ram. The Ramayana isn't asking you to be Ram or Sita, but maybe when we listen, we can observe our own actions. We should ask why we make certain choices. Sometimes our decisions aren't clear to others because they don't understand what we're dealing with."

I didn't understand what Baba meant then. When I examined my life now, who would know why I made the choices I made? The power of the story lay in finding our flawed selves and still trying to make better choices at every turn. The Ramayana was revealing all its secrets in the dust of Port Natal under the shade of the syringa tree. I was reading, and I could see my son was listening closely, and he wasn't the only one.

Those that came to see a broken Shivali thought that Uma was too bold, too wanton, like her mother. Her decision to love was the courage that I didn't have. Their bold looks, sniggers, and upturned noses told me what they thought of me. They were hoping to break me down or see me fail. But I was just a mother reading to her children. I thought I would change Lord Ram-ji's words slightly, so I said, "In life and death, my love for my children will never die." I knew that all my children were present, Hari, Madan, Mohan, and my precious Uma.

"You shouldn't be reading the Ramayana. Those holy words shouldn't be coming out from your mouth, *diyaan* (witch)!" This voice carried a disgust just for me, and just for this occasion.

"Don't you have any shame? Your daughter brought shame to us all by sleeping with a White man. Nobody wants you here!" That voice was one I intimately remembered. Night after night. Helpless and scared, I heard that voice grunt like an animal as I watched the flies on the ceiling or the dust on the floors.

"Killing yourself is a sin. She is a sinner twice over. And here you are, acting so pure and innocent. Your whole family is poison!" The voice mocked and spewed vile all over the shade of the syringa tree.

The voice came from the short, rotund, stooped body of the sardar. The sardar's stature showed exactly who you were dealing with. His skinny shoulders sat on a large, protruding stomach. His oily grey hair was slicked back, and his mustache was large and over-hung his lips. He alternated between clasping his hands behind his stooped stance and wagging his finger at me and the crowd.

"All of you are breaking God's law listening to this woman. She is not even observing the forty days after the funeral!"

The sardar was never liked by anyone on the plantation. He carried out the owner's punishments and had a few extra of his own. He thought he was better than us coolies and made it known to everyone through his whip and punishments. Using wives and unmarried women was his way of punishing the coolie men.

His voice was the sound of my pain and fear. All those nights made me hate myself and made my children into children of a pros-titute. My hatred for that voice gave me strength to continue reading. I just had a few more lines to finish, and I wanted the beauty of the story to drown out the vileness of the sardar's voice. I could feel the heat rising in Hari. *How much more could a child deal with?*

I held out my hand, palm upturned and facing Hari, and he sat back down. The damp and the dust fought for a place in my throat. I didn't want to stop reading, but the tears for Uma just rolled down my cheeks as I continued to share the story with all the people who loved Uma, who loved Hari and I, and those who didn't.

Now we were at the part of the story where the people ques-tioned pious, beautiful, and dutiful Queen Sita's chastity. King Ram couldn't take the shame and loss of faith of his subjects. He asked his warrior queen to leave, despite his love, despite his heartbreak. Chaste Sita walked into the forest and opened her hair, and the forest welcomed its daughter with open arms. She was a goddess, and not even God could abandon her. She decided how and when she would

THE STORY I TOLD MYSELF

interact with this world. Her courage in the face of disdain and dishonor was the story of this epic. Like my Uma.

"Stop reading and answer me! You are shameless, wretched woman!" The sardar wagged his finger in my face.

I could smell the tobacco on his finger, as it was almost sitting on my healed nose. This man whose hands I knew so well over the years disgusted me with just the tip of his finger. His sweat smell mingled with the tobacco creating the toxic sardar smell I knew well.

Those who came to watch me break strained their heads to listen closely to his words. Most people, however, were telling him to keep quiet as they listened to me finish the story and watched me close the book. I had carefully chosen today's turban. It was blue like Uma's river. The mantra that reverberated through my body, my mind, and the air around me said, "Enough. Enough. No more. Enough."

I dusted my coat and my dhoti as I stood up. "I feel no shame with you. You are the worst type of man, one that prays on desperate women and children."

His wife and daughter were standing to the side. His wife looked embarrassed. Her head was covered, but her pained, pinched face was still visible. His daughter looked confused by the glares people were sending to her father and the glances of pity her mother received.

"The shame I feel is that I told no one that you made me pay everyday so that my children could eat, even though I worked like everyone else on the plantation. My shame is that payment was made on your bed. You chose to keep a woman and her children frightened and trapped. You should hide *your* face and ask for forgiveness from me and my children," I said.

"Lies! Filth just like your daughter!" His face was contorted in anger, snarls hung on the edge of his lips as he lunged toward me, open palmed, ready to strike.

"How can you all listen to this and just stand there?" The sardar looked around at the crowd and lunged. A gasp came from the crowd as Hari stepped in between us. And it wasn't just Hari that jumped up. Many of the men, with Mohan and Madan leading the charge, rushed forward.

"You will not speak about my mother and sister!" Hari shouted as he grabbed the sardar's hand.

The sardar reached out with his other hand, wildly trying to strike anyone within range of his short arms. But the boys had already pinned his hands behind his sweaty back. It wasn't just the men that came forward. What women couldn't do with physical strength they did with their voices.

Savitri, my old friend from the ship, spoke. Her narrowed eyes and forceful stance made everyone fall silent. "Shivali is not lying. You made her suffer so that she could keep her children safe. I know she cried every night, yet she got up every morning, worked the fields, cooked, and lay on your bed every night."

Savitri looked at me and said, "Even though we were on the Blythedale plantation, Gopal and I knew it. We are all here today because of you, Shivali. No matter what this man did, you read the Ramayana for us. You brought us together under this tree. Shivali, you are our Devi, our Goddess. I'm so sorry we didn't say anything before. I'm sorry, Shivali, but I will speak now."

Mohan held onto the sardar, and I saw both anger and love seep through him as he spoke through clenched teeth. "This is my mother. She is the one who took care of me when I missed my mother and father. This is the mother who held me and let me cry. This is the mother who gave Madan and me a family."

Madan spat on the ground next to the sardar and said, "Mama gave us a reason to live and to believe that our lives could be better. This is my mother too. You are the dirt under her feet! Sometimes when I feel like God has forgotten me, Mama is the one I imagine when I close my eyes, and I know that I am not forgotten. Not by God, and not by my mother."

One by one men from the plantation stood up and claimed back my virtue from every vile word of the sardar. I had always thought that I was alone, that I had no one, but now I knew that we had a village, we had Hillary under the shade of the syringa tree.

Gopal shared, "He doesn't have a job at the harbor anymore. Everyone knows he's a snake. Richard's father fired him. Shivali, what do you want us to do with him?"

His daughter looked frightened as she hid behind her mother's sari. Even though this man was horrible, the little girl didn't deserve this. I heard that this was his third wife. She was the only one that had a child.

"Let him go, Gopal-ji." I nodded at the boys to let go of him, and I spoke to the sardar directly. "Please go far away from us. Don't come near us again. I have stopped the boys now, but I can't control what they will do if they see you again."

He still looked like he was ready to attack me. As they let him go, he lunged again, and Mohan's closed fist caught his mouth and nose. His face still carried bruises from their previous fight weeks ago, and Mohan was ready to finish what he started.

"Uma is dead because of this man! I am not letting him go without him knowing why he can't come back here!" Mohan punched him again, and this time teeth and blood landed on the ground.

"Uncle Mohan, please stop now. Didi hated fighting." Hari's words stopped this gentle man from doing something that would make him hate himself in the future. Mohan stared at Hari as he let the sardar go. The power and presence of this young boy couldn't be missed.

The sardar wiped his nose and mouth as he stood up. His white shirt carried his blood. He didn't look back or wait for his wife and child as he hurried away. His stoop was more pronounced, and his tummy jiggled in haste. I didn't feel bad for his wife. She knew what was happening, but his little girl didn't deserve this father. She turned around to look at me, her little girl fingers waving goodbye.

I would forever wonder why she waved at me. I closed my eyes and prayed for this little girl child. "God, keep her safe."

The air felt lighter after the sardar left. We could all breathe easier. The loss of Uma would never go away, but knowing that our people loved us, loved me, made it easier to face the future without Uma.

A lady much older than me approached and held my face in her hands. "Bless you, Shivali. I didn't know about you before today. Your story is many of ours. Your story is mine, but you have more courage than me. God Bless you, beti."

Chapter 18

Shivali's Shaded Syringa

"Shivali, are you listening?" Savitri shook me. "Where are you lost?"

I had been lost in the memory of Uma's death, and it still had the power to hold me tight. Sometimes sadness brought change. I lost my precious daughter and found my people in those times.

"Sorry, Savitri Bhen. I was thinking about something. What did you ask?"

"Are you ready to learn with these lazy boys?" Savitri's voice twinkled. The affection she felt for our boys shone on her face.

Madan piped up, "We're not lazy! We're going to be business owners!" He slapped Mohan and Hari on their backs. "The English better be ready for these Indians!"

Hari looked at everyone around him, his eyes bright with anticipation and a steely look of determination. "We'll start the school. Everyone will have a chance to educate themselves and pull themselves out of poverty and servitude."

Time had closed the hole that Uma left, but it would never heal completely for Hari. At least his joy had quietly returned. His determination was in full force. Hillary wore the shame of Uma's suicide mutedly nowadays. The shame never went away, just buried itself so deep that you hoped you could forget. There were still secrets whispered, but that was village life in Durban.

Richard would visit me and Hari at least once a month. He lived on his family farm for years after Uma's death. I loved to hear stories about Uma. I would ask him about the things that she loved to talk about or places they visited. It helped me get to know my Uma more. Richard told me about their visits to the harbor and the spring on the sugarcane plantation. He also told me about the times Uma would get angry with him.

"When I asked her why she didn't want more in her life, she got very angry, Mama."

Richard had become used to calling me Mama now. At first, I could see Hari frowning, but after a while it became normal for him too. Hari was slowly accepting Richard as his brother-in-law that could have been. Richard was already my son-in-law. He was my son-in-law the day Uma fell in love with him. He didn't know it. Uma didn't know it. I didn't know it. But it happened.

"She got so angry, and I have never seen her eyes open so wide! That's when I knew that she scared me, just a little bit!" he said with a laugh. I laughed with him. I knew that Uma well.

We got used to Richard coming on a Saturday each month, and I looked forward to it. He would bring something with him, some mangoes, some vegetables, and always flowers, orange and purple birds-of-paradise. I would normally cook something Uma liked, and together we would sit with our darling girl. Hari would eat with us and quietly listen, not saying much.

"Mama, I'm going to get some chicken tomorrow. Richard is coming. Maybe you can cook for us?" Hari said. That was when I knew that Hari had found his Uma in Richard too.

When Richard visited, every single time, I would have a moment of sadness.

"Why do you look so sad? I'm beginning to think that I shouldn't visit so often," Richard teased as I welcomed him into the house one blistering hot Saturday afternoon.

Hari stood by the door and rested his arm on the doorframe, trying to get some breeze. "I don't know about Mama, but I think about how it could have been if Uma and you were married, and you visited us." Hari's voice was so low, it was easy to miss the ache. "I think about what your children would have looked like."

Hari said what I thought about every time I saw Richard. "I think about that too," I said. "Would your little girl look like Uma, or your son like you or Hari? Maybe two boys?" The weight of this loss caught hard in my voice. I didn't know these children, and I already missed them.

Richard smiled, but his eyes darkened with sorrow. We reminded him of what he would never have with Uma. "Our children would have been here all the time. You would be their *nani* (grandmother), and Hari, you would have been the best *mamma* (maternal uncle)."

My baby girl would never have babies, but I knew if she had chosen to have babies with this man, he would have been a wonderful father, very different from the father that Uma and Hari had. I didn't think of their father much. He wasn't someone that affected me anymore. Too many years had passed, and the scared, frightened Shivali he married didn't exist anymore. The only person I thought of sometimes was my own baba. How he would have loved Hari and Uma, and I think he would have really liked Richard too.

Years had passed. The crowds were bigger, and there was no place to sit on a Sunday morning, neither under the syringa tree nor the tin shelter. It was wonderful to have people come every Sunday, and I wondered how long this would last. Some of the younger boys went to the beach every Sunday morning to sell either nuts roasted on the open fire wrapped in old newspaper or ice flavored with homemade syrups. We only saw them for chai and roti rolls. These boys were very responsible. They knew that everyone must contribute to the household. This small business made enough to buy some vegetables for the week and a few cigarettes to smoke behind the water tanks on the outskirts of the village. Some people had moved away to other parts of Natal. A few had even gone back to India.

After Uma's death, Megha's breakdown worsened and became permanent. She sat lifelessly for most of the day, staring into space or looking outside the window, not functioning in any meaningful capacity, including taking care of her two small, terrified children. They were scared of her and of what was happening to her. I wished I had helped more in the beginning and paid more attention to what was happening, but I was too deep in my own sorrow. I regretted that. Unni tried to care for Megha, but the care she needed was beyond him. Unni surprised us all. Even though we knew him as someone who boasted, spoke loudly, sometimes lied, and drank too much cane, he did what he could for the children. But they were small and needed a mother. After a while, the aunties and I took turns seeing to the children in the day, but at night, Unni had to take care of Megha and the children. All the while the children watched their mother slowly disappear in front of them.

After a few particularly hard weeks, Unni knocked on my door. He was disheveled, alone, and had a broken spirit.

"Unni, where are the children? And Megha?"

"I left the children with Megha for a few minutes. I'm going back quickly, don't worry. Shanba is watching Nithya. Megha doesn't do anything anyhow."

He knew I worried about the children and Megha. Unni's

shoulders had become stooped over the last years, and today they drooped with defeat.

"I wanted to tell you first what I'm going to do," he said. "We're going back to India, Mama." Unni called me Mama even though I wasn't much older than him. "I can't do this alone. Megha needs help. She doesn't look like she's ever going to get better, and the children need a family. I don't know where Megha's family is, but I think we'll go back to mine."

As much as I wanted to say don't go, I knew that I couldn't do anything for him. Life was so hard for us all, and it was almost impossible to take on more. Unni needed more help than any one of us could give.

"Come inside. This isn't something we should talk about at the door," I said. Unni came in, but still stood by the doorframe despite me asking him to sit. "Does your family know that you are coming?"

"No, but I'm sure they will welcome us. Besides, I'm the only son. I thought I could start my own life in South Africa, far from everyone."

What he had tried to escape in India, family, was drawing him back in again, and Unni didn't know how to say no. His stooped shoulders told the story of the responsibility he tried to escape, or maybe his inability to live on his own was the weight that pulled down his shoulders?

"Will they take Megha, Unni?" I was worried that they might only accept their son and grandchildren. A mentally fragile woman that they didn't know might be hard for parents and a family to take into their home.

"I don't know, Mama. They're hard people. But what can I do? I love Megha, but I can't bring the children up and take care of her alone. You all are strong, but I'm not so strong." Unni rubbed his hands together, pulling at his thumbs as he spoke.

I thought about their love story on the farm. How hard they

fought to get married. It was for Unni and Megha that we built our first temple. It was for them that we had our first wedding. The Unni in front of me wasn't sure what to do now. His Megha was slowly disappearing in front of his eyes, and he had no way of stopping it.

"I think you should get married again when you go back home," I said.

Unni's tears fell on his clasped hands as he spoke of Megha. I thought about the young girl that fell in love with Unni. I loved Megha. I missed her, and yet I wanted Unni to be happy too.

"I can't do that! I love her so much! And she's in there somewhere. I know it. I just cannot find her." He fell against the doorframe as he protested his love for Megha.

"Unni, I know you love Megha. I know Megha loves you very much. You gave her reason to live after everything that happened. But Megha's pain is too deep, and I don't know when and if she's going to get better."

I reached out for Unni's shoulders as a thought entered my mind. One that may not be good for anyone, but one that I had to share with Unni. I felt very guilty. I knew that I could have done more for Unni, Megha, and the children. My own grief wasn't an excuse.

"I'm about to say something that maybe very hard for you to consider, but think about it, please for your children's sake and yours." I wondered whether I should say more, but I couldn't stop myself. "Would you think about leaving Megha with me? You could marry again, and the children would be taken care of. Megha is so lost in her own world."

Unni's recoil from me was so instantaneous and with such a look of total horror that I wondered if what I was asking him to do was so horrible.

"I can't do that! Megha would never forgive me, and I would never forgive myself!"

"I know you want to do what's right, Unni, but Megha in this state is not helping you or the children. The children will never know her love as they grow, and they need a chance to live and thrive."

Would they be better off in a new land with a fresh start? I really didn't know what was right, but I thought Unni also deserved a chance to be happy.

"I can't do that, Mama. I won't leave her, even if she doesn't know what's happening." Unni's tears flowed more freely now. His words came with every sob and every tear.

This was a terrible choice. I shouldn't add more to Unni's pain.

"Don't worry about that now," I said. I had to calm him down. "You can leave Megha with me for a few days until you get everything sorted out. Let me also talk to Gopal and Savitri. They might be able to take the children for a few days. That will give you some time to make all your arrangements."

Unni agreed to this, and we decided he would bring Megha the next day. I spoke to Savitri on Sunday, and she and Gopal were happy to take the children. They didn't have children of their own. Savitri always wanted to be a mother. She was overjoyed to take the children. I hadn't realized that Unni had made plans for some weeks already. When we spoke about time to plan, I thought we had months, but Unni said the next ship to leave was in two weeks.

The children were confused by all that was happening. Their lives had changed after Uma's funeral, and they couldn't understand why. They looked frightened when they went to Savitri. I brought Megha with me so that they had some sense of stability. They knew her and Gopal.

"Come, little ones." Savitri hugged them to her breast. Nithya leaned into Savitri. Shanba was a little hesitant, and I could see the uncertainty in her eyes. She was a very smart little girl.

"Where is my father?" Shanba asked Gopal. She ignored Savitri.

"He's making sure that your trip to India is sorted out. Don't worry, he will be back in a few days, just over a week. Your mama will stay with Shivali Mama, and you and Nithya will stay with us until your father returns. Is that all right?"

Shanba just nodded at him and went to sit next to Nithya and Savitri. I don't know if she believed him or not.

I took Megha every day to see the children for the two weeks. The time flew and they were supposed to leave in two days. We needed to know what arrangements to make for Megha and the children. I asked Hari to go check on Unni. We hadn't heard from him in some time. I was also hoping and praying that he wasn't drunk somewhere.

"Mama, I think you should come to Unni's house." Hari had returned from Unni's house quickly. "Unni is not in a good state."

Oh my God! Not again. Not again.

Hari saw my face and knew exactly what I was thinking. "No, no, Mama! Nothing is happening. He needs to speak to you."

Hari grabbed me quickly, and my body relaxed as much as it could. We found Unni sitting in his one-room house, staring at the wall.

"Unni, what happened? Are you getting ready to leave? We must talk about what you want us to prepare for Megha and the children," I said.

Unni looked at me, tears slowly wetting his sun-darkened cheeks. The lost look in his eyes didn't match the excitement I thought I would see in his face.

"I am a bad person, Mama. How can a husband and father be such a bad man?"

"What happened, Unni? Did you do something?" Anger was my immediate companion, and I thought, I knew it! I should never have trusted him.

"I didn't do anything yet, but I don't think I can go back to India with Megha and my children. I think Megha is better off with you than me. Savitri and Gopal would be better parents to the children if they wanted to keep them. I wouldn't be a good father alone;

I know this. Megha is the one that did everything for them. These last months have been so hard, and I know that I haven't been good enough for them. Even if I remarry, I don't know if someone will love them like their mother would."

My anger drained as quickly as it rose. What was wrong with me? The situation was hard for everyone, but for Unni it was the worst of all. Who knew what was right? Unni remarrying? Unni not marrying but taking care of Megha and the children? Or Megha and the children staying with people who loved them? The decision he was grappling with was life-changing and almost impossible to make.

"Unni, son, breathe." I knelt beside him and held his head against my chest. He was heaving as heavy sobs wracked his body. "Are you sure this is what you want to do?"

"I don't know what is right, Mama. I'm scared that I won't be able to give my children the life they deserve. I'm scared that in India life will be hard for them. But I also can't stay here anymore. I have to go back home. Without my Megha, this is not home anymore."

That day I held Unni and let go of all my thoughts of right and wrong. Who knew what someone needed? I certainly wasn't one to judge anyone. I knew that I made a choice to keep my children safe, and it involved murdering their father. This man was asking for his children to be safe by removing himself from their lives.

Savitri and Gopal didn't hesitate to keep the children. They knew it would be hard, but there was also joy in finally making their own family. Megha stayed with me and Hari. She never recovered, and her mind was lost forever. Sometimes, it came back for a few minutes, a few hours, and then just as I would begin to hope, it would disappear again. The sense of loss was permanent. No doctor or priest could help her. The only time Megha showed any recognition was with the children. Even that waned over time. We made sure we went to see them often, and Gopal brought the children to us every weekend.

We never saw Unni again, but after about six months, Abdul-ji received a telegram from him with money. Unni never learned to write, but he had the postmaster write his letters and his telegrams. He never married, but he worked on his family farm and sent money to Megha and the children regularly.

Savitri and Gopal were born to be parents. They loved Nithya and Shanba. The children never wanted for anything. Not a mother nor a father. Megha was a part of their lives, so they knew that she was their mother, but Savitri was their ma, and Gopal was their baba. Savitri never let them forget that they had a "big mother," Megha, even though their big mother didn't know who they were. That was the woman Savitri was. Shanba had latched herself to Gopal. We all saw the love that Shanba and Nithya received from these new parents. Unni was the memory that lived on through the money that he sent to them, but they never saw him again. I wondered if they might try to find him when they were older. Gopal saved all the money that Unni sent for them.

"Why don't you use the money to help you and Savitri?" I asked.

Gopal worked with railways, and while they didn't starve, there wasn't a lot of money for anything more.

"One day, when the children are older, they will need the money for school, or a house. This money will be here for them. They must know that their father thought about them and that he did not forget them." That was the type of man that Gopal was.

Over time I thought about the decision that Unni made. It was so hard for him, but he never forgot his wife and his children. I wondered if they would have been better off or worse had he stayed. In my heart, I knew it was the best decision for everyone, including Unni.

Our community also grew with people coming from India to join us. They were called passenger Indians, and they were mostly traders and businessmen. Mr. Cassimjee brought his brother, and he opened another general store down on the South Coast, near the Sezela plantations. The Sitaram brothers also opened the first tailor shop in Durban. Soon more doctors arrived, and we even had lawyers from India!

"Did you hear about the lawyer from England that was thrown off the train?" Madan spoke of this young man Mohandas Gandhi, that arrived in Durban. "He is from India, but he knows the ways of the English. They said that he is standing up to the White men."

We were all sitting outside, enjoying the last of the warmth of May before the winter set in. Even Gopal-ji chimed in that evening. "We need more people to fight against these people and the way they treat us. Life under the White rule is becoming worse every day."

Mohan nodded. "You can't escape their prejudice. They want to keep us in poverty. Now we must have *passes* to go from one place to another!"

"No one is going to keep us in poverty, though!" Madan playfully smacked Gopal-ji on his back. The boys' dreams of a life meant that the printing press was soon up and running.

Even Tony from the bottom of the road bought the newspaper. "I wait for the paper every Friday!" he said.

"But, Uncle Tony, you can't read. You haven't come to school yet," Hari said gently. "Why are you wasting your money?"

"I don't care that I can't read now, but one day I will. Anyway, I would rather buy your newspaper, even if it's in English. I'm so proud of what you all have done."

These boys made me so proud. Every morning, I greeted the sun in the hope that I would be forgiven for all that I had done. The darkness in my soul was hard to get rid of, and I didn't think that it would ever go away. I could never forget Uma's body. But I was learning to live a little every day under the shade of the syringa tree.

Chapter 19

Hari's Paro

1908

The moment I saw her, I thought of Sakshi. My adult man's thoughts dipped into the well of memories of a small boy playing in the fields with his best friends. Ishapur was such a distant memory. I didn't remember anything specific, but I knew that I played with a girl called Sakshi and a boy called Ram. Some feelings were so woven into who I was that they would stay with me forever. Sakshi's face teased my memory. I couldn't recall how she looked. But I heard an echo of her voice in the passage of time and smelled her sweet small girl fragrance that changed with the years but stayed the same.

I hadn't thought of Sakshi or Ram in years, yet when I saw Paromala, I relived all those times with my childhood friend. There was something about the long plait of Paromala's hair, the way she stood with one hip slightly raised, and the way her eyes smiled that reminded me of the Sakshi from long ago. In that moment, Sakshi's face became Paromala's, and all the thoughts of Sakshi that had teased me forever were made a reality. Everyone called her Paro, and she was the most beautiful girl I had ever seen. My heartbeat danced erratically in my chest, hoping that Paro would join me.

I felt all this, but nothing showed on my face. I was an ocean of serenity—on the outside. Underneath, I was bouncing around like a mango falling from the tree! I was so nervous. I was scared that I would say something that would upset this beautiful lady. Everyone thought that I was very calm and that nothing caused me to get anxious. Most times, that was true. I stayed quiet, asked questions when needed, and helped where I could. That was what made people think I was calm.

But I also did what I thought was right. Mama taught us that kindness was important. Being available for others, rather than just yourself, was important. Never thinking you were better than others was important. She also taught us that setting boundaries was just as important. I had heard people say it could be difficult to be with me. I wasn't interested in gossip, and I asked them questions that were hard to answer. I knew this was true. But this was who I was—I was my mother's son. And hopefully soon, I would be Paro's husband—if she could like someone like me.

Aunty Savitri and Mama had told me about a girl that they wanted to introduce me to.

"Hari, Savitri Bhen knows this girl from the South Coast. She said she's a nice girl. I wonder if we should meet her." Mama's voice was very hesitant. "I don't want to pressure you into getting married. If you don't want to meet her, just tell me."

After Didi, Mama never broached the topic of marriage with me, but when the uncles and Aunty Savitri said it was time for me to marry, she hesitantly agreed.

"I would like to meet this girl, Mama. What is her name?" I wasn't hesitant. I always knew I wanted to get married.

"Paromala Sharma. Savitri Bhen knows her and her family well."

Didi said she didn't want to marry, but I was ready to marry Sakshi when we were children. I always knew that I would marry and have children. We struggled too hard, us three, for it all to end with me.

"Paromala's elder sister is married to Aunty Savitri's neighbor. That's how she got to meet her and to know their family," Mama said.

I was too busy working to even think about getting married, but once Mama put the thought into my head, I knew it would happen. I just didn't think it would be with someone as beautiful as Paro. My work had burned me so dark that I looked more like a laborer than a teacher.

I learned that Paro was born here in South Africa, deep down on the South Coast of Natal, a long way from Durban. Her grandparents had come on earlier ships in 1865 with their two sons and settled on the sugarcane farms near Braemar. Lots of towns down the South Coast had the same names as places in Britain. Mr. Cassimjee said the Whites tried to make this place look and feel like their home with their names, parties, games, and prejudice. Braemar was named after a place in Scotland, close to their queen's castle.

Paromala was the middle child of their eldest child, Durgaprasad, and his wife, KalaDevi. They had been free Indians for some time now. Once the ladies told me about Paro, the planning for us to meet started in earnest. Mama wanted to wait for a few weeks, but Aunty Savitri would have none of it!

"Why do you want to wait, Shivali? For what?" Aunty Savitri was adamant and very bossy, standing there with her hands on her wide hips. In all the ways that mattered, Aunty Savitri was Mama's big sister. She was Mama's didi. Mama needed someone to say no to her, and that person was Aunty Savitri. She didn't take any hesitation or defiance from Mama.

"It just seems like we're rushing so quickly. Shouldn't we wait to see if Hari is still interested after a few weeks?" Mama was still hesitating.

"Hari, do you want to wait?" Aunty Savitri asked me directly in front of Mama, daring Mama to say something contrary.

Aunty Savitri didn't share the relationship that Mama and I had. I could see an undercurrent that made Mama nervous and a little scared. It wasn't like my mother to hold back or to be fearful.

"Mama, what is worrying you?" I reached for her hands across the table. All this marriage talk was happening around the kitchen table while we were drinking tea and eating samosas that Aunty Savitri brought with her. The children were in the yard playing. We could hear them squealing and running. The home felt so full. It was the Durban winter. Not extremely cold, but colder than normal for us. Late July was the coldest time, and it was a good time for tea and samosas. The cold stove kept us warm in the winter months but broiled us in the summer.

"Nothing is worrying me, Hari Beta. I just don't want to push you into something you don't want to do. I never want to do that." I could see that Mama was reliving Uma Didi's life as she looked at me. "You should be sure that this is what you want."

"Mama, I'm ready to get married. I've always wanted to get married. I don't know if I'll like this girl or if she would even like me. She might say no. Then this discussion is for nothing!" I laughed softly and squeezed her hand.

She smiled and nodded, still sad.

"What do you mean, she won't like you?!" Aunty Savitri took the most offense at that. "She is lucky that you are even considering her. Paromala and her family should be grateful to have you."

You would have thought I rejected her! Aunty Savitri was furious that I dared to suggest this girl could say no to me. But Aunty Savitri didn't know Mama's story. She knew about Didi, but still didn't understand what that meant for us. She had a daughter that would marry someday. This little girl playing outside with her older brother should never be "lucky" or "grateful." She should want to marry the person wholeheartedly.

"This girl must like me and want to marry me," I said. "I don't want to marry someone who is forced to marry me. I don't want to get married like that. I want a partner in life, not a slave or servant."

I knew my voice changed; it quieted, and Aunty Savitri knew it was time to stop. She twitched her nose but held her tongue. There was still work to be done before Shanba married, but for now, we were good.

I met Paro two weeks from that day. It was late on a Sunday, and we planned to meet for a late tea around four o'clock. It was silly the details you remember. I always remembered times, dates, places. I would never forget that Paro and I met at her house deep in the Braemar sugarcane fields. We planned to meet later in the day because Sunday was Ramayana day. Mama finished reading earlier than normal, but there were no chai or roti rolls for us as it was still a distance to get to the farm. Too far in fact! Getting to Paro's home meant we had to take two trains. We took the first train from Durban to Umzinto, and then changed trains in Umzinto to get to Braemar. We were fortunate that we finally had a train. Uncle Gopal had a job with the railways as soon as they opened in Durban. These lines had taken longer to open.

We never did anything alone, Mama and me. We had a full crowd that went with us to see Paro and her family. The uncles came with Aunty Savitri and Uncle Gopal. Six people felt too much, and I said quietly to Mama, "I hope this is the first and last time we are doing this. All of us are too much for some people. We'll scare her! She might not want to marry me when she sees our crowd."

Mama laughed out loud and hurriedly tried to cover it with her hands. She looked so beautiful today. Aunty Savitri tried to get her to wear a sari, but Mama said no. I loved that about my mother. She was who she was. That was the kind of girl I wanted to marry. Someone who knew who she was. Mama's deep blue turban sat on her head. Her hair had grown out, but Mama kept it short still. Her dhoti was a deep cream, and her long shirt was the same color. Her coat was a shade lighter than her turban. She looked lovely. Her face had healed over time. Her nose never straightened, and some of her teeth were still missing, but you couldn't mistake the strength and beauty that brought.

Not everyone understood or accepted my mother when they met her. Our community loved her, but every new person that Mama met was like starting all over again. She stopped looking for acceptance a long time ago. She was a good gauge for assessing whether people were the accepting or judging kind. You couldn't hide from the turban and the dhoti. And you also couldn't hide from the teacher and community builder.

Paro's family knew what to expect. I usually expected a cautious approach to my mother. They were certainly cautious, but it was a caution that came with a first meeting, not from my mother's appearance. Paro's mother hugged my mother when she clasped her hands in greeting.

"Shivali Bhen, welcome to our home. I am so excited to meet you. I heard so much about you reading the Ramayana."

The stories of Mama had spread beyond our community. The story of Uma Didi and Richard had also spread. We were a family that came with a lot of baggage.

I was surprised by the number of people at Paro's house. I thought we were a lot with six people! Apart from Paro and her parents, the crowd included her two sisters and a brother-in-law and child, her grandparents, her father's brother and his wife and children, and her sister's in-laws. I felt claustrophobic just seeing everyone staring at me. Paro and I were certainly on show today, with Aunty Savitri being the master of ceremonies. She was the one who controlled the conversation and introduced everyone.

The moment I saw Paromala, the feeling of not being able to breathe stepped aside. She was the most beautiful person I had seen. The air stopped just for a fraction of a second, and the echo of a memory stepped through time to gently kiss my cheek, caress my heart, and give me my life partner. I always tell everyone not to judge, but I can't tell you why at first glance my heart became Paro's forever.

"Hari is very important in Hillary. He is the teacher and built the school. A very important man!" Paro and I were trying to catch glimpses of each other while Aunty Savitri spoke. Aunty Savitri was certainly making me seem better than I really was. This person she spoke of sounded more important than me.

The school was running; this was true. Richard and Mrs. Thompson taught Mama and me English, and we taught it in our school. Richard helped me to get a qualification in English that required writing an exam. It was so hard. Mama decided not to do it. The uncles were learning, too, but they decided to focus on the newspaper and let me focus on the qualification. I had Richard, but mostly Mrs. Thompson, to thank for this help. We sat for months, learning the basics and then applying the basics over the next two years before I sat the final exam. Mrs. Thompson had to get the Education Department of Durban to agree to let me sit the exam. I failed the first time, and Mrs. Thompson had to get special permission to let me take the test again. I passed. Not brilliantly. But I passed. Becoming a teacher took another three years after that. Now I'm a qualified teacher.

Mama and I taught the men and some ladies to read and write English. They didn't take an exam, but they could read. Now I was teaching the children. They would take exams soon. They would be able to do other jobs than just menial work when they were older.

Apart from the knowledge from books, my learning included Didi and Mama teaching me, without saying a word, the power and strength of women. My mother's courage to openly share her knowledge and teach both her son and daughter saved all our future generations. I knew even then that my children would be raised like my sister and I were. My children would not just sit under the shadows of the syringa tree—they would fly high above the tree canopy. This was my wish and my hope for the children of Hillary, especially for Shanba and Nithya.

"And he reads the Ramayana every Sunday. At such a young age too!" Aunty Savitri kept reciting all my accomplishments. I had taken over the reading of the Ramayana from Mama, although she still read when she felt the need to connect with the Ramayana and feel closer to the people of Hillary.

All the attention made it very tough for Paro and me to look at each other. We tried to steal looks in between, but the expectations of everyone made a simple glance especially hard.

"Mama, I would like to take a walk with Paromala to get to know her better," I said. The room quieted as I requested the opportunity to get to know this beautiful creature on my own. The only sound was the slurping of tea from saucers, the preferred way to drink tea—pour it into the saucer and slurp it up.

I could see Paromala's eyes from the corners of my own. Her twinkling mirrors were silently wishing the same, just afraid to ask. Her head was covered as per her custom, but I longed to see her hair. Her plait peaked from beneath her sari. Was it straight and silky or curly and soft? I wanted to take the sari off her head and touch her hair. What was wrong with me? I smiled to myself.

"That is fine with me, if it is alright with *Bhai-ji* (honorific brother) and *Bhain-ji* (honorific sister)," Mama said. She was referring to Paro's father and mother, giving them the respect of elders in the family. She made sure not to leave Paro's mother out of the permission. That wasn't common in our society. Permission came from the man not the woman. "Go ask your father" was common. Regardless of what your mother thought, usually she agreed with her husband, sometimes out of fear and other times out of ignorance.

"Yes, yes! Of course, Bhain-ji! The children must talk and get to know one another!" Paro's father hurriedly spoke, using the same respect when addressing Mama. He stood up and gestured to Paro to come forward.

Mama was quick, though, she turned to Paro's mother and asked, "Bhain-ji, are you happy for them to talk alone?" My future mother-in-law sent Mama a quick smile and nodded. Mama made it clear she was asking both of them, not just Paro's father. The look KalaDevi sent Mama said thank you without words.

"Why don't you both go to the garden and talk. You will be alone there." Paro's father held me by my elbow and led me toward the front door. "Beta, you and Paro take your time."

"Hari, remember we must still get home, so don't take too long!" Uncle Madan's wink brought playfulness into the room. "Paro, don't mesmerize him too much!"

I mock-frowned at him, but the smile he brought never strayed far from my lips.

The later afternoon was warm and had an orange glow to it as Paro and I went walking. We strolled in the garden at the front of the house. A large tree stump stood at the side of the house next to the washing stone where Paro and her younger sister washed their families' clothes. Mint loved the dampness and thrived all around the area. We sat on the stump, looking at the green fields far into the distance. It reminded me of when we first came to South Africa, green as far as the eye could see.

Paro's family had chosen to make their home just outside the Braemar sugar mills. They didn't farm sugarcane, though. They were wood and morning market farmers. Paro's father sold vegetables at the Durban morning market every week and wood to both the nearing mills and those far away. The train line was the lifeblood of their wood business, and it allowed them to send wood as far north as Eshowe, far past Stanger, up the North Coast. They made very little from this business. Illiteracy and deception from the English kept them with their head barely above water.

The evening light had just reached the tips of the cane, lightly painting it with a blush of orange. The atmosphere was magical, almost otherworldly. We sat next to each other in silence for some time. I sensed a tension curled up in Paro. I couldn't blame her; I felt a similar tension deep within me. I had to break the silence, or we would be sitting there forever.

"I'm twenty-five years old." These were the only words I could think of to say. If Didi were here, she would laugh so much and tease me. She always said I said the stupidest things when I was nervous.

I knew why I told Paromala my age. Most men were marrying by twenty-one and women by sixteen, so mid-twenties seemed slightly older to marry. I didn't know if age mattered to Paro. Mama told me that Paro was nineteen years old. Her family thought that this was also too old for a girl. The sweat gathered on my upper lip, made more prominent by the evening sun as I waited for Paro to respond to my declaration. She looked at me, head tilted, and eyebrows raised, slightly confused, but I think mostly amused by me. The corners of her mouth twitched upward, giving her face a mysterious look.

Maybe Paromala thought I had no other thoughts in my head. She wasn't wrong. All I could think of was her fragrance. I thought that I should just keep quiet. Paro and I sat softly for a bit, listening to each other's breath. When she stood up and started walking, I followed her. The grass dampened our footsteps. The trees bent their branches in embrace, and the flowers offered their scents to perfume the air around us. The air gently created its cocoon, holding the memories of our first meeting.

"Your age doesn't matter to me. I'm nineteen, and people already think I'm too old to even hold a pot!" this angel said as she stopped and looked at me.

Paro had a very disconcerting way of catching me unawares.

First when she stood up from the tree stump and now. She smiled when she said it. *Paro may be very funny, like Uncle Madan.*

"Besides, I think you have done so much in this time, when would you have had the time for me? I can take up a lot of time!" she said.

I was so excited when Paro looked directly at me. Most girls were taught to lower their eyes when they spoke to a potential suitor. Not her. I loved that she lowered her eyes for no one. Paro spoke as if we already had decided we liked each other.

"Can I ask you something, if you don't mind?" Paro continued walking, and I fell into step with her.

"Please do," I said. "Otherwise, we might be silent for our whole time together." I felt a bit more relaxed now. My blood slowly calmed down, and I could speak again without faltering over my words.

"Why does your mother wear a turban and a coat? We all know about the lady from Hillary with the turban, but it's strange for a woman. I'm curious. Especially here, in this country, everyone wears saris." Paro wasn't just asking *something*. She was asking a question that was fundamental to who we were, Mama, Didi, and me.

"My mama wears her turban and coat proudly because she doesn't care what anyone thinks about her or us. She doesn't do what others think is right. Mama does what she *knows* is right for her children, her community, and herself. When Mama, Didi, and I came from Ishapur, we came alone without a father. My mother had to be our mother and father."

Paro looked at me and all my nervousness disappeared as I spoke about my mother. "She wasn't only *our* mother and father. Mama took that role for so many on the ship. She took care of uncles Madan and Mohan like her own sons. You know, the younger uncles that came with us today. Uncle Gopal and Aunty Savitri are our family too. Everyone looks up to Mama. She can sometimes be hard and tough, but everyone loves her, and she loves them."

Speaking about Mama made me feel proud of her and who she was. "I'm marrying older because my mother never forced me to marry. She wanted me to be educated and to be a teacher. She didn't care that people said that she was spoiling me, or that I wasn't fulfilling a son's duty. Mama's turban is her reminder that she lives her own *dharma* (life path), and her coat is the courage that she wears every day."

As I spoke about my mother, my heart swelled with my love for her. It had been some time since I thought about when Didi died and worried so much about being alone with Mama and the hatred and fear that came with that thought. Today, my memories reminded me how lucky I was to have her as my mother.

"She sounds like a very incredible lady, and maybe a bit intimidating too," Paro said.

She looked afraid. And Mama could be scary, but she was also the kindest person.

"She just sounds like that. Believe me, she's far from intimidating, and she loves fully, with her whole heart. She makes people strong. You'll love her." My last words were whispered in a hopeful prayer. Paro looked at me, slightly nervous, and smiled.

"Paro, what is my name?" I said. It just occurred to me that Paro had not spoken my name once during our time together.

She looked down at the ground and said, "We don't take our husband's name in my family."

I couldn't lie. I was thrilled that she said *husband*. But I also didn't want a wife that was subservient to me. I took her hands in mine. Paro tried to pull away. Some of these families could get quite upset when skin touched skin, even if it were through holding of hands before marriage.

"Paro, if I can say your name, you can speak mine. In my home, my mother brought us up to be equals, boys and girls. My didi and I were equals for everything. I want a partner, a wife, not a slave or servant. My name is Hari. Please call me by my name."

Paro still looked around nervously, waiting for someone to jump up around us. Her upbringing held her back. Her future called her to take a step forward, hopefully with me.

"Say it, Paro."

"Hari." Paro whispered my name like an offering. "Hari."

"Paro," I whispered back. My heart knew I had found the person I could love.

We walked back into the house. It was late, and we needed to leave; the train schedule didn't change for budding love. But everything had changed that afternoon. When Didi died, everything changed. Today, my world changed again, and it would never be the same. Nor would I want it to.

"Hari, did you like the girl? She is pretty, na?" Aunty Savitri asked me on the train home.

"I liked Paro very much, Aunty." I didn't tell her that I thought I may love "the girl" already!

The marriage machine took over after that. Paro and I were going to marry in six months. That gave us time to get to know one another more. It was nice to have the time, but I just wanted to get married now. Going every month to see Paro was a delight, but it was far and that meant long waits and longing in between!

The moments when we saw each other were the sweetest. Paro was lovelier every time.

"Cut your hair and shave, Hari! You look like an animal." Aunty Savitri had now decided my appearance needed tending too. She was always fussing with Shanba and Nithya, and now she was obsessed with me!

Mama never bothered me with these things. They were too frivolous for the woman that cut off her own hair. I must admit that I wanted to look nice for Paro. I didn't want people to ask why a fairy was marrying a troll. Uncle Mohan helped me to pick out some clothes, and Uncle Madan polished my shoes for me. As a teacher, I looked decent, but now I wanted to look handsome for my girl. Paro said she liked my beard, so I kept it neater and shorter.

Our meetings had a routine. We would meet once a month on a Saturday. Sundays were difficult to manage and meant going after the Ramayana with very little time left for Paro and me to talk. Paro's mother always insisted that I eat lunch with the family, after which Paro and I spent the afternoon in the garden. The one time Uncle Madan went with me, he spent the afternoon with his friend who lived close by, and we went back together after five o'clock. I suspected Uncle Madan made up the friend. He just liked to sit alone in the sugarcane fields. The green could get into your blood after a while. We met at the station in Umzinto to go home. I was sure that he went to the racecourse there. The White landlords loved horse racing in this part of the world, even though it was far away from England. They kept themselves entertained with racing and grand parties.

Paro and I sat close. Very close, just not touching in case the family saw us.

"My sister was telling me about the newspaper. How exciting! How did you and the uncles do this?" she said.

I rubbed my hands together with glee! It was so much fun telling Paro about the newspaper. "I'm so proud of our uncles. These two boys ran away from home, worked on a sugarcane plantation, and now run a newspaper. *The Port Natal Weekly* is already in circulation."

"How long has the paper been running?" Paro's eyes shone as she leaned closer, but not too close.

"Three years or so. I can't remember fully. My uncles are some of the hardest working people I know! They have so much ambition. I know that they're driven by having something, some business of their own." I knew that feeling of wanting something, and someone, of my own.

"Very few people know how to read here," Paro said. She was right, but hopefully that would change in the future.

"When we first started, nobody could read the newspaper. The uncles would sell them to the communities around us. Those that could read, the doctors, lawyers, shopkeepers, and store owners, bought the newspaper every Friday, but they were just a handful of our people. It helped us that Mr. Cassimjee had a stake in the business. His friends bought the paper."

"What stories did the paper have?" Paro's eyes widened as she asked more questions. I loved her questions because it meant I could hear her beautiful voice for longer.

"The stories were very local, talking about what was happening in and around Durban, but recently Uncle Madan has started including stories about some of the protests directed at the English. Mohandas Gandhi, the lawyer from India, is fighting for Indians. He said that we're treated without any dignity, and he's right!"

"Even we heard about Mohandas Gandhi. My father said that people were talking at the morning market. Hopefully, things will change." A sigh followed her words. I wanted to show her a world that had more hope than pain.

"I think things will change. They have to. And we have people like the uncles who make sure that our people know what's happening. The more information we have, the more we can change our situation."

"But how will people know if they can't read the newspaper? I really believe in the paper, but I think it will not help if no one can know what is in it," she said.

This was true, and it was the same question the community asked all those years ago under the syringa tree.

"You're right. In the beginning, it was mostly the uncles, who had learned to read and write English, reading the stories to others. Mr. Cassimjee also did that at his shop. Often, people would go to the shop on a Friday just to hear him reading the top stories. At first, very few people from our area could read English, after all Mama and I were just learning. But they still bought the paper. They lined their cupboards with it, but they still bought it. Buying the paper was a matter of pride."

The newspaper brought many changes to our community.

"Families would plan to buy at least one paper. Few have money to spend every week, so some families took turns buying on alternate weeks. In some areas, people would contribute a small amount of money weekly and everyone who contributed had a turn to get the whole amount. They bought the newspaper like this, too, rotating among families in an organized schedule," I explained.

This became a local way to "bank" money and get a large sum at a scheduled time.

"But over time, more people learned to read English and read the stories for themselves. Our Hillary Community School and *The Port Natal Weekly* were the drivers of change in Hillary." I felt so proud of this community. "We're creating communities that have knowledge and information and who can fight back against the racial discrimination that is entrenching itself into this land."

"Listening to you speak about Hillary makes me believe there's still hope for a future free from this poverty and White man oppression," she said.

I hoped that Paro and I could build that future together.

Chapter 20

Uma's Final Gifts

Telling Paro about all that the community had built also made me reflect on how far we had come as the indentured Indians who worked on Mr. Thompson's plantation and lived in the line house. I was sure Dada would have been so proud of us, and I hoped Didi would have been too.

"Paro, what would you like to learn or want for yourself?" I said. Talking about the Hillary school and how it started made me curious about Paro's hopes and dreams. As I said it, I remembered that Richard asked Didi the same question, and he had told me how angry she got. I was worried now about how Paro would react. Should I not have asked her?

"I want to learn to read and write English. Can you help me? I want to read the newspaper too. I hear my father and uncles speaking about Gandhi-ji, and I want to read this too."

This woman wanted her own future.

"I want to be a teacher like you," she said. "But I want to teach small children."

Paro spoke so quietly I wasn't even sure that I heard her correctly. I took her hand, ready to let go if I scared her, or if some nosy family members saw us. She didn't pull away.

"Do you think I can become a teacher too? I want to help you and Mama teach others."

"I have a school where I teach everyone who wants to learn. It's my life's work. It's my joy. You give me a gift by asking. Of course, I will, Paro."

I was thrilled to hold her hand, but my heart was full knowing that Paro wanted to do something for herself and for others. I quickly kissed her hands before anyone saw us. We would have a wedding later, but this exchange felt like our vow to each other.

Going home with Uncle Madan was fun. He was full of stories gathered through all his travels and talks. He loved to talk with everyone! As we were leaving, Paro's *kaka* (father's brother) brought out a box full of vegetables from their farm for us to take home. Coriander, potatoes, tomatoes, leafy vegetables, and so much more. But the sack of cucumbers was just too much, and I said so to him. Besides, it was too heavy to carry on the train.

"Beta, you are our son-in-law, and your house is now like ours. Please take these and distribute them to your neighbors and family," he said, clasping his hands and offering us enough food for weeks.

All of this was more touching because I knew that Paro's family wasn't wealthy. I had fallen in love with Paro, and now her family had a special place in my heart too. This continued every time I visited, and they made me bring all *The Port Natal Weekly* editions that they missed. Everyone wanted to know more about what was happening with the Englishmen and their new laws. I would choose articles to read every time. I felt like a storyteller. I liked that!

When Paro asked me about Didi on one of the visits, I wasn't ready for the question. "I don't know if I can speak about Didi and what happened. It's too hard for me."

Usually, Paro and I stood very close when we spoke, hoping to accidentally touch each other. This time, I turned away. I didn't want Paro to see my tears or sadness.

Paro turned my face towards hers, her hands holding my chin. "Tell me about what she was like and why you loved her so much. Let's not talk about what happened."

Where should I start? What should I say about this angel who walked this earth for such a short time? Paro just stood with me as silent tears rolled down my cheeks.

"My didi was the person who always held my hand. She called me her Hari baby. I hated it because I was too big for that. She never stopped."

Paro smiled at *Hari baby*. I even smiled at that.

"What I wouldn't give to hear 'Hari baby' once more in her voice. She was the strongest of us all. She was so small when we left India, and she took care of me all the time. She was so bossy! She bossed me all the time. Told me what to do. But never let go of my hand, ever."

The memories were flooding back, bringing sweetness and sadness in equal measure.

"Sometimes, she held my hand or arm so tightly her fingerprints would remain," I said. Paro and I looked at my arm at the same time, perhaps hoping to see fingerprints.

"On the plantation, Mama was so busy. She worked hard, but so did Didi. She cleaned the house and took care of me, and when we left the plantation, she worked in the quarry." I looked into the distance across the sugarcane as the green carpet drew me deeper into my memories.

"Didi was quiet and thoughtful, and she had more courage than we knew. When she fell in love with Richard, she made the choice of love. She died for that choice."

"Oh, Hari! I'm so sorry!" Paro's hand flew up to cover her mouth in shock.

"She was the kind of big sister who knew I loved white guavas and would make sure that I only had those. My didi lit up everything and everyone around her."

Paro and I stood in silence. There would be so much to talk with Paro about Uma Didi in the future. But for now, Paro knew of the Didi that loved her Hari baby, held his hand, and gave him the best white guavas to eat, and that was enough.

Politics and the fight against White oppression was gaining hold among many men, and the uncles were becoming more entrenched in the politics of the day. Respect for Gandi-ji had grown among the Indian community, and grudgingly, the English knew that he was a force to deal with.

Uncle Madan couldn't stand to watch injustice. He traveled to meet Gandhi-ji in his settlement north of the Umgeni River, the river that ran from high in the mountains down to the ocean that rimmed the town. He spoke increasingly about getting involved with the Gandhi settlement. For now, *The Port Natal Weekly* took most of his time, but I could see that this would not be enough for him. Uncle Mohan went along "for company," and he also got to meet Gandhi-ji.

About three months before our wedding, the uncles came home to visit Mama and me. Generally, Uncle Mohan seemed quieter than normal. Uncle Madan, on the other hand, was very upbeat and filled with nervous excitement.

"You're very excited, Madan. What's going on? You got a girlfriend?" Mama said. It wasn't in my mother's nature to tease, but this son brought that out in her. She pulled his ear playfully as she spoke. Age had mellowed her a lot. Those sharp edges and sharper words had eased.

"Not yet, Mama, but the girls better be careful! I'm a successful newspaper man now!" Uncle Madan posed, chest out, chin tilted toward the roof, arms crossed, with a smile wider than the Umgeni River.

"I think Mohan will find a girl first. He's the pretty one," Madan said. He poked his finger into Uncle Mohan's ribs and got a sad laugh from him.

"Seriously though, I came to tell you that I am going to Pretoria. Many of the men are going to protest the laws that the government are creating to keep us in one area only," Madan said.

The pass system had been introduced, and we now needed a *dompas* (passport) to go from one area to another.

"They want to keep us from mixing with people from other races. Imagine us not being able to openly work and live with Zweli and Richard!" Uncle Madan banged his fist hard into the table.

I couldn't imagine that at all. Both were my family.

"I'm joining this group because we must stop this before the government tells us how to live our lives completely. Already they treat us like dirt, now they want to make that treatment the law." Madan spoke with so much passion.

The South African government was in Pretoria, in the province of Transvaal. It was far inland, very far from the coast of Natal.

"That's very far to go. You haven't gone so far away from home before," Mama said. She never tried to stop anyone, even when she felt nervous for them, but I could see she was apprehensive.

"I'll be fine, Mama," Madan said. All his passion melted into a love reserved only for Mama. "I'll be back in two months. Just in time to watch the small boy get married, hey Hari." He winked at me. "Don't worry, Mohan will go with you to see Paro. Besides, when I'm back, we need to finish all the wedding preparations."

"Just take care of yourself and let us know that you're fine. Don't worry about me," I said, and I meant it. I loved this man with all my heart. He wasn't my uncle; he was my big brother.

Our newspaper was started as a business, but it gave Uncle Madan a purpose. The jovial young man was still there, but now he also had a mission, and nothing would stop him, except his cousin and brother, Mohan. But Mohan would never hold him back. They had come far, these two. They had relied on each other for the last two decades. They were each other's strength. Nothing could come between them.

"You going to be alright, Mohan?" Mama asked as he stood there stoically. She saw the sadness in him.

"I'm fine, Mama. It's just that this is the first time we will be apart from each other in the last twenty years. I'm going to miss this mad child!" Mohan smiled as he rubbed Madan's hair and then gave it a playful tug.

"I'm going to miss you, too, Mohan. But before you know it, I'll be back. I have to do this. I can't stand on the sidelines. Zweli will help more with the newspaper too."

"I'll also help more. Uncle Mohan, you tell me what I can take on." I knew that I would have to help.

The months passed with Uncle Madan in Pretoria and Mohan, Zweli, and me carrying more on the newspaper. The school was also growing, so Mama took on more classes. She was getting older and tired more easily, but she wouldn't let up. Lucky for us, Aunty Savitri was very excited to plan the wedding, and having us all so busy meant that she could do what she wanted.

Mama would just roll her eyes and say, "Bhen, do what you think is right. Just don't make us look like fools!" That always made Aunty Savitri mock-mad and made my mother laugh.

The wedding was to be held in a temple in Sawoti, further along from Braemar on the train. The nearest big town or village was

Umzinto, a White settlement named for the river that ran through it. It was an old area of sugar money, yet the money all lay in the hands of the White farmers while those that worked the land barely survived. Like the Indian communities in Hillary and further up north in Tongaat and Stanger, these communities also built their own schools and their own temples, mosques, and churches. It was in one of those temples in Sawoti that Paro and I would be married. Families made sacrifices to have places of worship and celebration built. The same was true of the Sawoti temple.

Aunty Savitri wasn't happy. She thought it was very far for us to travel, which it was. It was also where Paro wanted to get married, so it was always going to be the right place. Our marriage was set for Friday morning. The priest said that the date and time was very good and that it would bode well for our marriage. Paro's family relied on the priest's recommendation, and they would do as he said without question. This didn't matter to me or my mother. All that mattered to me was that we got married, but I liked Paro's family. They were good people.

Uncle Gopal and Aunty Savitri made this wedding happen. Without them, we couldn't have planned everything. Uncle Gopal organized the cooking for both the Thursday night before and the Saturday after the wedding. Both days would be huge parties. I didn't realize that the wedding was so important for our extended family and for the community. The cook was planning to make a biryani for five hundred people—all the people from our village!

Biryani was always a festive meal for weddings, but I worried about the cost. We had the school and the newspaper, but the school didn't make money, and I got paid just enough for us to live on. The newspaper was making some money, but we had to share between five people. I didn't need to worry, Uncle Gopal said. He wanted to pay for the food. Mama wouldn't hear of it. I wouldn't have it at all, but this couple wouldn't listen.

"Shivali, you are my sister. Am I not your brother?" Uncle Gopal said.

What was Mama supposed to say to that? Uncle Gopal was calling Mama out on their relationship.

"Of course, Gopal-ji. But this is too much!"

"No, Shivali. It's not too much. It's not enough. Let us do this. Savitri and I didn't have children, and now we have Shanba and Nithya. You made that happen for us. We would have loved to have done Uma's wedding too. Let us help with Hari's wedding. Besides, we feel like Paro is our daughter-in-law too!"

"Mama, let Uncle Gopal do this for you and Hari. For us," Uncle Mohan said.

He was the one that convinced Mama and me. He looked at Mama like that eighteen-year-old boy she had stabbed all those years ago, ready to fall into her arms and sob his heart out. He was saying let us be part of this; we are family.

Uncle Madan returned on schedule and unharmed, thank God! But he also came back changed. A purpose that had been brewing for years had taken shape, and he would become the political voice in Hillary and in Port Natal more broadly. This passion both intrigued and scared me. It made Uncle Mohan nervous, too, but I could see pride lurking under his anxiety. These two—a businessman and a politician. Who would have thought the two ship would-be thieves had it in them?

Uncle Madan's return freed up some of my time, so I had some time to plan things for the wedding. Some things had just gotten pushed and pushed because of time. One of those was Paro's wedding sari and jewelry. This was the groom's family's gift to the bride as part of her wedding. Mama and Aunty Savitri had been pestering me for weeks to go shopping, but I just didn't have the time. The pressure mounted and came to a head when Aunty Savitri threatened to pick out the sari and jewelry herself, and Mama put her foot down.

"We can't let her pick a sari! Paro would have to live with the most frightening clothes and colors if she did. Savitri loves red and gold. The more gold, the better. We need to go!" Mama said.

Richard came to visit us earlier in the week when we had planned to shop, about three and a half weeks before the wedding. Richard had never married. I didn't think he ever would. He didn't live on the sugarcane plantation anymore. He bought a piece of land further inland, near a place called Underberg, close to the beautiful Drakensberg mountains. Once, years ago, Richard described this place and its unparalleled beauty. "Sometimes a cloud covers the tops of the mountains, and it looks like she's wearing a veil, just like a bride," he said.

Richard remembered Didi's beauty when he spoke of those mountains, covered with the most gracious greens and a background of the clearest sky human eyes would ever see. He said the skies reminded him of Didi's smile. "Hari, when I close my eyes and sit in the silence, I feel the echoes of the mountains reflecting her laughter. I feel like Uma is all around me."

His house was close to a river, and every morning a thick fog held the land in its embrace. For Richard, Uma came to gently kiss him good morning in the fog. As Richard described his garden, I hoped that Didi found solace there. She loved beautiful flowers, and she loved gardens. I hoped the fog found space to dance with joy in that Underberg garden. I knew Didi found comfort in the orange and purple flowers that still grew in my garden.

When Richard came to say he was leaving for Underberg, Mama was the one that cried. I didn't expect her to cry for him, but like always, she surprised me. No, it was more like she absolutely turned everything I expected of her on its head. For Mama (and me), Richard held a piece of Uma that was missing from our lives. Being close to him gave us that Uma. Richard leaving felt like Uma Didi was leaving again.

"I'm not leaving forever, Mama. Underberg is just a few hours away. I'm still going to visit you and Hari. You're my family," he said.

Richard kept his promise to us, and he kept his promise in death to Didi. He bought her the land next to a river, with beautiful gardens and away from prying eyes.

I thought the wedding and our planning might have been too painful for Richard, but he was with us regularly talking and planning. This time he came with boxes. One large square one and one slightly smaller, thinner one.

"Hari, I'm telling you that you can't say no to what I'm about to say," Richard said.

Given what Uncle Gopal had just done with paying for the food, I was very nervous about what Richard was about to say. I wanted to say no immediately, but I was also curious.

"I can't promise I won't say no, but tell me." My heart was beating rapidly.

"When Uma and I were talking about getting married, I always imagined what she would wear. Uma told me that she would only marry in a sari, and she hated red, but you know that because she said that you didn't like red either." His eyes reflected his memories, and tears filled the space between his eyes and his voice.

"My darling girl also never had any jewelry, and I hoped that when we married I would give her bangles. She told me that in your culture, the man gives the bride a gold and black bead *Mangalsutra* (marriage chain) to signify their union."

I knew right away what Richard had done. "No, Richard, please don't embarrass me by saying anything further. I can't take anything more from you."

"This is not from me. Your didi would want you to have a gift from us. She would want your bride to know how much she is loved by her sister-in-law."

The sobs were heavy and loud, but they were from Mama as she hugged Richard. "My Uma is here, Richard. How do you know how to make me feel close to her?"

"Because she's a part of me and you and Hari. She never went away. We can't touch her, but she touches our lives all the time."

Richard opened the first box, and sitting in a nest of tissue paper was a light, orange-colored sari with a border of the darkest orange. Delicate, tiny gold threads were woven into the sari, and the border had purple thread tenderly nestled among the gold. If Didi were a sari, she would look just like this.

"Where did you get this from?" Mama asked with tenderness as she hesitantly caressed the cloth.

"When the wedding date was set, I had it made for Paro. Uma would have done the same."

"This is so beautiful," I said. I was glad that it was just Richard, Mama, and me at home. It felt too intimate to have everyone look at this sari. It was like the three of us were looking at Didi. The ceremony would be complete because my didi could be a part of my happiness, even though I couldn't be a part of hers.

As Mama reached to close the box, Richard stopped her. "Wait, Mama." He opened the second, smaller box, and inside in a sea of blue sat a Mangalsutra and two heavy-looking bangles.

"I would have given Uma something similar for our marriage, and I know that Uma would want you to give these to Paro," he said to me.

This was all too much. My didi was here with Richard giving me all these tokens for Paro, but all I wanted to do was ask Didi to hold my hand as I took this step in my life. Richard had given us so much; he gave us a side of our Uma that we didn't know and now these gifts that would be a part of us all forever.

"Don't say no, Hari. Please let Uma and I do this for you and Paro. We want to be a part of your wedding too."

I said yes to Richard, and I said yes to Didi.

The wedding in Sawoti was beautiful. Paro's family welcomed us with such grace and love. Mama and the ladies stayed home. The custom was for the women to wait at home to welcome the bride. I wondered why she did that. It wasn't like her to abide by tradition. I wanted her with me.

"Mama, why don't you come with us? This tradition doesn't make sense."

"I want to be the first to welcome Paro into our house. For that, I must be at home. You have everyone with you, but I'll be the only person here to welcome my new daughter. Let me stay."

I didn't argue with her. I also wanted her to be the first to welcome my bride home.

Mama bought a new coat for the wedding, and she wore a deep orange turban. She looked regal as she circled a tray with a lamp slightly in front of me and blessed me with a *tilak* (dot) on my forehead and a kiss in my hair.

"Bring our Paro home, Hari. Bring my daughter home."

But the biggest surprise for us all came from Megha Aunty. That she would participate was never a question. But no one thought that she would understand what was happening. When Mama kissed me, Megha Aunty stepped forward, took the tray, and repeated what Mama did. "Go well, Hari. I will wait to welcome your bride."

Everyone was dressed so well. The uncles were dapper in their suits, and the aunties teased them that they were looking for brides too! As was the tradition of the day, the bride changed midway through the ceremony into the clothes and jewelry we brought for her. Shanba played the role of sister handing these to Paro.

When Paro emerged dressed, the crowd gasped. No one had ever seen such a sight. Paro didn't just look beautiful—she radiated from deep within an ethereal, spiritual presence, and everyone around us felt it. Richard and I shared a look. Didi was here too.

Uncle Madan nudged me and whispered, "Lucky Aunty Savitri didn't choose the sari! The gasp would be for a different reason then!"

Uncle Madan could lighten any moment, and I had to laugh. Richard heard him, too, and grinned broadly. This felt right. I was marrying this lovely woman, my family was around me, my didi was blessing us, and my mother was waiting for us at home.

Sawoti was far, and our trip home was too long, especially after a long day. But it gave me time with my Paro before the village got a hold of her.

"You look beautiful, Paro. I can't believe that you married me."

Paro smiled, and for the first time, placed her hands on my face, cupping my face in both hands. "Finally, Hari, we can start our lives together. It's me who can't believe that I found you!"

"You both are very lucky you found each other! Stop making me jealous now!" Madan said. Privacy wasn't an option. Even intimate moments were shared.

"I think you need a wife now, Madan. You're getting jealous at other people's marriages!" Uncle Mohan's side comment made us all laugh. The ice was broken between the uncles and Paro, and they would be her fiercest supporters—besides me, of course!

Paro's entry into our home was just as spectacular as her entry at the ceremony. She stopped everyone's gaze, and my mama hugged her so hard it was clear that Shivali welcomed her daughter. Another piece of my mother came together.

These days with Paro learning and teaching were the most beautiful days. Who was the teacher and who was the learner? Paro taught me humility with her gentle strength. I taught her the alphabet. Her happiness in each moment anchored me in our life, and I taught her how to write her name. I taught her to read the Ramayana, and she instructed me in how to interpret a story for life and not just what was in a book.

Time passed quickly with Paro. She joined the Hillary community school and became literate, wrote her exams, and became a teacher too. You couldn't stop gossiping in our village community, though. Some people grumbled about why Mama was letting her daughter-in-law study and work. Mama didn't care and neither did I. We walked our own path always; this was no different. But it was Paro who led the way. She was fearless. Even when she was scared, she would still do what she thought was right.

Oh, my Paro! If only you had met my Uma Didi, you would have loved her and she you.

Epilogue

Uma's Grove

1923

This was a place of sugar and spice. Spice was no longer a new bride. She had settled into her home, integrating into a new life, and blending into the landscape. Life could be hard in this land of white gold. Everyone was trying to build their lives here. A new generation was emerging from the depths of green to play different roles in this place. Some were workers of old, but many were professionals, businessmen, and even politicians. Very few thought of going back to India, and some even came back after leaving.

Our Hillary community was made up of mostly brown with some black and white—the colors of the people of this land. And the school was a place for all, but times were changing. Richard got more and more nervous and angry looks when he came to visit now. The English government had made too many laws to keep us subjugated. The newspaper's success had brought White scrutiny, especially with the stronger political role that Uncle Madan played in our community.

My children, Gorak, Sona, and Inder, learned in the Hillary school. They heard stories of warrior queens, of ships that crossed dark oceans, and of men who were brave and strong. They learned how to read and write the language of the laws in the land. Uncle Madan was determined that our children must understand what was changing around them. He and Uncle Mohan introduced a paper with cartoons and comics for children, and we used them in the school. Uncle Madan had become intense, but he had also managed to activate the community around him.

Uncle Mohan decided to marry a lovely girl from close to Paro's home. It caused quite a stir because he was old, in his forties, when he married. He needed to settle down, though. Uncle Madan had always been Mohan's anchor, but he had found his passion. Uncle Mohan needed to have someone else to pour his love into now. Uncle Madan would always be his brother, but their lives had diverged from one another.

When our children were born, Paro made sure that school wasn't just about learning but also about joy and fun. She always brought the light. Mama and I could be quite heavy, but Paro had enough lightness to balance us both out. Thanks to Paro, our school held concerts with plays and music. We all knew that generally we were terrible music and drama teachers, but it was so much fun! The first songs at our concerts were religious hymns, but slowly more popular music was included. The sound of children's laughter blessed the school. The presence of learning and joy celebrated its creation.

When the school turned twenty years old, we had to celebrate. It was such an achievement to have built the school, but for it to also thrive was wonderful! Mama said that she also wanted us to leave something for the community to enjoy forever. The community decided to plant a fruit grove, and Richard suggested that we plant a guava grove. There was such intense debate on how many trees to plant! It was Megha Aunty who unexpectedly said, "Maybe you should plant nineteen, one to celebrate each year of Uma's life." So it was decided—a guava grove of nineteen trees. I wondered if anyone would even remember why there were nineteen trees in the future. Mama said it didn't matter; we knew.

We only planted white guavas. The best kind of guavas. Richard bought the trees for us, and the planting day was happy but slightly sad for us all. We would never forget that an innocent life was lost here. It wove itself into the fabric of the community, and sometimes we knew it was a faint shame that people carried. The day we planted the grove was a redemption of sorts for many of the people. Each tree planted was done with a prayer for Uma, the school, and the community. My mama held Richard's hand tightly as she whispered her prayer for Uma. Our religious leaders led the prayer for the school, and Uncle Madan prayed for our community.

Nineteen white guava trees now nourish the school of Hillary and stand in silent witness of the love of a boy and his sister, the love of a man and his beloved, and the love of a mother for her children.

That day, after we planted the grove, I watched my children with so much wonder, and nostalgia, and pain. Gorak and Inder adored Sona. And Sona was their big sister. Their Didi. I saw us in them, and yet they were so different. They lived openly, without hiding and without fear. Hopefully, they would never know that secrets could slowly twist all that was good into an unrecognizable pain.

Mama was very partial to Paro, even though Mama kept this close to her chest. You could see her love in her soft gaze, in her gentle words, and most importantly, in her love for her grandchildren. She missed Uma so much, but all her love was poured into Paro and the children. Paro was a mother who loved fiercely, and I was a father who demanded no sacrifice.

Life marched on, and love lived here every day.

Manufactured by Amazon.ca
Acheson, AB

13572745R00155